"Amos Walker and Travis McGee would understand each other. So Estleman goes on my very short list of the peer group I can read for pleasure."

John D. MacDonald

"The Walker books are among the most enjoyable being written today in the classic private eye field...impressively crafted, at once sentimental and cynical."

San Francisco Examiner

"EVERY BRILLIANT EYE is Loren D. Estleman's sixth Amos Walker novel, and his best."

The Detroit News

"Estleman is good. Very good."

San Diego Tribune

Fawcett Books
by Loren D. Estleman:

EVERY BRILLIANT EYE

GUN MAN

KILL ZONE

MISTER ST. JOHN

MOTOR CITY BLUE

THE STRANGLERS

EVERY BRILLIANT EYE

Loren D. Estleman

FAWCETT CREST • NEW YORK

A Fawcett Crest Book
Published by Ballantine Books
Copyright © 1986 by Loren D. Estleman

Library of Congress Catalog Card Number: 85–10711

ISBN 0-449-21137-1

First published by Houghton Mifflin Company. Reprinted by permission of Houghton Mifflin Company.

The author is grateful for permission to quote three lines of "The Tower," from *The Poems of W. B. Yeats*, edited by Richard J. Finnegan. Copyright 1928 by Macmillan Publishing Company, renewed 1956 by Georgie Yeats. Reprinted by permission of Macmillan Publishing Company, Macmillan London Ltd., and Michael B. Yeats.

Manufactured in the United States of America

First Ballantine Books Edition: March 1987

For my mother and father

1

I DROVE THE LAST TWELVE MILES BACK TO DETROIT ON the heels of a late-summer rainstorm that had the drains gurgling and my wipers swamping brown wash off the windshield from the tanker in front of me. I'd have passed it except it was doing seventy on the double nickel and I needed the help to get home without attracting red flashers.

The truck was the first good thing that had happened to me all weekend. I had picked up a computer software salesman on a routine tail job in Drayton Plains Friday afternoon. It was now three-thirty Sunday morning and I hadn't been out of the car except to grab a burrito and visit a service station, having gotten my fill of the back side of Toledo and points in between while my subject ran his samples for vice presidents in Purchasing and took their secretaries to various motels to continue his pitch. If I'd been working for the guy's wife it would have been a productive weekend. But his firm had hired me to find out if he was running his own game and so far as I could tell he

1

hadn't left his assigned route. I had made the mistake of calling in my report and now they were shipping out a company man to pick up the baton. Sunday morning canned is a lousy place to be.

I left the tanker at the Chrysler interchange and drove along shining funereal streets to my neighborhood, slowly now to catch Julie London's last few whispered phrases on the radio. She was singing about apple trees and sunlit memories like someone who had been living underground a long time. I sang along.

That year as in all the others I was living in a bedroom, bath, kitchen, and living room under a roof that had needed shingles since Hiroshima. Now the Japs were building better cars than Detroit, but the roof still leaked when there was snow on it. Replacing the shingles had come fifth on the list of things I had promised someone I'd do when I bought the place. Leaving me had come first on hers.

I parked in the driveway, too wasted to pry open the garage. The stale air inside the house stirred when I fanned the front door. I wound the clocks, read my mail, and put my investigative talents to work on the refrigerator. Inside were a can of beer and a slice of pizza growing gray penicillin like old bums' whiskers. I wasn't in a mood for either. From the cupboard over the sink I hoisted down a bottle of Scotch and a barrel glass. I ran water into the glass from the tap. My hand shook when I unscrewed the cap from the bottle.

That was enough for me. I screwed the cap back on and drank the water and put away the bottle and glass. Thirty-six hours in a car with just the radio for company would have anyone's nerves dancing. But I wasn't taking

2

chances. Instead I put on some coffee and smoked my last cigarette.

The percolator and the door buzzer went off together. On my way through the living room I glanced at my great-grandmother's Seth Thomas. Ten after four. I got my .38 out of the drawer in the lamp table before undoing any locks.

The redhead standing on my stoop wasn't pretty. She was too tall and bony in an expensive blue dress that fit her like a sail and she sprayed her hair in hard waves so that it looked like combed copper and when she smiled, every Shrove Tuesday, her gums showed. But she never had to bruise her nails on a doorknob where there was a man around. She modeled fashions for the two major local magazines and entertained convention scouts for an area hotel chain while the cops were busy rousting the street trade, which shows how much they know. Her heavily inked eyes took in the gun.

"They should tear down the big tire display outside town," she said. "Put up a sixty-foot revolver in its place."

I lowered it. "It's ten after four, Irene."

"Thanks. My watch stopped and you were the only friend I could think of who tells time."

"We're not friends."

"You and Barry are."

"Is it Barry?"

She said it was. I stood aside, closed the door behind her, and tucked the revolver into its drawer. She stood in the middle of the room lazily running her hands up and down her upper arms. It was a cool night for August and she wasn't wearing a jacket. "Cold."

"The furnace hasn't been running. I've been away."

"Is the bar open?"

I went back into the kitchen and turned off the coffee and introduced some Scotch to some water in two glasses. Good intentions never live long around me. My hand was steady now, anyway. When I returned carrying the drinks she was sitting on the sofa with her legs crossed. She had thick ankles and no flesh on her knees. I handed her one of the glasses and stood holding the other.

"That's better." She set down her glass a third empty on the chipped coffee table. Looked around. "Is this how you live?"

"The chandelier's out being cleaned, sorry. What about Barry?"

"You haven't seen him lately or you wouldn't have to ask. He's drinking again."

"I didn't know he stopped."

"For five weeks. He fell off so hard he's still bouncing."

"That's the problem?"

"It's the symptom, as they say. I don't know what the problem is. You're the detective."

"Right. Not a psychiatrist. Where is he?"

"Getting drunker someplace."

"The bars are closed."

"The blind pigs are just warming up. He spends most of his time at a place called the Inner City Action Council, over the A-1 Hardware on Clairmount."

"Whatever happened to 'Joe's'?"

"Those civic betterment names sound good in court," she said.

I said, "He's looking for an extra smile under his chin."

"He needs taking out of there before he gets one."

4

"He'll just turn around and go back in. Unless I hide his artificial leg."

"You're his friend."

"If you had any of your own you wouldn't draw that like a knife." I ate some Scotch. "How long's he been showing up at this place?"

"What month is it?"

"Uh-huh. Why's tonight worse for him than all the rest?"

She ran a finger around inside her empty glass and tasted it, but I wasn't taking hints today. She put the glass back on the table, not gently. "I'm getting out. My clothes are in the car. I've been sitting on them across the street for an hour waiting on you."

"So get out. Who's standing on your foot?"

"My old man taught me never to leave a campsite without cleaning up first. I want to see him in good hands before I go. Hands, anyway. You don't live with someone a year and then just walk without seeing he gets put back up on the shelf."

"Ten months," I corrected. "And two weeks."

She smiled then, uncasing her gums. When she did that she looked like a horse. Not a showhorse; a stomper. "You never did like me. That's why you haven't been to see Barry in so long. Somebody somewhere must've spiked you pretty good."

"You going to be here when I bring him back? If I bring him back?"

"No." She stood, hauling up her shoulderbag strap the way they do. "Tell him Irene said to have a good life. I've got friends who will put me up till I find a place. He shouldn't look for me."

5

"I'll be sure and tell him."

She thought about it a second, decided it wasn't worth getting mad over, and said, "You'll notice a change in Barry."

I waited, and I was still waiting when she went out, leaving me to close the door behind her. After a moment I emptied my glass and retrieved my keys from the kitchen table.

I should've asked.

2

THE CAR WAS GETTING OLD. THE STEERING WHEEL SHUD-
dered above fifty and when the lights stayed red too long
the carburetor coughed and swallowed its tongue. It needed
parts worse than I did, but I still owed my mechanic for the
fuel pump he'd installed last May. In the world of self-
employment my busy periods were slower than most people's down time. I nursed the Olds through a string of
lights on Calvert and blew out the carbon when I hit
Dexter. The streets were wet and empty, like my stomach.

Barry Stackpole went back longer with me than anyone
else except Lieutenant John Alderdyce of Seventh Squad
Homicide. Barry had been a correspondent covering the
U.S. push into Cambodia from the bottom of a shell crater
when I fell on top of him. One leg, two fingers, and a
broken skull later, he was a syndicated columnist with the
Detroit *News*. His beat was organized crime, and he owed
the missing parts to a modest sort named Vincente "Big
Bang" Bagliano, whose son was now in charge of the

7

Neighborhood Watch program in Birmingham. They buried Big Bang in hallowed ground a couple of years back when he choked to death on a raw oyster.

After his release from the hospital, Barry had been a clay pigeon for a while, getting his mail at his office in the *News* building and never living in the same place longer than two weeks. But the current generation of *capos* was substituting dollars for dynamite and with the streets belonging to the lead pipes and scuffed leather jackets no one was much interested in the organized variety anymore. These days he was renting a house in Harper Woods, and the last time I had heard from him he was writing a book.

None of whatever had happened to him since was really Irene's fault. It never is. There is an Irene waiting somewhere for every one of us, to hand us a martini mixed in the same room with a bottle of vermouth and pillow us with her breasts and say, there, there, they just don't know what they've got in a man like you. The trick is to recognize her and cross the street when we see her coming. By which time, of course, it's too late.

Back when Rosa Parks Boulevard was still Twelfth Street, before the '67 riots, it had sometimes been called Sin Alley, but that was just newspaper talk. Detroiters who were still thirsty when the legitimate bars closed at two knew it as The Strip, a place where a drink or a woman could be had any time of the day or night. You know it. They might call it the Tenderloin or the Combat Zone in your city, but during an election year or ratings sweep weeks the local TV stations in towns three thousand miles apart could swap footage and you wouldn't see any difference. You know it by the neon and by Aretha Franklin wailing out of the open windows and by the black girls shivering on the corners in their short skirts and high boots.

Then the cops hit a blind pig over the Economy Printing Company at Twelfth and Clairmount and it was all over in a kaleidoscope of flame and spraying glass that had lasted a week, killed forty-three, and taken the National Guard and the United States Army to hose down. It's still The Strip, but the neon's gone and there are boards over the bottle-smashed and fireburst windows, and following the general rush from the bars to the after-hours places the street is as quiet as a dead cat in an alley. Except for the hookers on the corners. We'll be rid of them when we're all nuclear dust.

One of them was crossing in front of the A-1 Hardware on her way to the corner when I parked at the curb and climbed out. She stopped, looked at me, and said, "Lost, mister?"

I studied her, patting my pockets for a cigarette I didn't have. She had on a glistening black plastic raincoat that came to the tops of her thighs and nothing underneath. Sandals and orange-painted toenails to match beads the size of crabapples in her ears. Her lipstick was orange too and her brown skin looked purple in the light from the store's display window. She wore her hair cut close to her head. She reminded me of someone and I didn't like it.

"What're you," I said, "fourteen?"

"You want fourteen? I can do fourteen, mister."

I shook my head and walked past her toward the open door next to the hardware. Behind me she said, "I wouldn't go up there, mister."

I looked back at her. "I bet you would."

"Not if I showed up in the dark as good as you, mister."

"I'm not a mister," I said. "I'm a private dick."

She laughed, with a tinkle that was worth ten dollars all by itself. "We be good together, then. I'm a public pussy."

Gray light from a greasy fixture at the top of the stairs slid down the rubber-clad steps between a brick wall on one side and painted plaster on the other. The stairwell smelled of marijuana and old sex. I had climbed fifty miles of stairs just like them and I was still in the same place. At the top I followed a narrow hall with a bare hardwood floor to a door at the end with an L of light showing around it. When I knocked, the door came open three inches. I looked at a chain and an eye behind it in a black face.

I said, "Inner City Action Council?"

Nothing. A radio behind the eye was playing so low only the electric bass wrinkled the atmosphere.

"I'm just in from L.A.," I tried. "Scouting for the Lakers. Guy I sat with on the plane said I could get a drink here."

"I don't play." The door closed.

I put my ear to the panel. The door was reinforced oak and I couldn't hear anything. But I couldn't count on that working both ways. I retraced my steps down the hall. The boards reported back.

Downstairs I stood in front of the hardware store and wished I had a cigarette. I was still wishing five minutes later when three couples boiled out of a doorway across the street and came my way at an angle. I could see their yellow shirts and electric blue blouses before I could see anything else. And six sets of bright teeth. They were talking in high affected whines and laughing, but when they saw me they clammed up.

In the pool of light on the corner of Twelfth, the girl in the raincoat stood smoking a cigarette and trying to handle it as if it weren't a fencerail. I walked that way. Just as I got there a twelve-year-old Thunderbird with a broken muffler and Woody Woodpecker painted on the passenger's door burbled to a stop against the curb in front of her. The window came down and an Afro poked out the opening. "Let's see what you got, sweets."

I said, "Dangle, darling."

Two eye-whites rolled at me.

"Court's closed all day," I said. "You'll miss church waiting on bail."

"Hell, whyn't you say so in the first place?" The window rolled back up and the heap chugged on, its exhaust roaring off blank-faced buildings on both sides of the street.

"I thought you said you was private," said the girl.

"I did. I am."

"That's restraint of trade, mister."

"Our lawyers will work it out. What's your name?"

She smiled. "Candy."

"Yeah."

"Okay, Thelma."

"Thelma, how'd you like to make twenty bucks standing up?"

"I don't know. I never tried it."

I gave her the twenty and my arm. She took both as if they were her first in weeks.

3

THE THREE BLACK COUPLES WERE CONVERSING LOUDLY with the eye behind the door when we topped the stairs. I thought at first they had drawn the same bare wall I had, but then someone laughed, mostly squeezed air, and I knew they were just stoned. On the way up with Thelma I had taken off my hat and stashed my tie in a pocket. People tend to remember such things long after features are forgotten.

By the time we reached the end of the hall the door was closed, but then it opened without the chain and we crowded in on the far side of the group going in. I felt like an albino flea in a box of raisins. But the lights in the room were low and the only illumination in the hallway was the globe over the stairs on the other end. The sentry shot the bolt behind us and diddled the chain into its socket and I was inside.

"What's it today?" the door-jockey asked Thelma. "Candy or Tiffany?"

She gave him a look that ought to have shrunk his shorts. "I'd tell you go fuck yourself, but why rub it in, right?"

It slid off him. Most things would, including falling pianos. He was a big man from the waist up, with a dollop of coiled hair on a head that was otherwise bald and a big belly and melons of muscle on his upper arms under a shirt a size too small, but his legs were bent and withered as if by a childhood disease. He could be tipped off them if he didn't get in the first shot. I steered Thelma away.

"Job's over, angel," I said. "Hunt heads if you want."

"Maybe I'll just drink. I get caught working this place they mail my legs to Cincinnati. This a union shop." She left me for the bar.

You never know what to expect in those places. Some of them look like any other saloon, others like an Arab carhop's wet dream. Naked girls in chains for barmaids are not unknown. Usually, though, the mere prospect of a place to sluice down when the lights go up in the legitimate spots is enough to draw cash customers. This one was set up like a meeting hall, with a bare plank floor and lunch-room tables arranged in parallel rows and folding wooden chairs on both sides, and that's probably what it was during the day. But at night all but the fluorescent ceiling tubes on the ends went out and the table at the far end blossomed thick glasses and bottles with off-brand labels.

The room had started out as adjoining apartments with a common wall. Nothing had been done to cover the seam where the two color schemes met. About sixty people were seated elbow to elbow at the tables and standing in clots in the corners, fingering their glasses and bobbing their heads in time with the music throbbing out of the ghetto-blaster

13

on the bar. The whites of their eyes glittered like scattered bits of glass in the gloom.

They knew I was there, of course. You can fill all the tambourines you want with talk about how we're all the same under the color, but that jungle sense dies kicking. I moved to the bar and asked for a double Scotch rocks.

The man behind the bar wore his hair in Stevie Wonder cornrows and a moustache and beard that looked like soot smeared around his mouth. He had on a white shirt with the tail out over a black sweatshirt. The black rubber butt of a revolver stuck out of his pants where the shirt split in front. "You with Thelma?" he asked.

"Yeah."

"Kay." He fisted some ice out of a portable cooler into a glass and poured from a fresh bottle. "Five bucks," he said, pushing the glass my way.

I laid a twenty on the long table. While he made change from a pasteboard shirt box full of curling bills I said, "Barry Stackpole been in lately?"

"Don't hear much names back here."

"You'd remember him. He's white, limps a little. Wears a glove on his right hand most of the time and he doesn't use the hand much."

He took a five and a ten out of the box, smoothed them, folded them, and poked them into his shirt pocket, watching me. I shrugged.

"Try that corner," he said.

I didn't know how I had missed seeing his sandy head when I came in. He was sitting at the end of the far table with his back to the bar and his Dutch leg propped on the rung of a chair on the other side. Most drinkers seek the dark and he had that fluorescent-washed table all to himself. I started that way with my drink.

14

"Say, man?"

I looked back at the bartender.

"No refills, man. Drink up and take your buddy and split. I got no insurance against breakage."

"That fifteen should cover the fixtures."

Evidently the hat check girl was off tonight. I set my hat and drink on the table next to Barry and sat down. He didn't look at me. He had a glass half-full of amber liquid in front of him with lumps of ice floating in it and he was playing with a flat tin ashtray, pushing down the lip with his thumb so that it flipped up and landed upside-down on the table with a racket like raining hubcaps. The table was littered with butts and flakes of ash. I watched him do it a couple of times.

"I'm disappointed," I said then. "I expected to find you face down in a pile of empty shot glasses. Instead it's tiddlywinks."

He looked at me for the first time, focused, and grinned baggily. "Hey, Amos. I'm trying to get it to land right side up. Bastards loaded it."

He was farther gone than I'd thought at first. His speech was okay—if anything it got more precise when he was tanked—but his head swayed and there was a glaze over his eyes that turned them from crisp blue to murky gray. While I was looking at him he picked up his glass in his right hand and drank from it. He wasn't wearing his white cotton glove. The skin was shiny where the third and fourth fingers ended at the second knuckles.

I said, "I haven't seen you use that arm in years."

"I've been exercising. A doctor told me I'm using muscles meant for something else. He didn't approve. They don't approve of anything, and wind up jogging into the paths of butchers' vans at forty."

15

"You doing anything with it besides bending it?"

"My column's set through next week. I'm on vacation."

"What about the book?"

"The book's deader than Lazarus. Take a necromancer to raise it." He swirled the liquid in his glass, watching the lumps of ice collide. "This is honest liquor."

"It's stewed barbed wire."

"What I mean. No phony aging or blending or storing in musty kegs in some Mick's basement. Just the quick burn and that feeling you've got the world on your belt. Irene send you?"

"Yeah."

"I guess she said she loves me or something."

"She said to tell you good-bye."

"Yeah?"

The conversation was going nowhere on a tankful of fumes. I looked around. The bass was still buzzing out of the portable radio on the bar. A pretty brown girl in a white jumpsuit with her straight black hair in bangs was standing in front of it, moving unconsciously with the beat and listening to a party in denims telling her about his childhood. You would sneak glances at her over your glass, admiring her trim lines and the way her white teeth flashed when she laughed, and then you would walk out behind her and she'd glance back and give you some hip action and the rest would be all business. I wondered what had happened to Thelma.

I said, "I didn't know you were still seeing doctors."

"Ongoing thing, chum." Barry fingered the ashtray. "Until they pat me in my pasted-together face with the well-known instrument. I go in, say hello to the pretty nurse-receptionist—they're all pretty these days, and none of them dates patients—show the man in the white blazer

16

how my stump is doing, pick up my new prescription, and blow. Make an appointment for next week on your way out, Mr. Stackpole."

"Prescription for what?"

"Headaches, pal. You ever try to chew a piece of tinfoil with a fresh silver filling in a back tooth? That's my head when it's cold or rainy, or when it's muggy or snowing or when I flush the toilet and forget to jiggle the handle. Not that the aching ever goes away. It's there, like Muzak. Our skulls weren't built to accommodate steel plates."

"I've got a papercut on my trigger finger," I said. "Haven't shot anybody all week."

He grinned down at his drink. "Okay. No violins today."

We drank. The overhead light threw pale double shadows on the table.

"This dump remind you of someplace?" Barry asked.

"A high school cafeteria with ethyl added."

"There was a place in Saigon just after the Cambodia bugout. We got shitface there. I left for home the next day. What was it called?"

"Minh's."

"That sounds like it."

"They were all called Minh's," I said. "And it didn't look anything like this. There were candles on the walls and a fishnet behind the bar."

"I didn't say they looked alike. Half the clientele was Cong. They made your back crawl. You feel it?"

"At least twice a week, and in better places than this."

"What it looks like," he started, and stopped. "I did the program, you know."

"Program?"

"A-goddamn-A. Meetings in church basements and like you said high school crematoriums."

"Cafeterias," I said. "No, you were closer."

"All the meeting rooms look the same. Long tables like this and folding chairs and fluorescent lights and scrawny old ladies with rhinestone glasses and blond streaks in their hair, not at all what you expect of a burned-out alkie. It can't compare with a redwood bar and rosy light from a Budweiser sign and a juke and a twelve-year-old bartender in a red coat and bow tie who calls you sir and are you ready to go again. If they put the guys who design bars to work on the rooms where AA meets, we'd lick alcohol abuse in a month."

"Except for funny cocktail napkins. They can lose the funny cocktail napkins."

"Funny cocktail napkins are the key to the whole thing. That's the ridiculous note that makes the rest of the symphony sublime, like the flaw the Chinese used to build into their porcelains. Boxer shorts with evening dress. Without funny cocktail napkins the whole beautiful plan falls to shit."

"I can see you've given this a lot of thought."

"Mostly I've been sitting here wondering if I should blow off the top of my head like Hemingway or just climb into a warm tub and do a vent job on my wrists."

I gave that all the space it deserved, sipping my drink. "Any of this have to do with Irene?"

"No, I tried her first. When she didn't bore me to death I figured I was harder to kill than that. Maybe I'm all right. They say people who do it don't talk about it."

"They're wrong as usual. A thing like that generally takes a pep talk. This personal, or you want to make a statement?"

"Forget I said anything. Just another lush in love with his own funeral. Tell Irene I'm okay. Having hot flashes."

"Irene's gone."

"I forgot."

I was aware then of the room stirring. I've gone back over it since and I'm sure the patrons were moving before the first blow. That jungle sense again. Then the noise started, like gunshots, and I went over in my chair, knocking Barry out of his, which took some doing because he was sitting there loose like a sack of mud. But I hit the floor on top of him and clawed my gun out of its belt holster. There was a lot of yelling and running and someone in the room shouted something about the police in a proprietary tone and then I knew the noises weren't shots but the reports of a sledgehammer striking the heavy door.

4

"CAN'T BE A RAID," BARRY WAS MUTTERING. "THEY HIT the place last week."

"You can't trust cops. Can you walk?"

"Is my leg still on?"

I looked and told him it was. I leathered the gun and untangled my own legs from my folding chair and got a double handful of Barry's jacket and hauled him up with me. At least he was helping and not short on bones like some drunks I'd handled. The crowd, which had moved instinctively toward the door when the racket started, was now surging in the other direction as shreds of paneling began to fly. We moved with it. A yellow shirt with a Superfly haircut was standing in front of the window with a .45 pistol in one hand and a gold badge in the other, telling everyone to stay in his place and keep his hands in sight. He was one of the bunch I'd come in with. It's an old trick; get inside and if you're not out in ten minutes it's assumed you've observed a buy after hours and the time has come to go in with the hammers. He looked at me with Barry hanging on.

"Maybe next time you spend your mornings squeezing cantaloupes in Greektown," he said.

I said, "I've got to get my friend to a doctor. He's sick."

He glanced at Barry. The whites of the cop's eyes were bluish and he had an old burn scar on his right cheek, crackly looking like the skin of a roast duckling. Something fluttered across his features then. Recognition? Barry's picture appeared atop his column daily. The cop said, "He should do his drinking in better places."

The door came apart then with a noise like ripping cloth. I saw the bouncer go down with a plainclothesman kneeling on his back and more suits and uniforms tumbling through the torn space. A big sergeant had the bartender spread-eagled on his palms against the wall behind the bar and was reading him his rights with the bartender's gun screwed into the nape of its owner's neck. The cop in the yellow shirt moved his eyes that way. I hit him with the room.

It wasn't bad, considering I'd had to use my left while supporting Barry with my other arm. I caught him square on the corner of the jaw and he dropped like a ripe peach. The leather folder containing his badge flopped to the floor. I picked it up. He was lying on top of his gun but I didn't need that.

The invaders had fanned out and started breaking the crowd into sections with that combination of arm-wrenching and bellowing through bared teeth that always seems to wind up "proceeded to separate the offenders" on the report. I put Barry's head through the open window and shoved at his rump with both hands until he got the idea. Climbing over he banged an ankle against the window

21

frame with a loud crack and I winced, but he kept going and I remembered that ankle was fiberglass. I followed him out.

The cool air smelled funny after the smoke and fumes inside. We were standing on a fire escape that still had some red paint clinging to the rust, over an alley with a police cruiser parked in it splashing red and blue light over the brick and asphalt. We started down. Barry supported himself on the leprous railing.

"Freeze! Police!"

I looked at a shiny visor at the bottom of the stairs with a square beardless jaw underneath and a revolver gawking at me in two outstretched hands. I flashed the gold buzzer.

"You in tandem?" I barked.

The barrel pointed skyward. "Sir?"

"Oh, for—you got a partner?"

"No, sir."

"Go around front and give them a hand. I've got an injured officer here. Move!"

He hesitated for less than five seconds, then obeyed, his footsteps swallowed in darkness. He was a month out of the academy, tops.

Barry and I skidded the rest of the way down the iron stairs and went up the alley behind the uniform. The usual crowd of civic observers was gathered in front questioning the parentage of the officers escorting the first of the hand-cuffed parties out the door into the county wagon. I let the folder and badge slide down my leg into the mill of feet and helped Barry into my car on the passenger's side. I was losing him fast now that the physical part was over. Getting the door closed without sacrificing any more of his limbs involved propping him up with one hand and then with-drawing it and slamming the door fast, like closing a closet

22

full of bowling balls. If the latch didn't hold I'd be scraping him off the street after the first turn. As I browsed the front of the Olds through the crowd into the traffic lane I glimpsed a big black detective in a green corduroy suit frowning at the car in the rearview mirror. Probably looking for a busted taillight or an expired plate. They are always working. •

5

TRANSPORTING BARRY FROM THE CAR INTO THE HOUSE was one for the Egyptians. I opened the garage and drove in and left him dozing in the seat while I got the side door open and turned on the lights. He tumbled out when I pulled on his door but I caught him under the arms. I locked my hands around his chest and tugged. He kept saying, "Wait, wait a minute." I didn't have a drunk's minute; no one has, except another drunk. I backwalked him to the door, leaving a double black line from his heels on the concrete. He was ten pounds lighter than I, but he kept wanting to melt through my grip and I had to stop every couple of seconds to hike him up. His jacket and shirt were bunched under his arms. The bee-sting I had between my shoulder blades from the long drive north spread to my discs and the bad Scotch was thrumming in my skull. Walker, you need a vacation.

The trip through the kitchen into the living room was more of the same. I let him down once to rest and get some bedding on the sofa. He was snoring when I came back. Finally I sat him on the cushions and lowered his top half and raised his legs parallel and peeled off his shoes. I had the right one off before I remembered that one wouldn't make any difference to him. The artificial foot was a glossy flesh color and looked like a shoe tree, attached by a ball and socket to the leg. I wondered if he was in the habit of taking the leg off when he slept, then decided it didn't matter and spread the blanket over him. Tomorrow I'd start taking home stray cats. The neighborhood brats would call me Crazy Amos and throw things when I pedaled past jangling my bicycle bell.

I popped three aspirins, switched off all the lights and locked all the doors and turned on the shower. My suit smelled of cigarette smoke and Toledo. I hung it up for the cleaners and looked at my face in the clouded mirror and then killed the shower and went to bed. I'd have fallen asleep in the stall and drowned under the spray, but that didn't worry me half so much as not being able to think of a good reason not to.

It was still dark out when I heard bumping noises in the living room. I lay listening for a while, the way you do. The luminous dial on the electric alarm clock said I'd been asleep forty-five minutes. It didn't feel like any more than forty-four. I got up and fumbled into my robe and slippers. The light found Barry standing in the middle of the room with his knees against the coffee table and a litter of the usual coffee table junk around his feet. His hair stuck out in spikes and half his shirttail hung down under his jacket like a comic drunk's in a nightclub act. His eyes weren't comic. He looked scared as hell.

"Where's the bathroom?"

"That way. Want help?"

25

He shook his head and turned and wobbled the way I'd pointed. While he was inside I went into the kitchen and plugged in the coffeemaker. It had been perking for a couple of minutes when the bathroom door opened. He had tucked in his shirt and smoothed back his hair and his eyes weren't so scared. He saw me sitting in the easy chair and said, "I guess we did some talking before."

"Don't draw that old gag on me, Barry," I said. "You remember the serial number on your family's first television set."

"Last night's foggy. Or was it this morning? I thought maybe I dreamed it. Something about a berserk P.I. committing two felonies to spare a friend a night in the house of doors."

"You got a high opinion of yourself. They weren't going to lock you in and let me fly."

"It's been a long time since I saw you in action. You looked good."

"You didn't. You still don't."

He passed it. "Is that coffee I smell? As I recall you brew a decent cup."

"These days so does everyone. Have a seat." I got up.

"Can I use your phone? I have to call Irene, let her know where I landed."

"Irene's smoke, brother. Powdered. Put an egg on her shoe and beat it."

He got it then. I wasn't sure he ever would. "Good for her," he said. "She took a lot more than she had to."

"Screw that. Sooner or later every guy gets the Irene he deserves. I'll fetch the Joe."

"Joe." He smiled. "Anyone ever tell you you talk like an RKO soundtrack?"

"Old movies talked like everyone else. I just never changed. I've got plenty of aspirins," I added.

"They're just candy to me."

I poured two cups black and brought them out on a tray with napkins. He was sitting on the sofa amid the tangled bedclothes. I took the chair and we sat sipping and not talking. If they don't want to you can't make them. Ticking, the old clock made a double knocking noise like a man walking with one wooden shoe. It had been the first expensive present my grandfather had bought for his mother. He had given up a new set of wooden wheels for his Model T to get it. I didn't know where either of them was buried.

My guest drained his cup and set it down with a rattle. He wasn't any less drunk, just steadier about it. "I think I can sleep now," he said. "To hell with all this gab about caffeine. It's just reverse publicity on the part of Brazil, like Hitler burning the Reichstag and blaming it on the communists."

There was nothing in that for me, and so I finished my coffee and put the tray away and washed the cups. He was under the covers again when I came back through the living room.

"When you want ears," I said.

"Yeah."

I went back to bed. I heard him moving around on the sofa for a little. Then I didn't.

I woke at ten with the sun in my face and no memory at first of what had happened a few hours earlier. I'm not Barry. It came back to me in little polite waves while I was sitting on the edge of the bed wondering what day it might be and if I should dress for home or the office. Finally I

27

decided it was Sunday and shuffled into the bathroom for a hot shower.

When I came out wearing my old house clothes, the sofa was deserted. Barry had folded the sheet and blanket and stacked the pillow on top of them on one of the arms. The stuff that had fallen off the coffee table had been replaced.

In the kitchen doorway I froze at the sight of the scrap of paper on the table.

The table was cheap gray printed Formica over softwood, admirable for concealing coffee rings and setting off notes like this one and others. One I remembered particularly had been written on yellow stationery with a spray of orange flowers in one corner: "Amos—It didn't work out. C." There hadn't been enough words to make it hard to remember after nine years. Just five, six if you counted the initial. Which were as many weeks as had seen me haunting Detroit Police Headquarters, General Service division, Missing Persons detail, until the summons came. Walker *vs*. Walker. That was gone, but the note was still somewhere in the house, waiting to pop up unexpectedly while I was looking for something else, like a frightening picture in a child's book that he can't resist flipping through.

This one was even shorter. It had been written with one of the thick black markers I use for reminders to myself. "Sorry and thanks." The printing was Barry's. You learn to print fast when most of your stuff comes in over the telephone and you want to be able to read it later. He had used a white paper napkin that looked as if it had ridden around in a pocket for a while, all sharp creases, with funny pictures on both sides.

6

I DIDN'T SEE HIM AGAIN FOR ALMOST A MONTH. MY OLD angel, Midwest Confidential Life, Automobile, & Casualty, had a lock on my time for most of that period, which I spent babysitting some fairly sophisticated rental surveillance equipment in a utility closet next door to an apartment in Belleville. The woman was claiming permanent disability on an accident involving a top-heavy file cabinet and her back, but you wouldn't know it by the several hundred feet of film I took of her dancing her way back from the elevators after an all-night date or the eleven hours of taped telephone recaps of erotic encounters with a quality control foreman at the GM assembly plant in Westland. It was strictly leverage. No Wayne County jury in these times was going to find for a Fortune 500 company with branch offices in six states over a fifty-year-old file clerk with a mother in a convalescent home. I was buying my client an out-of-court settlement.

I got a lot of reading done in there with the mops and

cleaning fluids and decibel-level indicators, mostly funny caper novels by a writer who thought crooked cops were more lovable than honest private investigators, and the *News* and *Free Press*. Barry ran a long series in his column on the lifestyles of various local public servants, contrasting them with those of the assistant administrators who did most of their work, and it got pretty funny, especially when he described the office of a high official and mentioned the new silk wallpaper that couldn't be cleaned and so when it got soiled had to come down, all several thousand dollars' worth of it. But when election time came and went they'd all be right where they were now, papering the walls with virgins' hair or something equally rare and costly. To understand the workings of Detroit's government in a recession you have to read a book about Boss Tweed with James Brown shrieking on the stereo.

Which was just another measure in a composition as old as Cadillac's bones. Barry's writing was getting back some of its old sting, and he had a fresh picture at the top of the column that showed more of his age but none of the fright I had seen in my house. His kind of square good looks were coming back into fashion. There was a cosmetic surgeon in town who had to smile every time he saw the shot. After the explosion he had had to reconstruct that face from photographs and then graft skin over the seams. He hadn't got it quite right, of course. They never do. It had taken getting used to, like a new typeface on a newspaper you've been reading for years.

The owner of the face walked into my toy office on West Grand River while I was filing my copy of the report to the insurance company in my battered green cabinet. He had on a beige linen blazer, fashionably rumpled, over an open-necked champagne-colored silk shirt and gray trousers and black shoes with perforations in the toes. No tie. It had been years since I'd seen him wear one. Ten, in fact. The occasion had been my wedding.

He looked around, at the veteran desk and the dusty Venetian blinds and the mismatched file cabinets and the rug that was just something to cover the boards and the general no threat of an invasion of privacy by photographers from *Forbes*. "Joint looks the same. The wallpaper's new."

"It's just paper. I'm not running for office this year." I squawked the drawer shut and grasped his good left hand. He had the kind of grip you don't get punching keys all day.

"Thought you'd like that one," he said. "There's talk of subpoenaing my notes for that whole series. Another grand jury's sniffing around the City-County Building."

"They'll get how far with you?"

"The usual. I'm packing a toothbrush in my wallet these days."

"What brings the boy reporter out this way?"

"I've been trying off and on to call you for a couple of weeks. The girl at your service is quite a conversationalist. Did you know she was once married in Oklahoma?"

"Nearly everyone has been, though not necessarily in Oklahoma. I've been working. I do that when I'm not scraping friends out of blind pigs and piling up priors."

"Must've been two other guys. Thirsty?"

"Depends on who's buying."

"The Press Club gave me back my card. That's how good I've been lately."

"Toss me my hat," I said.

We took a cab to the brick building in the demilitarized zone a block over from the city's two warring newspapers.

On the way he made a bet with the driver on the Lions in next Sunday's exhibition game. He knew every hack in the city. I never could figure how he got along in Detroit without owning a car. "What would I get?" he'd asked once. "Chevy? Everyone'd think I was in hock to GM. Ford? Chrysler? The same. I buy a Jap machine and they ride me out of town on a rusty axle. Going public here is like being married to a jealous tramp with a butcher knife."

At the door he fed his computer card into a slot, waited for the buzz, and led the way inside. He caught me looking around for armed guards and said, "We're important as all hell, we scribblers. A feature writer gets a coconut bounced off his skull in Beirut Tuesday, and Wednesday the *News* springs for automatic coconut-catchers. Most of the scoops in here wouldn't know a satchel bomb if it landed in their margaritas."

"So they wouldn't. I didn't know it was required."

A kid waiter in a vest and black bow tie showed us to a horseshoe-shaped booth upholstered in red vinyl. Barry handed him the menus, explaining that we weren't eating, and ordered a Coke. I did the same.

"Don't do that to me," Barry pleaded. "You make me feel like the idiot uncle everyone humors."

"Bourbon and branch, then," I said. When we were alone: "You've been dry now how long?"

"Eighteen days. I started tapering off right after I left your place. You handed me a scare, pal."

"How is it?"

"Dull as hell. Like going back to black-and-white when you're used to full color. Most of the friends I thought I had aren't. The ones I still have tell me they liked me better sloshed. I've started going to meetings again, though, and that's sort of interesting. Sit back and listen to the mating calls."

"Any of them yours?"

"Not this year. Oh, they come on to me, the divorced mothers who didn't open a bottle until the kids were in bed and the secretaries who used to come floating back to their desks from lunch. As a snorting hunk of raw masculinity I'm told I don't spoil too many breakfasts, and women who have given up saucing get that rabbity look, like ex-smokers eyeing a buffet table. But a relationship like that has all the suspense of blind lovers strolling hand in hand. You know they're going to walk in front of a truck. You just don't know when."

"I guess the head still hurts," I said.

"Sometimes I think it's what sees me through."

The waiter came and set down our drinks and went. Barry took the plastic straw out of his and tapped a drop off it on the edge of his glass and ditched it in the ashtray. He nodded at the waiter's back. "They're getting younger."

"No, we're just pulling away."

"We're not even middle-aged," he said.

"Age is a sliding scale. You want to talk about something or just shoot clouds? I feel like I'm fielding flies here."

He sipped Coke. He was sitting with his back to the wall, watching the drinkers at the bar making airplanes of their hands and the neat white-shirted bartender sneaking looks at himself in the mirror behind the stacked glasses. "I'm taking a leave of absence starting tomorrow. Six months, maybe a year. Jed Dutt will fill in on the column."

"The book?"

"Yeah. I need the distraction, take my mind off the crisp

33

clean clatter of ice in a glass. I can do the column drunk but a book is something else. It requires concentration."

"I guess there are worse reasons to write."

"None I can think of. But I'm desperate. Also I want to get the thing written. I don't care if it never sees print, which it probably won't. Problem with newspaper work is you can never say you've finished anything. You settle for what you've got because it's two minutes to deadline—it's always two minutes to deadline, no matter how early you start—and then you turn it loose and it flutters for a few hours and then it's something you throw away, what's that filthy newspaper doing on my nice clean slipcover? But when you've done a book you've finished something. No one can take that from you."

"Well, good luck with it."

He smiled then. It was the old Stackpole smile, folding deep lines at the corners of his eyes. Welcome back. "I wasn't fishing for platitudes. You're maybe the only person I can tell all this to without getting dumb questions back like what's the book about. Come to think of it, for a sleuth you're not too curious."

"I'm on a break. Does it matter what the book's about?"

"It does and it doesn't."

I dug out my pad and pencil, wrote something, tore off the page, and gave it to him. He looked at it and I said, "That's a book editor I met once. You know the firm. You can mention my name if you want. It won't do you any good."

"I bet it will." He put the sheet in his breast pocket. Then he picked up his glass and rattled the ice. "We haven't done our toast in a long time. I miss it."

I lifted mine. "Cold steel."

"Hot lead." He sipped, made a face, and set the glass down. "Oh, Keith Porter's dead."

"Keith Porter?" I was lighting a cigarette. I blew smoke at the ceiling and flipped the match into the ashtray.

"That's right, you never met. He shipped home about the time you and I got to know each other. He was a cameraman with the Press Corps in Nam. He was in Lebanon last year and El Salvador the year before that, with CBS. All those bullets and car bombs. His wife wrote me from Colorado. He electrocuted himself with a power drill in his workshop."

I shrugged.

He rattled his ice. " 'The death of friends, or death of every brilliant eye that made a catch in the breath.' "

"Yours?"

"Yeats. I came across it in a book the other day while I was looking for something else, you know the way you do. Can't get rid of it."

"What's it mean?"

"The lights are blinking out, buddy. Every night there are a few less than there were the night before." He set down the glass sharply. "Let's go out in the sun."

I killed the rest of my whiskey and we went out, leaving half his Coke on the table. There was some sun, blinking milk-eyed through shifting thin sheets of cloud. We shook hands in front of the building and I stood there waiting for a cab and watched him step into a parking structure on his way back to the *News* building. His limp was barely noticeable.

If I had it to do again I wouldn't let go of his hand.

35

7

THE LAST WEEK OF SEPTEMBER BROUGHT IN ONE OF THOSE airless spells we get just before the first nip of autumn, the kind that glues your shirt to your back and clouds the sky with barbecue smoke one last time before the grills go back into the garage under the snow shovels. No one complains about it, much. It's like an old man cursing on his deathbed. Then one night you go to sleep turning your pillow to the cool side and wake up to find a skin of frost on your bedroom window, and for the next eight months it's galoshes and flannel. No measure of time seems briefer or harder to recapture in the dead gray of January. But while it's here you enjoy the women in their thin cotton dresses and that last week of complacent certainty you're going to live forever.

It was cookie season. The day after I left Barry a man who identified himself as an editor with a local magazine called demanding I investigate the personal finances of a writer who wrote uncomplimentary books about Detroit.

36

He was certain the writer was in the pay of the Baltimore Chamber of Commerce. I just got through hanging up in his face when the telephone rang again and I advised a woman who claimed her neighbor had deliberately run over her cat to try the Humane Society. She asked if I'd pay for the call.

Two days later a woman in her sixties, with marcelled bright orange hair and blue-tinted glasses, wobbled into the office carrying an earthenware pot with three feet of marijuana plant growing out of it. She said it belonged to her tenant and she wanted me to stake out the empty apartment across the hall until he got back from California and make a citizen's arrest. I asked her why she didn't go to the police.

"I went," she said. "They sent me here."

"Who'd you talk to?"

"A lieutenant named Alderdyce."

I doodled a caricature of a baboon on my message pad. "Why not make the arrest yourself?"

"I don't have time. I have to cook and clean and cut the grass. I used to have a gardener that came in twice a week but I had to let him go. Neighbors complained about his language. You're not a swearing man, are you?"

I referred her to another lieutenant named Fitzroy and held the door for her and the plant.

The telephone went off again the following Monday while I was flipping butts from my ashtray into the clanking blades of the antique fan.

"Let me guess," I told the receiver. "Eva Braun's living in your neighbor's gazebo."

"What? Is this A. Walker Investigations?"

The voice was a not unpleasant masculine rumble. I said I was Walker and the voice said, "This is Arthur Rooney of the law firm of Walgren and Rooney. If you're free tomorrow morning I'd like to discuss retaining your services in a matter involving a client."

I sat up a little straighter. "I've heard of your firm, Mr. Rooney. Are your offices still in the National Bank Building?"

"They are. Sixteenth floor. Can I expect you at nine?"

"Let me check my calendar." I held my hand over the mouthpiece and blew some loose ash off my desk. "I seem to be free, Mr. Rooney."

"Very well."

It's a strange living. The space cadets are enough to drive you to barber college and when you do draw a sane one, nine times out of ten his story will be so familiar you'll want to skin Form B slash 27 off the stack and ask him to fill in the blanks. But you sit and listen and try not to squeak your chair and agree that Billy shouldn't have left home in his father's Dodge with the mortgage money or that the last people who rented the house on Vernor were insensitive to turn loose a sick donkey on the living room rug and then skip out on the last two months' rent. You take your money up front like a bus driver and say thank you for coming in, I'll call when I have something. Step to the rear, please.

The temperatures broke during the night. The morning air was brisk and damp and light fall jackets were starting to appear downtown. I parked my car—it was humming like a Swiss waiter now, thanks to Midwest Confidential and a new carburetor and crossover—and walked two blocks to the National Bank Building in Cadillac Square, carrying my brown topcoat, which needed a press. A pneumatic hammer was stuttering somewhere in the direction of Gratiot. Everyone was working today.

38

I almost put on the topcoat when I hit the lobby. The air conditioning was on, as it would be until the calendar told them to turn it off; federally funded institutions are all the same. I straightened my tie and smoothed back my hair with the help of my reflection in the slick marble facing on the wall, checked the directory just for luck, and rode the elevator to the sixteenth floor in the company of two young security guards and a white-haired woman in a tailored blue suit. When the doors opened the woman and I got out together.

The reception area was hidden behind a smoked-glass partition with WALGREN & ROONEY stenciled on the door in silver letters. I held the door for the woman, who nodded at me quickly with a tight red-lipsticked smile and a flicker of curiosity in her gray eyes. She paused before going in. "Are you here for one of the junior partners?"

I said I had a nine o'clock with Rooney. She covered up well, went through the door and set her purse down on the curved reception desk and scissored long red nails through a pad with an alligator cover. She wasn't as old as her white hair suggested, maybe forty. Silver high-heeled sandals climbed trim ankles and as she bent forward the back of her snug skirt pulled taut across a handsome backside. She turned her head and caught me looking. She smiled again.

"You're Amos Walker?"

I said I was. She went on smiling and looking at me and lifted the receiver off a yellow telephone intercom. "Good morning, Mr. Rooney. Mr. Walker is here. Yes, sir." She hung up. "Mr. Rooney will be right out."

I thanked her and wandered over to read some framed civic improvement citations on the pastel wall opposite her station. In the glass of one I saw her watching me from behind the desk. I was the meat of the menopause set now.

A couple of parties in dark suits carrying brown leather briefcases came in from the elevators while I was standing there, asked if the mail was in yet, and walked down the short hall on the other side of the desk without once glancing in my direction. If I was waiting I wasn't worth it and if I was worth it I wouldn't be standing around no reception rooms.

After five minutes or so a tall man with very broad shoulders under a gray pinstriped suit came around the corner of the desk with his right hand out. "Mr. Walker? I'm Arthur Rooney. Good of you to come."

I grasped the hand. It was warm and dry and his grip was very firm. In corporate law it better be. Whatever shanty Irish there might have been in Arthur Rooney's genes had been carefully scraped off and carted away in the dead of night. His face was square, evenly tanned, and his brown hair, tinged with silver, came forward in a crisp shelf over his brows. His eyes were a level amber, wolf's eyes. They were the only thing remotely predatory about him, to look at. He had a blue silk pocket square to match a necktie with a knot the size of a grapefruit and a deep dimple underneath. Why do they wear them if they don't know how to tie them?

He asked the receptionist to hold his calls and we walked down the hall and around the corner into a large office with oak on the walls and a window looking down on the square. Far down, dwarfed by the glass towers surrounding it, the cupola of the old county building stood lifting her ruffled skirts clear of the asphalt and concrete.

"The old lady of Randolph Street," Rooney said, thrusting his hands deep in his trouser pockets. "When I was with the circuit court I kept my office there after everyone else had moved into the City-County Building. They didn't care about cost when she was built. You can bet some public servant squeezed himself a tidy little retirement out of the overrun. It was worth it. This less-is-more crap has got out of hand. Stand an ice cube tray on end and call it architecture."

"Why'd you leave the bench?"

"I gag easy. No one calls me Judge after he's known me five minutes. It's on the letterhead, but who reads letterheads? Sit down, Mr. Walker. Coffee?"

I said I was fine and inserted my hips into a chrome scoop chair with padding that was too coarse and grainy to be anything but leather and crossed my legs. Rooney cocked a hip onto the near corner of his desk and folded his hands around the bent knee. He was one of those.

"I'll get right to it," he said. "I called you because you came recommended by a couple of lawyers whose opinions I respect and because you're a friend of Barry Stackpole's."

"This is about Barry?"

"As you may know, Walgren and Rooney is of counsel to the Detroit *News* in matters relating to copyright and libel. This office has advised Stackpole on the several occasions he has been summoned to testify in civil and criminal cases linked to his reporting. That he has seen fit to ignore that advice and spend a number of weeks behind bars and an unestimated amount of his personal income on fines and costs in consequence is entirely his business."

"It is about Barry."

"I understand you've been in contact with him within the past week."

"Just about a week," I said.

"Did he seem in any way troubled? Persecuted?"

I got out my pack and raised my eyebrows. He nodded. I dealt myself a smoke and we did the business of me looking for a place to put the match and him scooping a small glass tray out of a drawer. I balanced it on my knee and said, "You told me over the telephone you wanted to hire my services. Why don't let's talk about which ones you want and then we'll discuss what Barry was wearing last time I saw him and how often he changed the sock on his artificial foot. Or not, if we decide I'm not what you're looking for in an investigator."

He pursed his lips, looked at his hands on his knee, unfolded them and slid off the desk and walked around behind it and sat down. He looked older there and a lot harder, the way he must have looked presiding in court. We weren't lodge brothers anymore.

"You'd have made a better prosecutor than a defense lawyer," he said. "It's that passion for specifics that wins convictions. All right. Stackpole is missing. He took leave from the *News* a week ago and now his editors are unable to locate him. I thought that as his friend you might know where he is or, failing that, that you might know where to start looking. In either case our client will recompense you for your time."

"I guess you tried his house."

"It's locked up tight. His phone has been disconnected by his request and the post office is holding his mail. The bars he frequents have been notified to hang an eye out for him and to call this office when he appears. So far they haven't called."

It was okay until he got to the part about hanging an eye out. Speech is like clothes and you don't wear tennis togs to the office. I guess he thought it made him regular folks, like a candidate for president has his picture taken in his shirtsleeves spitballing with workers at a construction site, hardhat and patent leather pumps. To which, nuts. I said, "What makes him more popular now than he was five days ago?"

He ran a polished nail along the edge of his big desk. "Let's just say some people want to talk to him."

"Uh-huh." I took one last drag, squashed out my butt, set the ashtray on the desk, and stood, refolding my top-coat. "Thanks for the dope on the old county building, Mr. Rooney. I'll be clanking along now."

"Oh, sit down, Walker. Our work isn't so different after all. You get into the business of client privilege and pretty soon you're demanding a writ before you'll tell someone the time by his own clock."

I sat. He unsheathed a slim pen from the onyx holder on the desk and tapped it.

"The governor has ordered a grand jury investigation into the personal finances of certain city officials. The probe will touch on some specifics Stackpole covered in his recent series. Tuesday—the day after you were seen drinking with him in the bar of the Detroit Press Club—the jury issued a subpoena for his records involving the series. When he failed to produce them by the end of the week the jury called for their seizure and summoned him to appear. He has until Monday to do so or be found in contempt.

"In the past, the media have found it in their best inter-est to encourage a reporter to lie low until the end of the grand jury session. In this case, however, the *News* will be fined a thousand dollars for each day Stackpole fails to appear. The editors have therefore directed me on my ad-vice to put you on his scent."

Put you on his scent. There it was again, like a Dead

End Kid in a three-piece suit. I said, "It stinks, Mr. Rooney, if you don't mind my saying so. Barry had to have been served, which is a little tougher than getting the leopard down off Kilimanjaro. Even if he weren't, he's too good a reporter not to know all this is going on. If he hasn't shown before now he has reasons."

"He was served, depend on it. His flair for theatrics is well known to this firm, and it's just possible he's waiting for the last moment to come forward like Houdini from his watery grave. The other possibility, that he has no such intentions and is somehow unaware of the seriousness of the situation, is why I asked you here. A thousand dollars a day won't shut down the presses at the *News*; they spend that much on paper clips. But these are parlous times for print journalism, which in the public trust ranks somewhere between politicians and used car salesmen. Even television journalism places higher, and that's a contradiction in terms. The editors would like to project the image of cooperation with the authorities, particularly in such matters as incendiary as municipal corruption.

"Put bluntly, Mr. Walker, the First Amendment has its tits in a wringer on this one and your hand is on the handle."

"Me, Becky Sue Mattressback, from Rattlesnake Bend, Utah, in the driver's seat of democracy." I lit another pill. "Walgren and Rooney has been in practice for a couple of years. The first thing a legal firm does after airing its shingle and ordering stationery is put an investigation agency on retainer, preferably one of the big stainless steel jobs with all the options. The only thing I've got going for me is I'm a friend of Barry's. You don't strike me as a hunch player, Mr. Rooney."

"I'm not. When I was told Stackpole hangs around with

a private detective I put that agency we retain on you. I have your war record and your work history going back to your apprenticeship with Dale Leopold at Apollo Investigations."

The smoke from my cigarette was bothering him. He leaned back in his chair and tilted his head a little to keep it out of his eyes. I didn't do anything to help him.

"It's been a long time," he said. "I was in criminal law then and I've handled plenty of cases since. Walker is a common name. I didn't make the connection until I read your name on that old police report, identifying you as sole witness to Leopold's killing.

"I was Earl North's attorney, Walker. I defended the man who killed your partner."

I said, "I know."

8

THE SMOKE GOT TO BE TOO MUCH FOR HIM FINALLY. HE rose and walked over to the window and looked down on the old lady of Randolph Street. It was one of those dramatic moments they teach you to milk in law school—forget the statutes and precedents and bastard Latin, it's housewives and credit plumbers you'll be trying to impress. He said, "I wasn't going to bring it up. When you didn't say anything or show you recognized me I thought it was best things stayed buried."

"The only thing that got buried was Dale Leopold."

"North was at the end of his tether. He had a bad marriage, a job he hated, and an affair he couldn't end because he didn't have the character and because he didn't have the character he was convinced he was less than a man. When he found out his wife had put a detective on him he started carrying a gun. The Freudians could tell you all about that, draw diagrams. One day he stopped and turned."

"Bullet pierced the right ventricle, death was instantaneous, the report said." I tipped half an inch of ash into the tray. "Only it wasn't, really. It always takes a few seconds. Dale had time enough to realize what had happened. He wasn't carrying. You hardly ever need a gun on the wandering spouse detail."

"You were, though," said Rooney. He had turned from the window. "I think that was the factor that swung the jury's sympathy to our diminished capacity plea, your wounding him after Leopold went down."

"The black shoulder sling was a sweet touch. Yours, I bet."

"It's just a job, Walker, sometimes not so nice to look at. Cases like that are why I went into corporate law after I took off the robes. I thought it might be cleaner. It's not. You deal with a higher class of criminal, but a crook in pinstripes and a rep tie is still a crook. I suppose you hate my guts."

"I don't hate anyone's guts, Mr. Rooney. It's a waste of good emotion."

"Next you'll claim you weren't the anonymous character who kept sending North postcards on the anniversary of the shooting. He wanted me to get a court order to stop you, but by then I wasn't his lawyer anymore."

"If he's still getting them, they're not from me." I killed my stub. "You're not throwing me work because you feel bad about having helped spring a murderer. Guilt doesn't work in this office. It clashes with the thousand-dollar rug."

"Definitely not. Don't misunderstand me. I'm not apologizing for giving an accused party the representation to which the Constitution entitles him. If the case came across my desk tomorrow I'd handle it the same way." He took his place behind the desk again and resumed tapping the

47

pen. "I remember being impressed with your testimony on the stand. It took me two days and three expert witnesses to defuse its effect on the jury. Nothing I've read over the past couple of days has changed my conviction that you're a fairly solid individual and an honest man with some sort of personal integrity. Granted, you have a frightening capacity for liquor and for smart-mouthing your way into deep shit, but there are worse faults and I like a man who wears the ones he has up front. *Plus* you know Stackpole. *Plus* you make a religion of keeping confidences, and this is just the sort of thing that wild-eyed harridan the *Free Press* would admire to slather over its front page: '*News* Columnist Evades Grand Jury.'"

"Someone ought to analyze this team thing," I mused. "Throw two newspapers into a pit with the smell of blood all around and even the briefcases start waving pennants and chanting slogans. Say I grab this bone and I find Barry, which you've never tried to do or you wouldn't be talking about it like it's already done, and he doesn't want to come back, which he won't or he would have already. What then?"

He stopped tapping. "Are we speaking hypothetically, or do you know where he is?"

"You've been breathing that legal air too long, Mr. Rooney. Real people don't talk around a corkscrew."

"So *you* say." He smiled grimly at his little joke. "Well, either way you would have to bring him forward or report his whereabouts. Otherwise a contempt case could be made against you for harboring, if the jury wanted to get ugly."

I said, "That's law. You and I both know there's not much law in it. Anyway, I've done jail. I could do it again."

"It's been my experience that people who say they're

willing to go to jail have never been to jail. But I think you mean it. If you would arrange a meeting with Stackpole I would consider your responsibility discharged."

"I set up a meet, you show up with court-appointed officers and park him in protective custody, read that hoosegow."

He fondled his pen a few seconds longer. The Freudians would have had fun with that, too; they spoil everything. Then he socked it back into its holder.

"I won't insult you by insisting my word is good," he said. "Sitting on that elevated seat gives you a perspective on the legal profession you don't get in Ethics 101. Have Stackpole contact me. After that whatever decision he makes will be his alone. I might add that I haven't made this many concessions since I last set foot in a courtroom."

"Welcome to the real world, Mr. Rooney."

"The one I've been living in is no seminary. You'll do it?"

"I'll shake it and see what falls out. Good reporters know how to fill in their tracks, and Barry's the best I know in a town full of Joe Pulitzers."

He laid his hand on the telephone intercom. "I'll have my secretary draw you a check. You require three days' fee in advance, I believe. Maybe you'll want to give some of it to Dale Leopold's widow."

"She married her dermatologist and they moved the kids to Houston. I need it more than they do. It's just a job, like you said."

"Helen, make out a check to Mr. Walker for seven-fifty? Thanks." He pegged the receiver. "I'm glad to hear it. I was afraid you'd be one of these tiresome knights-errant."

"Knights can always eat their horses," I said.

Dale Leopold. Not a big man, but he looked it until you got close, which no one did because he was a little hard of hearing from the police firing range and yelled everything. Formerly Sergeant Leopold of Missing Persons detail, General Service division, Detroit Police Department, retired on a medical because of his hearing. A head-buster from war days when the 4-Fs used to swarm into the beer gardens on East Jefferson and whistle at the servicemen in town on passes in their crisp uniforms and brush haircuts and the squad had to come in and sit on their faces until the MPs arrived. Dale Leopold of the flinty cops' eyes and brittle gray fringe that ended exactly where his creased brown fedora began. All chest and gut and no hips. Not a nice man but a good one. Two years out of uniform he could stroll into any squad room in the state and help himself to coffee without a break in the conversation around him, or could until Vietnam ended and the rooms filled with ice-eyed young men with longish hair and hard flat stomachs. He'd fit in again now that they were older and softer outside, but inside hard as tile. But he was bones.

I rode down with him in the elevator that day and we walked through the chill lobby and out into the warmer autumn air and got into the car together and drove away from there. Funny how you can love someone without liking him and work with him and love someone else in another way without liking her and not have a marriage worth telling anyone about. After the note I didn't remember much of the meetings with lawyers, but I remembered Sergeant Leopold in his blue uniform shirt starched platter-stiff, borrowing detectives' desks to fill out his mountains of forms and shouting in that dead cops' chant that everything was being done, etc. Catherine Walker, Sergeant

Leopold. Five-seven and self-conscious about her height, stoops a little walking, weight one-twenty, black hair, brown eyes. Pouts when she's thinking. Dimple, right cheek, chin slightly square, white half-inch scar left side of forehead at the hairline. Fell out of a tree and landed on a red wagon when she was ten, Sergeant Leopold, she was a tomboy. Appendectomy scar, right abdomen. Birthmark on her right hip, but you won't need that in your report, Sergeant Leopold. Nothing? Okay, I'll be back tomorrow. Thanks for your time.

Missing Persons, with pictures of teenage runaways on the walls, high school shots; substitute a ratty sweatshirt for the ruffled blouse, dirty the hair a little, paint a sneer on the smiling lips—that's our little Sheryl, Officer. She made the Honor Roll last year. A fat black woman sitting beside a desk listening to a young patrolman with pimples telling her a little boy answering her son's description just floated to the surface of an undrained swimming pool in an apartment complex in Taylor, the woman watching his lips closely as if trying to read them. The quietest conversation I had ever overheard. Six weeks of that, then the summons, and then the call to Sergeant Leopold, yanking the report. "Sorry to hear it, Walker. Come see me when it's done. No, not here. This is my last week. Got a pencil?"

A brown fedora lying bottomside up against the curb, a bald head on the asphalt, gray eyes growing soft and muddy in a slack face. Rule One: Never get emotionally involved in a case. Rules Two through Ten: Observe Rule One.

Jed Dutt was standing in front of the elevator when I got off at Barry Stackpole's floor in the *News* building. He had a lanky frame he did nothing whatever to maintain and a backward-leaning stance that accentuated his slight pot, a tallish man who combed his hair back from a thinning widow's peak and wore half-glasses on the end of his long nose and polka-dot bow ties and gray wool sweaters with patches on the elbows. He looked like a professor in a small college. He pulled a long freckled hand out of his pocket and laid it in my palm.

"Glad you called first," he said, withdrawing it. "All hell's busting loose up here, as when isn't it?"

I pocketed the tag the female guard had given me in the lobby. "As if I could get into Fort Horace Greeley without calling first. What sort of hell?"

"Heat."

We were walking down a paneled corridor hung with prize-winning articles and photographs in frames toward the partitioned cubicles where the columnists and department editors worked. Dutt's vocabulary didn't go with his place on the Entertainment desk. He had been police beat until the chief barred him from headquarters for taking the chief's picture dozing on the sofa in his office. Now he interviewed blonde TV sitcom starlets and strung-out forties band singers on tour. Just by way of transition, his first column as Barry's replacement had been about a crooner in his sixties appearing that weekend at the Hyatt Regency in Dearborn who had got his start four decades earlier with the help of a free-lance entrepreneur named Willie the Hammer.

The farther we went the noisier it got. A white-haired editor I recognized was standing in the opening of Barry's cubicle, reading the Bill of Rights from memory and tapping out the punctuation on the quilted chest of a large fat man in a tight brown suit and a gray felt hat with the brim turned up all around. The fat man was yelling something back and waving a folded length of paper while a trim young black man in a Wayne County Deputy Sheriff's uniform stood off to one side with his hands on his belt, jaw working at a lump of gum. He was waiting for a lull and didn't look in any too much of a hurry to get one. They had attracted the same small crowd of bored interested non-involved reporters that a fire in a steel wastebasket draws at two hours to deadline.

I put on my cop's voice. "What the hell is this? You're drowning out the presses."

"Fat chance," said the editor. "They're clear out in the suburbs."

The man in the hat looked me over. His chins were glistening blue and the whites of his eyes had a pinkish cast. He had Sen-Sen on his breath and I could live next door to him ten years and not know him any better than I did in that instant. "Who're you?"

"My question, friend," I said. "You're the one with the lungs."

"Spengler. I'm an officer with the governor's grand jury." He flashed a state buzzer in a leather folder.

I said, "I've got one of those too. So far it hasn't got me into a theater on Gidget night."

"Private, huh? Well, I got me a court order to go through the papers in that office and take away evidence pertaining to the current investigation." He got it all out in a breath.

I held out a hand. He hesitated, then laid the fold of paper in it. I glanced at the fine print and he snatched it back. "Looks legitimate."

"Damn straight."

"Better let him in," Dutt told the editor.

"Fucking Democrats." But the white-haired man

stepped aside. Spengler and the deputy rumbled into the office. The rest of us stood at the opening. There was room for only two inside.

"Hold it." The deputy threw an arm in front of the court officer.

The enclosure wasn't any neater than I remembered. Barry treated shelves like gunnysacks, stuffing rather than stacking books and manuscripts into them, and the overflow mounded the desk and the packing crates he used in place of file cabinets. A piece of twisted metal the doctors had dug out of his chest after the explosion, encased in Lucite, held down a sheaf of curling receipt slips on the computer terminal that had replaced his typewriter. The same old telephoto snaps of old men named Carlo and Don Cheech covered the walls.

Nobody there was looking at any of that. Those eyes not blocked by Spengler's bulk were on the two-foot stack of papers and looseleaf notebooks standing in the center of the floor with a hand-lettered sign on top:

DANGER!

WIRED FOR DEMOLITION

A length of flat insulated wire circled the stack twice and vanished into the bottom drawer of the desk.

"Bluff," Spengler said. "Them newspaper snoopers." But he didn't move a grain of his two-sixty.

"Primacord."

The fat man quarter-turned my way. "Huh?"

I said, "They carried it in coils over Khe Sanh in 'copters whose pilots could set down in a field of crackers without a crunch. It's volatile stuff."

Spengler's little eyes went back to the stack of papers.

A pale pointed tongue came out and slid along his lips. "Aw," he said. "Aw."

"It'll take out this floor and some of the Lively Arts," I went on. "The book section anyway."

"What do they want to go and mess around with that stuff for?" His voice got shrill. "Can't a guy do his work without he gets shipped back in an envelope?"

The deputy lowered his arm. "I'll radio police headquarters, get the city bomb boys down here."

"Well, I ain't paid to babysit no bombs." Spengler pointed a finger the size of a zucchini at Jed Dutt. "The stuff stays till we get back."

"Peddle your fat butt, Lionheart. It's private property until you get ready to serve that order."

"You got God in a box, smart guy. You went to college."

The two intruders went out of there on a crackle of applause and Bronx cheers.

"They don't make them like that anymore," I told Dutt.

"Only five times a week and twice on Sundays."

As the white-haired editor shooed the reporters back to their desks, Dutt said, "That sign's been giving me the willies. I'm afraid to use the office."

I stepped inside and pulled the end of the wire loose from the drawer. It ended in two frizzed tails of shredded copper, like the ones you hook to the antenna terminals on a television set, which is what kind of wire it was. He stared at me over the tops of his glasses. "How'd you know?"

"Nobody who lost pieces of himself to a dynamite charge is going to be fooling around with Primacord. Can I look through this stuff?"

"We got orders to cooperate. I can't let you take any of it out of the building, though. House rules."

"I won't be able to read all of it here," I said.

"The line is we can bend all the regulations we want out there, but in here they're stone city." He touched his bow tie. "Seen our new copying machine? It takes a few minutes on your way back to the elevators, but it's worth it."

I grinned. "I'll be sure and take the time."

He put his hands in his pockets, nodded. "You get anything on this would look good in print." He let it flutter.

"Yeah."

He nodded again and left me, his rounded shoulders and back-tilted posture describing a lazy S.

I rolled Barry's swivel around the desk and sat down and started picking through the stack. I wasn't going to find anything. I didn't know for sure if the series he'd been working on had anything to do with why he had gone underground, and knowing him I figured the papers were a decoy anyway. If there was a danger of them falling into public hands he'd have destroyed his notes and relied on his phenomenal memory. I was bobbing for wax apples.

Five minutes in I bit into real fruit.

9

I DIDN'T KNOW THAT'S WHAT IT WAS WHEN I FOUND IT, OF
course. You hardly ever do, which is why it's called de-
tecting. Before I got to it I skimmed through a dozen sheets
of dog-eared copy paper bearing the typewritten beginnings
of several columns, watching Barry grind down the leads
to that famous Stackpole edge—he never composed on the
computer, refusing to share his dynamite with the office
system until it was ready for show—tried to make sense
out of his pencil scrawl on some loose sheets torn from his
telephone pad and gave up on that. There were check stubs
made out to cash in unspectacular amounts, a reminder to
himself to buy Irene something for her birthday, random
figures in columns; the usual impedimenta of life in an
imperfect world. It will take more than machines with
memories to make us give up our little scraps of paper. He
had apparently emptied his drawers to build a convincing
pile for the Spenglers he knew would be dropping in.

When I got to it, it was a three-ring folder bound in

slick black plastic with the name of a local heating and cooling firm stamped in green on the spine and cover, one of those things they give you when you buy a new furnace, containing your guarantee and operating instructions and numbers to call when you screw them up. They always outlast the furnaces and usually wind up holding family recipes and newspaper clippings. This one was jammed tight with double-spaced, neatly typewritten sheets. It weighed at least three pounds. When I flipped back the cover, the title page went over with it and I was looking at the first page.

In August, after the defoliants have done their work, the trees around the harbor stand naked and it looks like November in Michigan. Only it's August in Southeast Asia and with no shade to protect it the water gives forth crawling waves of heat like sun on concrete and those fish that are too large to loll in the shade of the sunken timbers lie on the surface with their sunburned fins turning white.

I peeled the title page away from the cover.

Cold Steel, Hot Lead
by
Barry Evan Stackpole

"Barry, you bastard," I said.

I had suggested the title to him when we were in that hole in Cambodia, and at the time, with Charlie spraying orange tracers into the bushes all around us, it had seemed a pretty good joke, the way a chance reference in a certain context that wouldn't make you smile on a straight sober

morning blows the roof off a late-night party after everyone's stopped counting his sloe gin fizzes. It had been our
toast for a long time and had come to mean nothing more
than throwing spilled salt over a shoulder. I'd thought. All
the while he'd been writing the book and, no doubt, grinning every time he typed the title at the top of a fresh page.

I riffled the pages with a thumb, reading the numbers.
They went up to 462. I'd be the best part of my retainer
making copies, and dollars to bullets there was nothing in
it that would lead me to where Barry was cooling leather. I
cast a glance behind me to make sure the doorway was
empty, popped open the steel rings, folded the block of
pages inside the topcoat I'd been carrying all day, and replaced them with a like quantity of blank newsprint from
one of the shelves in the office. Then I returned to the
stack.

It gave up a number of scratch sheets with unidentified
telephone numbers written on them, a fresh-looking manila
file folder containing dated clippings from old copies of the
News and *Free Press*, and a trio of Detroit Metropolitan
telephone directories for the past three years. He'd once
told me he never kept personal address or telephone books
because they were always getting lost, and that when his
mental Rolodex failed him, every other Leap Year Day,
there was usually a directory handy. He never forgot an
unlisted number. Half the time I had to look up mine. I
took down some of the scribbled numbers into my pocket
notebook and opened the most recent directory and copied
some of the ones circled there in ink. I felt like a goat in
the city dump.

There was nothing else for me. I rebuilt the heap, replaced the wire and warning sign so as not to disappoint
the bomb detail, took a last quick look around for pur-

loined letters, and left the office carrying the folder full of clippings and the package wrapped in my topcoat. The editor who didn't like Democrats sat in his cubicle next to Barry's, scowling at someone's story on his VDT, and a woman reporter at one of the open desks was changing from high heels into brown loafers. She had slim feet and wore no stockings. Jed Dutt fell into step beside me from somewhere on the way to the copying machine. "Anything?"

"Couple of telephone numbers," I said. "And this." I handed him the folder.

He read the clippings as he walked. I adjusted the coat over my left arm, bunching it to conceal the square corners underneath. It was getting heavy.

He said, "Some of these stories are mine from back when I was on cophouse. They go back a few years. What's the connection?"

"If I knew that I wouldn't have to make copies. I think best on my keister."

"It's that pressure on the brain." We stopped at the machine and he watched me lower my coat carefully to the floor before laying the clippings face down on the glass cover. "That knob controls the number of copies. Just push the button when you're ready to print."

"Thanks.

"And you better carry that stuff you're hiding out in the open when you pass Lady Patton in the lobby. Otherwise she'll call out the troops."

I looked at him.

"I got off police beat just in time," he said, with his shy grin. "When you start to think like a cop it's time for a change."

He left me. I stood there for a moment rubbing the back

of my neck. Then I started twisting knobs and pressing buttons. There was something to be said for not being in show business while Jed Dutt was on the Entertainment desk.

The building wino was using the upholstered bench in my waiting room to kill a fifth of Annie Greensprings. He was a gray-stubbled black man who wore a blue knit cap and brown jersey gloves with the fingers out and an olive-drab army overcoat the year around, which was okay because I was pretty sure he didn't wear anything underneath. I didn't ask him how many customers he'd scared off while he was sitting there. He wouldn't have remembered anyhow. "Out," I said. "There's an astrologer next door. You can gaze at the chart of Venus and plan your next vacation."

He got up, looking at me with glistening spaniel eyes, and shuffled toward the door I held open. He smelled of dago red and a stopped-up toilet. When he was almost in the hall I said oh hell, clawed out my wallet, and jammed a five-spot into his slash pocket. The look it bought wasn't worth it. It never is.

Inside the cloister I picked up my mail and went over to the desk and boomed down my armload of papers and skinned through the envelopes. I was very popular with Publishers Clearing House and the *Readers Digest*, and the quick-print place I had do my business cards and letterheads had sent me a 5 x 7 greeting card with a cartoon of a chicken being held upside-down by a hairy fist clamped around its legs and the message inside: "*Now* will you pay?" I peered at the fine print on the back. It wasn't a Hallmark so I filed it under the blotter with the others.

I hung up my coat, which was showing wear from all

the carrying around, and took my seat behind the desk, dialing my answering service as I shuffled through the newspaper clippings I'd copied at the *News*. Two of the pieces, dated several months apart, were about bodies found in the trunks of cars parked at Detroit Metropolitan Airport. They could have been connected. They could just as easily not have been. One good way to relieve traffic congestion at the airport would be to direct the cars with stiffs in them to their own part of the lot: Visitors, Passengers, Corpses. There was an article about a Detroit police inspector taking early retirement after eighteen years with the department, dated last January, a long Sunday magazine profile of a local labor union chief, dead two years, and a scattering of three-inch fillers on various assaults, shootings, and hits-and-runs in the metropolitan area. A five-year record of random violence with nothing but a manila folder in common. On the face of it.

"Just one message, Mr. Walker," said the girl at the service. "From a Lieutenant Fitzroy at police headquarters."

"What did he say?"

"Something about an old lady and a marijuana plant. It's rather involved."

I grinned. "Thanks. I can figure it out."

After hanging up I puzzled over the clippings a little longer, arranging the white copy sheets side by side on the desk. Then I tried shuffling them, but that didn't light any bulbs either. Finally I restacked them and slipped a paper clip over one corner and put the sheaf in the drawer with the brass knuckles and my diploma from the Willie Sutton School of Dance. I lit a cigarette and pulled over Barry's typescript. Paged through it, stopping here and there to read.

I am sitting in a hollow bunker with an ARVN who has spent two tours here. We are not talking, conserving ourselves in the heat, when one of the new Cobras clatters overhead at treetop level, thorny with machine guns and rocket launchers, raising dust and dead leaves. Particles fly into our eyes and tears join the sweat on our chins.

"I always did hate choppers," says the ARVN, thumbing off the safety on his M-16.

The M-16's muzzle velocity is not great. In the echo of the sloppy action's rattle we hear distinctly the clanking of the bullets striking the Cobra's armor plate.

The helicopter hovers, seeming to shudder, more from surprise than from pain. The blades change pitch, the tail rotates, and the machine's squat nose, splotched brown and green, swings around, its cannon and Gatlings trained on our little bunker.

For a time the earth ceases to turn. The great steel dragonfly floats on air as thick as bath water, swaying a little, not enough to hinder its aim. We remain unmoving.

After a minute—it seems much longer—the Cobra turns and resumes its flight. The beating of the blades recedes into a steady thrum, and long seconds pass before we know we are hearing it no longer.

We breathe.

My fingers were making the sheet crackle. I laid it down gently and moved my cigarette over to the tray on the desk and broke off a column of ash reaching clear back to the filter tip. Then I got up and cracked the window. September air trailed cool fingers into the office. I burned some fresh tobacco and watched the traffic flashing past down West River through the little gap between the corner of my building and the gravel-strewn roof of the lower one next door. I watched the cars until they looked like cars and not like armed helicopters. Then I sat down again and drew out the copied newspaper clippings and dialed Barry's number at the *News*. The telephone rang seven times before Dutt speared it.

"Still think the place is going to blow up without music?" I asked.

"No, I just can't work around a mess I didn't make personally. Anyway, the Detroit bomb squad swung through and chased the goblins out from under the bed and Spengler took away the stack."

"I hope you wished him luck with it."

"He should rupture himself lugging the stuff over to the City-County Building. What's keeping me from another column about yet another black playwright whose titles won't fit on any marquee in the city?"

"Your byline is on one of those pieces about body drops at Metro and on that feature thing about the labor leader, whatsizname, Kindnagel," I said. "Any of the others yours?"

"No, those were strictly blotter. Kids come in fresh from journalism school and a viewing of *All the President's Men* and the editor hands them a rape in a student parking lot at Wayne State. I've got my notes on those two I wrote right here. What do you need?"

I paused. "That cop thing again?"

"Reporter's instinct. They pass it out at the graduation ceremony in the obituary department, or they used to. I figured you'd call after you had a chance to look at the stuff."

"What's the tariff?"

"Same as before. An exclusive if anything comes of it, or I collect another time."

"Eminently fair. They ever identify that John Doe at the airport?"

"About a week later. It was a hot news day, my follow-up got bumped. Woman named Pearl Cochran from Lathrup Village positived him at the county cold room." Paper rustled on his end. "Philip Anthony Niles. Her brother. Ran a body shop in Royal Oak, along with a tab with one of the friendly finance boys downtown, a Cuban named—I like this—Amigo Fuentes. Police took him down and cut him loose after forty-eight hours. He was out of town that week."

"He still in business?"

"You're asking me, Entertainment? All I know is he was managing a junkyard at Fourteenth and Myrtle that year."

I wrote it all down. "What about Kindnagel?"

More rustling. "No connection I can see. He was in on the ground floor of the Labor Zionist Movement locally, helped organize most of the Jewish laborers in the city while everyone was watching Bennett's bullies kicking Reuther and Frankensteen down the steps of the Miller Road Overpass. Maybe the most nonviolent union takeover in this town's history."

"I forget what he died of."

"Just plain living, as I hope to. Went in his sleep about the time the article ran. One time when those jerks on the Sunday side were right to sit on a piece for six weeks. Sold every copy but the ones on file. He was ninety-two. Everything else is in the story."

I thanked him and broke the connection with my thumb. Holding down the button, I thought for a beat, then let it pop back up and tried John Alderdyce's extension at Detroit Police Headquarters. I got him on the first ring.

"Hornet?" he barked.

"Housefly, I think," I said. "But it's not bothering anybody up there on the ceiling. How's the homicide rate?"

"It's doing fine, same as my flu. We're the ones losing ground. What is it, Walker? I'm expecting Sergeant Hornet with a bullet from a picket fence on St. Antoine."

"What's a picket fence doing on that street, collecting limericks?"

"That bang you hear is me ending this conversation."

"Second, John. I need a line on a side of beef you boys pried out of a trunk at Metro two years ago. His name was Philip Niles."

He sneezed, blew his nose loudly, and said, "That it? Sure you don't want the ballistics on the Abe Lincoln burn? Call Records, goddamnit."

"Second, John."

"That's just what you've got, friend."

"Does it happen you know an Inspector Ray Blankenship, who took his papers early from Homicide eight months ago?"

A little time passed. Voices droned a mile away. He never closed the door to his office when he was alone in it. "What about him?"

When it came, it came hard and fast. I said, "I don't know what about him yet. That's why I'm asking. I never heard of the guy, and I thought I knew all the inspectors in the department."

"They kicked him up on retirement, to goose the pension. They do that when they like you upstairs. I hear. He was lieutenant in charge of the detective squad at the Fourteenth Precinct. As of three this morning, though, he's nothing. He ate his service revolver. They're still scrubbing up."

10

"I HAVE TO ASK THE QUESTION," ALDERDYCE SAID.

But he didn't ask it. I parked the receiver in the hollow of my shoulder and set fire to a Winston. Waving out the match: "I'm on the bottom step of a missing person. He had a newspaper squib about Blankenship's retirement in his possession. Right now I'm just scratching at pebbles."

"Would I know this missing person?"

"Yeah."

He waited. Then he blew his nose again. "It's not my hot handle, so who cares. It's not even Fitzroy's anymore; they're closing it out as suicide. What'd you do, pull the son of a bitch out with your teeth?"

This last was directed away from the telephone. I heard Sergeant Hornet's wheezy fat man's voice and the word "bullet." To me, Alderdyce said: "If it's okay on your end I'm going to hang up in your face now. My hobby calls."

"Blankenship was Fitzroy's?" I asked quickly.

"Yeah, but you don't want to talk to Fitz today. He's

67

awful mad at you for some reason I'd rather not know anything about. Sergeant Grice was the dick on the scene. He's poking at a kill on Montcalm today. A bag lady. They're going after the derelicts this season." Click.

I cradled the receiver gently, the way a mortician lowers the lid on a coffin when mourners are watching. Montcalm, the part of it where a murdered derelict was likely to turn up anyway, was a two-minute drive from 14th and Myrtle, where Jed Dutt had said Amigo Fuentes' junkyard was located. I cleared my desk into two drawers—the one on top was too shallow to hold Barry's memories of Vietnam and Cambodia—and rolled on out of there. My wino was curled up in a fetal position on the floor next to the stairwell, snoring and hugging his green bottle.

Montcalm. The name conjures up images of crisp blue snow on a craggy peak with pines carpeting the slopes. The reality is a stretch of broken pavement with the lines rubbed off and the signs on the corners, where there still are signs, rusting around bullet holes. Three out of five Detroiters own guns, and one of them is going off somewhere every night. The curbs are lined with long low cars with tailfins and syphilitic decay around the wheel wells, a clot of gaunt young blacks in bomber jackets and Levi's gone the same greasy shade of gray leaning on the fenders of every third one. They are there every hour of the day and night, cuffing one another's shoulders and laughing through their noses with their eyes hooded. They live in a world where time is measured in empties and scar tissue.

I cruised with my foot off the pedal, letting the slant of the street pull the Olds along and flicking my eyes right and left, looking for official cars. The scenery was mostly the backs of buildings with rough yellow concrete stoops and green and black plastic garbage bags leaning in door-ways. Nothing ever fronts on streets like Montcalm. It's as if sixty years ago the architects knew there would be nothing to look at.

After six blocks I spotted a county wagon backed into an alley with its big red dome rotating lazily. A cruiser from the Tactical Mobile Unit was parked across the street, and on that side a black unmarked car with twin whip antennas blocked a hydrant. There were plenty of other places to park, but if they can they will leave them where no one else is allowed to leave his. Give some guys a cap and a whistle.

I pulled up behind the blue-and-white and crossed the street on foot just as a lot of suit and coat with a man inside came out of the mouth of the alley. His face was a weak lime tint and everything about him said cop except the color. "Got a cigarette?" he demanded.

I shook one out of the pack and lit it for him. He took a deep drag and started hacking. Then he puffed again, coughed some more. Spat phlegm.

"Bet you'd quit if you didn't enjoy them so much," I suggested.

His eyes moved over me for the first time. They were watering in a narrow young-old face under a snapbrim hat with a wide silk band. He wore a thin matinee moustache that looked inked-on against his pallor. He said, "I don't smoke."

I played with it a moment, then put it away. "Sergeant Grice?"

"Down there." He jerked the crown of his hat toward the alley. "You with the department?"

"I'm private."

"Okay. I had to ask. One more set of footprints won't make any difference on this one."

I put that away next to the other and walked past him. The alley fell off at a thirty-degree angle from the street, running out of pavement at the bottom, where it curved into a welted parking area behind a drugstore with a padlock on its back door and plywood where its windows belonged. Deep ditches lined the drive, making it too narrow to admit anything but foot traffic. A group of men stood at the bottom. Halfway down I lit a cigarette for myself, and I didn't want it any more than the guy I had just finished talking to had.

I had smelled that stink a couple of times before. That meant nothing; when it comes to that particular odor you are always a virgin. Every man in the group had a cigarette in his mouth and was puffing up thick clouds. I was still coming when one of them, an officer in uniform, broke and strode past me double-quick time. He lost his smoke as he came but didn't stop to crush it out, letting it roll. As he passed I could hear him breathing through his mouth in little sobs.

The trio remaining included another uniform, flat-nosed with flinty threads glittering in a thick horseshoe moustache, a round-faced Oriental I recognized from the coroner's office in jeans and an orange zip-front jacket, and a black plainclothesman in the regulation three-piece suit that went like hell with his brilliantined hair and ducktail. The light shone blue off his high pompadour. They were watching a pair of white-coated morgue attendants in gas masks carefully separating a bundle of rags from a settling of wet newspapers and bloated cardboard cartons against the drugstore's block foundation. A hand stuck out of the

70

rags, its fingers fanned out stiff like spokes from a wheel. A cloud of flies boiled over the debris.

"Don't expect lightning to strike on this one," the Oriental was saying. "We're going to have to go in with masks and decontam suits, and when we're finished cause of death will be as good as a guess."

"I already know cause of death." The black detective leaked smoke out the side of his mouth. "Lateral laceration of the carotid, left to right, probably from behind, victim bled out in minutes. Just like the others. What do you figure, three weeks?"

"About that. You could've passed within two feet every day for the first couple of weeks and not noticed it in all that junk. After that you could hardly avoid it."

"Neighborhood dogs led us to this one," put in the uniform.

"Sergeant Grice?"

The detective turned my way and my stomach scaled my ribs. His right cheek was a map of sharp broken creases like crumpled cellophane. The last time I had seen that burn scar, the face that wore it had been in the path of my flying fist. He was the undercover cop I'd knocked out in the blind pig on Clairmount a month before.

He said, "Who's asking?"

He hadn't recognized me. I did some business with the ash on my cigarette. Covering up. "My name's Walker," I said. "I'm a private investigator on a missing person case. They told me at headquarters you caught the squeal on the Blankenship suicide this morning."

"He the missing person?"

"It takes some telling. Can we go someplace where we can't see the air we're breathing?"

71

"That's the first sensible suggestion I've heard since I got on this detail."

The white coats had managed to scoop the body into a zipper bag and were transferring it onto a collapsed stretcher. We headed uphill, trailing the uniform and the medical examiner. The atmosphere got sweeter by degrees. As we walked I told Grice about the clippings in Barry's file folder. He listened with his eyes on the ground.

"Blankenship snuffed himself, all right," he said. "Just because I'm fresh off a year and a half on Vice don't mean I can't see the pattern. He had a busted marriage and at forty-eight he was washed out as a cop. Maybe your man just likes to collect newsprint."

"I have to wonder why Blankenship walked two years shy of a full pension."

"Burnout. The Fourteenth is a war zone."

"He could've put in for transfer."

Grice took a last drag and snapped away his butt. We were at street level. The detective with the hat and moustache was standing by the unmarked car with the uniform who had left just as I reached the parking area, comparing complexions. Grice said, "Maybe getting in your twenty is like climbing a mountain. The last two feet are the hardest. His record is so clean it hurts your eyes. Prints on the gun were his and the lab says he'd fired a gun recently. His wife's staying with her sister in Grand Rapids and has been for the past week. And I'm pulling a double shift like it's loaded with rocks. I don't feel like crawling into anyone else's head. Especially when he don't have one no more."

"Where's it go from here, I.A.D.?"

"It don't go. Internal Affairs don't bother itself with civilians, which is what he was since January. The gun he used was his own, although it was the one he carried all the

72

time he was in plainclothes. He'd turned in his departmental piece."

"Did you know him?"

"To look at. Not to talk to." He was studying my face. The whites of his eyes were just as blue by daylight. They reminded me of skim milk. "We met? You look familiar."

"I'd remember," I said. "Is the widow coming in?"

"I guess. To dot all the *i*'s."

"When she does, would you have her call me? I'd owe you one." I gave him a card.

He poked it into his handkerchief pocket without looking at it. "If I remember, and if I happen to be wearing the same suit." He grinned suddenly. "Look at that, will you?"

His gaze was grazing my right shoulder. I turned around. I was looking at the opposite side of the street, anonymous but for a glass door in the building on the corner with DETROIT POLICE DEPARTMENT lettered on it in light blue. The interior was dark behind the glass. "You mean the ministation?"

"Yeah. One of Hizzoner's bright ideas when he took office. A cop on every corner. If the old lady screamed, which she wouldn't of because her vocal cords would of been slashed first thing, they would of heard it there, which they didn't because it's been empty for a year. Someone has to pay for that silk wallpaper downtown."

Barry's column was more widely read than I'd thought. I said, "You told the M.E. this bag lady wasn't the first. I haven't read anything about any others."

"That's because no one wrote about any of them. No one looks at the street trade when they're alive, why should they bother when they're dead? This one's number six. It's really number five, on account of she was drawing flies when last week's turned up in a doorway on Sherman, but

73

we number them by the reports. *I* do, anyhow. Right now it's just some dead bums and bag ladies, my speed. It gets out we got another mass murderer loose, the case gets taken away from me and handed to those flashy killers in Major Crimes. I'm just the dirty-stick boy on this detail. Suicide? Dead wino? Call Grice."

"You feel that way, how come you left Vice?"

He showed his teeth again. "Prestige. You sure we don't know each other?"

"No way we could. I haven't killed anyone lately and I don't have any vices. I appreciate the time, Sergeant. I owe you, like I said." I turned away quickly.

To my back he said: "You wouldn't if you'd tell me where it was we met. Wherever it was I don't remember enjoying it."

11

THE JUNKYARD—THEY CALL THEM DETROIT CEMETERIES most other places—swallowed the whole block behind a twelve-foot board fence with HAGMAN SALVAGE painted on it in red letters as tall as a man, and an entrance on Myrtle. As I nursed my crate along the broken-asphalt driveway, picking my way between glittering carpets of shattered glass and twisted bits of molding, a yellow crane attached to an electromagnet shaped like an enormous suction cup lifted a late-model Buick with smashed fenders twenty feet above the aisles of stacked auto shells and set it almost noiselessly on the conveyor of a crusher busy knuckling an Oldsmobile two years younger than mine. The grinding, squealing inevitability of that machine made you cringe, like a hellfire minister holding forth in a church with no exits. The place smelled of dried mud and scorched metal.

The office was a tiny shack made entirely of corrugated roofing wired together at the seams, with a hole cut for a window. A pair of men standing in the open watched me park next to a dusty pickup bearing the salvage company's name and get out. One of the two was a squat black in his early sixties, with iron-gray hair curling up around the edge of his green billed cap and an impressive belly spilling through his open workshirt over his belt, rivulets of sweat making tracks in the fine coating of dust on his skin. His companion was a Hispanic, short and thin, sporting a lion's mane of wild black hair and a Fu Manchu moustache. He had on a frayed denim jacket over bare brown chest, jeans with threads showing at the knees, and expensive steel-toed workshoes that had seen plenty of combat. He could have been thirty. He was probably closer to fifty. You treat the two ages two ways, so I played it safe and split the difference.

"I'm looking for Amigo Fuentes," I told him.

His eyes were black under lowered lids. "Are you a policeman?" He tried hard not to pronounce the *y* like a *j*.

I said I wasn't and showed him my ID. His glance raked it swiftly.

"Her parents send you?"

I went on looking at him and put away my wallet. "You're Fuentes?"

"Let's go inside. Cleon, bust them bolts if you got to, but yank that transmission. Man wants it by fi' o'clock."

"Yas," said the old black man, and left us, slapping a ballpeen hammer against the side of his leg as he walked.

"Domb shits, these niggers," Fuentes said over his shoulder. "Wanted Liquid Wrench to pop the bolts on a car was here ten years when I take over."

"Good help's hard to find."

"Ain' it the truth." He snapped on a dropcord suspended over a steel desk, blinding me with 200 watts of sudden naked white light.

76

Something struck me hard across the stomach. When I doubled over, a hand snaked behind me and jerked the revolver from my holster.

The light went out. Green and yellow dots burst before my vision and glimmered away, like stones sinking in a deep pond. Fuentes was standing beside his desk with my Smith & Wesson in one hand and a jack handle in the other. I sucked for air and probed the sore spot on my abdomen.

"Man wearing a piece walks different," he said. "You're estupid, Mr. Michigan State Police Licensed Private Investigator. What you think, you come see me wearing a piece, I'm estupid too? Domb *cubano*, he going to shit when he sees you carry? Tell her parents is not my brat."

His voice was a whining singsong. I breathed and said, "I've heard better Alfonso Bedoyas. You do any Jane Withers?"

He laid the gun on a stack of yellow invoices and slung the jack handle clanking onto the desk. "You take a tap good, I think. Maybe you ain' so estupid after all. Maybe her parents don' send you neither."

"The gun wasn't for you. It's that kind of neighborhood. No, her parents didn't send me. I don't even know who she is. I'm looking into the murder of Philip Niles, who turned up at Metro Airport a couple of years back with a twenty-two slug in the back of his head."

"Shit, Niles. Ask me about Cortez. They keep going to bring that up like a millage election till they nail me. I don' kill Niles. I kill Niles, I don' get my money. Is not good business. Even the cops see that finally."

"Bodies in trunks are a signature," I said. "Feed it to the press and they'll cough up 'gangland-style slaying' a hundred times out of a hundred. It happens you're in a

77

game that sometimes finds it necessary to cut losses by making examples of those players who forget the rules. I'm not talking about the salvage game."

"Sure, I shoot him from Miami, where I'm staying that week."

I laughed in his face.

A brow got dark. His fingers touched the desk with the jack handle on it. Then he shrugged that exaggerated shrug they shrug in hot climates. "Hey, we're just two guys talking. Man don' pay on time, he gets more time. He don' pay on time, he don' walk so good. One out of fifty, sixty, maybe he gets dead, somebody slips or gets caught up in the moment, you been around, you know how that goes. But Niles, he got a good business—going concern, one partner only. You can' make cash? Sign here, I got me a hook in Royal Oak. I don' kill no one, understand, but more I don' kill a man's got prospects."

"He ran a body shop," I said. "How much can there be in taking wrinkles out of fenders?"

He uncovered a bandit's grin with a glint of gold in it. "You ain' been to Royal Oak, see the operation?"

"What about it?"

"You don' do your homework, don' ast me will I do it for you. What's a private pig want with Niles, anyway? His wife think he making it with the angels?"

I passed it. "You said they keep bringing up Niles. Who else has been around asking about him?"

"Some blond Anglo about your age. Was in last week. I tol' him what I tell you. He don' get no jack handle, though."

"Why not?"

"Hey, I got pride. I don' hit no old ladies or cripples. Man limped."

78

The crusher ground away on the other side of the lot. A windshield gave with a noise like a wave breaking on rocks. He said, "Okay?"

I stirred. "Okay, thanks. What do I owe you? Oh, yeah." I slung a fist low into his midsection.

He jackknifed, spraying spit. His lungs creaked and his hands closed and opened, closed and opened spasmodically. For a long time he held that position, saliva running off the point of his chin. Then he looked up at me slowly. Gold glinted.

"You get one," he gasped. "Don't lean on your luck. After that I come for you with dogs."

"Amigo," I said, "your accent's slipping." I picked up my gun and walked out of there and got into my car. As I backed around, the crane was feeding a fresh half-ton of steel and glass into the crusher, which went on masticating without a burp.

12

DETECTIVES IN BOOKS ARE ALWAYS SQUAWKING ABOUT not having any leads to go on. In real life they beef about having too many. Birdseed on the windowsill of a room where a man was murdered could be a dying clue. It could just as easily be food for the birds. I had a room full of left shoes and broken pencil points and cryptic messages and a thousand ways to go, any one of which could wind up costing Walgren & Rooney and the Detroit *News* a bushel of cash and not buy them anything better than a bloodhound tracing a missing man's boot back to the place where it was made. What makes you good in the work is a nose that tells you early when the trail's going sour.

I wished I had it. I took lunch in a coffee shop on Michigan Avenue, one of those places with a circular counter and a bouncing front door and stools that don't get a chance to stop spinning between customers coming and going, and laid out what I had so far. I had a Detroit police inspector, dead apparently by his own hand; a proprietor of a Royal Oak body shop, dead by someone else's; a Jewish labor leader, dead by death; a live Cuban manager of a Detroit junkyard who lent money with no questions asked and who had obviously seen Al Pacino in *Scarface* thirty times and taken notes; and a sprinkling of newspaper clippings that had as much to do with one another as *Alley Oop* and the stock market forecast. All of which could have been just junk from a reporter's drawer. Except for one thing.

A guy answering Barry's description, blond hair and bum leg, had been to see Amigo Fuentes within the past week, asking about Philip Niles. Or a guy that didn't look anything like Barry, but that happened to share a couple of his characteristics, had been asking about him. Either way we were two people who had suddenly found a man who had been dead two years worth knowing about.

I paid the counter girl, a blonde in her late thirties with tendrils of hair corkscrewing down both sides of her face, and asked if there was a telephone.

"We had one, but the boss had it ripped out. Customers making calls blocked traffic at the door. Thanks, mister." She tucked my dollar tip into the front of her uniform.

"Your hair's coming undone," I said.

She glanced quickly at her reflection in the stainless steel behind the counter. "Don't scare me like that, mister," she said, straightening. "I spent a half-week's pay getting it to look like this."

"It looks nice."

She smiled. "Yeah?" Then she whisked my plate from in front of the hack who had taken my stool and asked what he was having.

I drove around until I found a bank of open-air telephones on a corner and parked in front of a mailbox. A black woman in a light blue uniform as wide as a bus braked a three-wheeled scooter flush with my left rear fender as I climbed out. I had to look a second time to see the scooter.

"You can't stop there," she said. "Unless you got something to mail."

I gave her a hinge at the honorary sheriff's star in my wallet and lifted the receiver off one of the telephones. She sat there a minute, her little two-cycle engine making flatulent noises, then *phut-phut*ted down the street to stop next to a diesel truck cab that was taking up two meters. I put the receiver back on the hook and swung up the metropolitan directory.

Jed Dutt had told me Niles's sister, Pearl Cochran, lived in Lathrup Village. There was only one Cochran listed in the Birmingham exchange with a Village address, a Kevin Cochran on Catalpa. I tapped out the number.

"Hello?"

"Mrs. Cochran?"

"Yes?"

"Pearl Cochran?"

"Yes?" It was one of those high-pitched voices the unluckiest of us end up married to.

"Philip Niles's sister?"

She might have drawn a quick breath. You can't ever tell over the telephone. A hand got cupped over the mouthpiece and I heard muffled voices. Then she came back on the line. "Who am I speaking to, please?"

I told her. "It has to do with a missing person case I'm working on," I added. "I'd like to talk to you about it if you have time."

"I'd rather not."

"I have reason to believe the man I'm looking for was investigating your brother's murder when he disappeared."

"Mr.—Walker?" she said. "My brother is dead, Mr. Walker. Nothing we would have to say to each other will change that. I've reconciled myself to the fact that he was killed and that that gangster who killed him is still at large. It's taken me nearly two years. You'll understand if I say I don't want to rip open that old wound."

"Is someone in the room with you, Mrs. Cochran?"

"My husband was. He's left. He and Philip never got along. I think his murder was a source of some satisfaction to Kevin, but we don't discuss it. This is painful," she added.

I breathed some air. *Mrs. Leopold, I have bad news, the worst.* "I understand. One more question. Can you tell me if your brother's body shop is still in business?"

"The last I heard. It's on Campbell Road between Eleven and Twelve Mile. Acme Collision. Philip's old partner operates it."

"What's the partner's name?"

"You said just one more question. Wally Petite. That's his legal name, Wally. Not Walter."

"Thanks, Mrs. Cochran. Sorry I bothered you."

"I'm sorry too." She broke the connection.

The telephone stand didn't have a Yellow Pages. I got Acme's number from Information. A Kentucky twang answered. When I asked for Petite it said, "Sec," and I was listening to a hammer banging metal a long way off. A lot of seconds later the telephone rustled and someone said, "Petite."

I told him what I'd told Pearl Cochran and asked for an interview. There was a space during which I could tell the banging had stopped, then: "I don't see what good it could do, but I suppose I can spare you a few minutes. Tomorrow morning at ten?"

I said tomorrow morning at ten would be fine and we said good-bye. His voice had no inflection at all. I blamed it on the instrument.

I tried a third number, but my luck wasn't holding. A tape recording as old as my wallet growled and ground down and asked me to leave a message before the beep. I didn't bother. I drove away from there. As I left the light at the corner, the meter maid was still idling next to the big truck with her ticket pad out, waiting for the first of the two meters to go into violation.

Lou Gallardo worked out of a green Quonset hut on Pinecrest in Ferndale, with a partition between his four-by-four office and the storm door retailer he rented from. SPEEDO REPOSSESSIONS AND TRACES, read the steel tape on the red fire door that had stood open for as long as I had been coming there. I went in without knocking and found Lou on the telephone with one brown wingtip propped atop a stack of blank Michigan Secretary of State driver's license application forms on a gray steel desk that showed the marks of a thousand struck matches. A red sock showed above the wingtip and two inches of hairy ankle showed above that. He had on green pants on top of the mess. A snappy dresser is Lou.

He showed tobacco-stained teeth in a broad grimace of a grin when he saw me and waved at the wooden kitchen chair on the customer's side of the desk. I transferred a month's back run of the *Free Press* classifieds from the chair to the floor, moved a ceramic ashtray containing a smoldering stump of cigar to the far corner of the desk, and accepted the invitation.

"Sure, the jimmy's a legitimate expense," he was telling the person on the other end of the line. "I busted the point off mine gaining entrance to the guy's garage. Sure, he can sue. But no one wants to get called a deadbeat in open court. Yeah, I got the Caddy out back. Piece of shit. You can eat your lunch in the time between you stomp on the accelerator and the pistons get the hint. GM ought to be ashamed to call it a Cadillac. Time was—yeah."

I smoked a cigarette and watched him until I got exhausted and directed my attention elsewhere. Lou put more physical energy into a telephone conversation than any six bullfighters on a Sunday afternoon in Pamplona. I was admiring an assortment of burglar tools in a wooden ammunition case on a shelf behind his head when he banged down the receiver. I hadn't heard a good-bye.

"Last time I take on a goddamn accounting major for a client," he said cheerfully. "How the hell are you, Amos?"

"I'm eating." I pointed at the box of tools. "You can get ninety days for just having those."

"I bought 'em off a detective in the Detroit B-and-E Bureau. He didn't bust me. What brings Bulldog Drummond sniffing down Perspiration Lane today? You looking to go legit, get into repo work?"

"I'm too old to learn the long way around those new locking transmissions, Lou. I need some dope on a smash-and-smooth shop in Royal Oak. Acme Collision, on Campbell Road. I figured you'd have it if anybody did."

He leaned back in his swivel and pulled a drawer out of a black pebbled-iron file cabinet in worse shape than my green one. After thumbing through some tabbed cardboard folders he drew one out and put his foot down on the floor to make room on the desk. I watched him reading. He was a compact five feet with a sprinter's frame going to fat and a perfectly round head with a matting of blue-black hair and a series of longitudinal creases in his cheeks that broke into an accordion when he smiled. His brow glistened, and although it was early afternoon on a cool day he had already sweated through his green-and-red-striped shirt. He could slide a car out of the police lockup under the guard's nose and tell you where the refrigerator light went when it went out. If he had any ambition he'd have been the best P.I. in the state.

"Thought so." He held up a sheet. "Acme is the elephant's graveyard for boosted wheels. It's where hot Buicks go to die."

"Chop shop?"

"Calling Acme Collision a chop shop is like calling the Vatican a country church." He passed me the sheet.

It was a computer printout off the Royal Oak Police Department's central system, listing the serial numbers of dozens of stolen vehicles traced to Acme's address. It was an original, not a Xerox copy. I handed it back. "So how come they're still in business?"

"Evidence. Car comes in, it's stripped and pieced out over a six-state area in a few hours. By the time any part of it is traced to Acme the owner's been paid by his insurance company, why should he come down, identify a greasy fuel pump? The Acme people are back on the street. Cops watch them for a little, they bump out fenders and go home at the end of the day with clean noses. Cops go back to what they were doing before and it starts in again. It's a honey of an operation. If I weren't so law-abiding these days I'd get in my résumé."

"Not you, Lou. You're strictly ten bucks in the maid's apron pocket and five minutes alone with the boss's ledger."

He remembered his cigar and stuck it in his face. Tilted upward it gave him a jaunty look, like the famous Roosevelt profile or Ed Muskie before New Hampshire 1968. "Think you know me, huh?"

"Six years ago I *was* you." I tapped the printout sheet. "Where do you get this stuff?"

"I'm a detective, son. Lessons cost extra."

"What've you got on Wally Petite? He runs Acme."

"Only what I hear. He was chief mechanic in the service department of a car dealership downtown till he set up in Royal Oak three-four years ago. Hasn't got all the grease out from under his fingernails yet. Was a time there just after the new law when pit monkeys with state certification could name their own price. His was a full partnership."

"What about his late partner? Philip Niles?"

"Before my time." He relit the cigar, which had gone out. "I was stealing cars for Reliance in those days. Cheap bastards still owe me forty bucks out-of-pocket expenses."

"It's a big club."

He grinned around the chewed stump. "Where'd those big shiny operations be without sleazes like me and bloodhounds like you?"

"Stinking up somebody's tin hut with a four-for-a-quarter stogie, probably." I got up. "It's a start, Lou. I'm into you."

"I'll take it out in trade sometime. You haven't told me what it's about."

"That's right."

"Oho, a client with ears."

On my way out I spotted the red light on his telephone answering machine. "Oh, you need a new recording. One you got sounds like a lady moose in labor."

"I'm coming up on my second year on this tape." He

reshuffled the papers in the folder. "You going up to Royal Oak?"

"Tomorrow."

"Watch for low-flying engine blocks. Those choppers play for money."

13

THE DOOR TO MY OUTER OFFICE WAS AJAR. I WENT IN ready to give my wino the guided tour into the hallway and looked at an elderly party seated on the bench with his feet flat on the floor and his hands folded on the crook of a Malacca cane with a brass tip. He wore a straw Panama tilted two centimeters over his right eye and a tan suit of some light knobbly material and gold-rimmed glasses and a short white beard trimmed neatly to conform to the angle of his jaw. The neck of his lavender shirt was open, exposing a corner of one of those nitro patches heart patients wear, that feed medication into the system constantly. He looked at a big gold watch on his left wrist, stood up with difficulty, introduced himself by the name of Harold Konschuh—something on that order—and announced that just because a person was retired didn't mean his time wasn't valuable. Quite the contrary.

I apologized and unlocked the inner door and held it as

he went through, taking little nibbling steps. I was behind my desk before he made the customer's chair. He lowered himself into it and said: "I thought you'd be older. I picked your name out of the book because Amos sounded like someone of my generation."

"I'm not, sorry." I drew a pencil out of the cup on the desk and began thumbing the eraser.

He settled and resettled his cane tip between his feet. "I want you to take a picture of Mr. Ford for me."

"Mr. Ford?"

His mouth twitched. "Henry Ford. He visits me in my house nightly and stays to all hours. An old man needs his sleep. The police won't listen to me. I want you to take Mr. Ford's picture so I can show it to them and then they'll make him go away."

"Are we talking about Henry Ford the Second?"

"Did I say Junior? There is only one Henry Ford."

"Henry the First is dead, Mr. Konschuh."

"*I* know that! Tell *him*!"

I reversed ends on the pencil and doodled on my calendar pad. "Approximately how long has Mr. Ford been bothering you?"

"Eight months. It started right after I left Ford's. They made me retire because of my heart. I was an engineer there for thirty-eight years." His head tilted back sharply. His glasses flashed.

"What's he do, moan and rattle chains?"

"That's only in the movies. My doctor has me down to one cigar a day. I generally smoke it just before bed. If Mr. Ford is there at the time he blows out the match. He didn't hold with smoking, you know."

"I didn't know."

"That's why there were no ashtrays in the Model T."

90

"Try a lighter."

"I did. He hid it. The rest of the time he just sits there in my good leather chair giving me that provincial look, like a Maine farmer sitting on his front porch. It's very unsettling."

"I can imagine." I made another doodle. "I'm on retainer to someone else right now, Mr. Konschuh. I'll have to pass."

"I'll pay you well. I've made some sound investments over the years and I have no one to leave it to."

"Sorry, Mr. Konschuh."

He refolded his long pale hands atop the cane. "A man needs his little pleasures, Mr. Walker. I haven't many left. The situation is intolerable."

His beard quivered. I did some more scribbling, then laid down the pencil and got up and opened the top drawer of the file cabinet. From it I drew a Pentax 35-mm. camera, fiddled with the slides and buttons for a moment, and put it down on his side of the desk. "I've set the meter for indoor light at evening," I explained. "You focus by looking through here and turning the lens until the image clears. Work this lever to advance the film. It's all loaded and ready to go. When you've got your picture, have it developed and bring the camera back here. We'll discuss payment then."

He stood, pressed his fragile fingers into my hand, and went out with the camera under one arm. It took him five minutes to reach the hall even with me holding both doors. I saw him safely down the first flight of stairs and went back inside. I didn't expect to see the camera again. I had dropped it out a window of the Pontchartrain Hotel a year or so back, cracking the case and shattering the lens. It was ideal for the picture he wanted to take with it.

I paid a couple of bills, called my service for messages —I didn't have any—and went home carrying Barry's typescript. I was through for the day.

14

THERE ARE RESTAURANTS IN SAIGON THAT IF YOU visit them in civilian clothes and no MPs are present can make you forget for an hour that you're not home. The hanging plants look familiar and the music is western and the percentage of waiters who don't speak English is not that much higher than in many establishments in New York or Detroit. I am dining with a Laotian woman whose tilting features and straight black hair pulled back with combs make her resemble an American Indian. She wears pearls and a low-cut gown of some black unreflecting material and my evening with her is costing me two hundred dollars American. Everything is higher in Saigon.

As we start the second course a girl of perhaps fifteen, in a sleeveless flowered dress caught on one ivory shoulder and a red sash around her waist, her face painted like a doll's, enters the restaurant and stops at a table. The G.I. seated there tells her to go away. She starts to talk. He shouts it and throws something from his plate at her. It bounces off her face. She goes to another table where two servicemen are sitting. One snaps his napkin at her, stinging her in the eye. They are laughing as she turns away, rubbing at the eye with a knuckle. The laughing has a relieved sound.

She is approaching yet a third table when the headwaiter appears and closes a brown hand on her arm, jabbering away in a harsh dialect quite unlike the one in which he greeted us. At length he releases her with a shove. Glaring, she leaves, her platform shoes clomping.

"What was all that?" I ask my companion.

Through it all she has continued sipping a tall gray drink through a straw. She casts a cool glance in the girl's wake. "A country whore," she replies in good English. "She is not licensed to work the better restaurants."

"She doesn't appear very good at it in any case."

She shrugs, stirring her drink. "The Americans call her Kitty Catastrophe."

It is the first time I have heard her stumble over a word in English. "Why do they call her that?"

"Tonight she has business with an American soldier, tomorrow he is dead. Mines, gunfire, bombs. It has happened four times. Tonight, love. Tomorrow, death. Four times, four deaths. She is famous for it now.

"I think she must starve," she reflects.

The door buzzer razzed. I looked at my watch. Eight-fifteen. Sunlight was slanting in through the east window, throwing a bright yellow trapezoid across the table in the breakfast nook, one corner drooping Dalilike over the edge

94

onto the floor. I drained my coffee cup and reshuffled Barry's script and went into the living room to answer. I was wearing pajamas and a robe and slippers.

I had a dream on my doorstep. The dream had on a tailored beige jacket and matching skirt that caught her at mid-calf, with a slit up one side and a row of brown leather buttons along the slit and an ivory-colored silk scarf around her neck, or maybe the scarf was beige and the suit was ivory-colored; I have trouble separating those shades. I wasn't much looking at the outfit anyhow, but into deep blue eyes with a lavender tinge. The make-up was minimal and her hair, pinned up, was the color of light reflecting off gold through a sheen of clear water. It was all packaged by someone who knew his work and couldn't be rushed. It was a dream I'd had before and I smiled in my sleep.

"I'm sorry to bother you at home, Mr. Walker. I should have called." The lavender-blue eyes barely flickered over my attire and unshaved condition. "Louise Starr, remember? We met last spring. I was Fedor Alanov's editor."

I got the smile off my face somehow and my body out of her path. "I remember, Mrs. Starr. I'm not that far gone yet. Come in."

She entered, turning her head only slightly to look around. I scooped a smeared shot glass off the coffee table from the night before and sat her down on the sofa and asked if she'd like a cup of coffee.

"I'd prefer juice if you have it," she said. "In New York I have to drink coffee. I haven't developed a taste for it yet and I'll bet I've drunk ten thousand cups."

"I have orange juice. But it's the frozen kind."

She smiled and said that would be fine. I left her to get the juice. I damn near bowed.

In the kitchen I searched through the cupboards until I

found a juice glass of one of those pressed designs that are supposed to look like cut glass, one of a set of six that Catherine had bought when we were moving in and that I hadn't used in years. It looked okay, but I washed it anyway and dried it and filled it from the pitcher I'd prepared earlier that morning and brought it to her on a tray with a paper napkin. I didn't have any linen ones and it was the first time I'd regretted that.

She sipped, smiled her approval. "That's refreshing. In New York they feel obliged to serve it to you with the pulp floating in it so you know it's fresh squeezed. Now they're telling us the pulp is good for you. If I want an orange I'll peel one myself."

"Everybody worries about everybody else's health. It's the times we live in. Are we going to talk much more about orange juice? I'm running low on ammunition."

She laughed lightly, genuinely, and said, "I'd forgotten your dry humor. Where I come from, everyone just thinks he's funny." She ran a gently tinted nail up the seam of the glass. "I'm here on business, but I don't want to talk about it just yet. Am I keeping you from something?"

"I've got an appointment this morning, but not for another hour and a half. How's Tolstoy?"

"You didn't know? That's right, you couldn't. After we went to so much trouble to protect Alanov and ensure that his book got finished, he paid us back our advance and went with another publisher. Our lawyers are talking to his lawyers. In the end we'll get the bill for their lunches and no Alanov. We don't need him anyway. We've got Andrei Sigourney. He's one of the reasons I'm in town. He's having trouble with his novel and I'm his shoulder to cry on."

"He's going with the name Sigourney?" His real name was the reason I knew him and Alanov and Louise Starr.

"It's what he's comfortable with. He's visiting his grandmother these days," she added, and sipped at her juice.

There had been evidence that he had had more than her shoulder in the past. I didn't press it. Instead I said, "He's one reason you're here. What's another?"

"Yes, your appointment." She set down her glass and looked at me. The room was full of jasmine, as any room would be that contained her. "I'll talk to you about it if you'll sit down. Standing like that with your hands in your robe pockets you look like George Sanders."

"I'm in no condition to sit with ladies, Mrs. Starr. I'm a razor and a clean shirt away from that."

"Dear, I didn't think anyone troubled about such things these days. I'll wait, if you want to go ahead and shave and get dressed. My plane landed two hours ago. I haven't been in town long enough to make any appointments I'd be late for."

"I'll just be ten minutes," I said. "There's more juice in the refrigerator and some magazines there on the table. No *Publishers Weekly*, sorry."

"Thank you. I'm all right on my own."

I didn't argue with that. In the bathroom I hung up the robe and washed and scraped my face until it shone. I brushed my hair and looked at the gray and opened the medicine cabinet and considered a bottle of cologne in a box wrapped in green and gold foil, a present from a grateful client, then closed the door on it without touching it. I put the robe back on for the short trip to the bedroom and selected a powder-blue dress shirt and the pants to my gray suit and put them on. I wiped off my shoes with Kleenex and returned to the living room. She was still on the sofa, reading that week's TV magazine.

"Those are some pretty old movies you've circled," she said, laying it aside. "I would have guessed you're a buff. You talk and act just a little like a character in a black-and-white film."

I broke a pack of Winstons out of a carton in the drawer of the telephone table and held it up. She nodded with a smile. "It has its advantages," I said, stripping off the cellophane. "Sometimes it pays to let the people you meet in this business think you're into some kind of trip. When they think they've pegged you your job's half over."

"It's not all an act, though, is it? You're really that way."

I lit up and sat down in the easy chair, said nothing. She got the hint.

"Someone called my office a few days ago and spoke to my assistant," she began. "I was in a meeting at the time, but when I learned who it was I called him right back. He was writing a book and he wondered if we'd be interested in publishing it. He said you'd given him my name."

I uncrossed my legs. "Barry Stackpole?"

"He's syndicated across the country. A book with his name on it carries a guaranteed sale of fifty thousand. His biography alone—Vietnam, the attempt on his life that crippled him, his personal enmity with known gangsters—would assure it a sale to a major book club. I want that book, Mr. Walker."

"So buy it."

"That's the problem. I told him to send me what he had and we'd talk contract. Right after I hung up I realized I'd been foolishly cautious. I should have had an agreement drawn up then and there, sight unseen. Like all dying enterprises, the book business is getting highly competitive.

There was no telling how many other publishers he was talking to.

"I tried to call him back, but he'd left or he wasn't answering his phone. I've tried several times since with no luck. Someone at the *News* told me he was on a leave of absence. This morning I rented a car at the airport and bought a map and drove out to his house. It's locked and his lawn needs mowing. I thought maybe you'd know where I could get in touch with him." She leaned forward a little with her hands in her lap. She wasn't wearing a wedding ring.

"What day did he call?"

She thought. "I was with the board that day. Monday. Late Monday afternoon."

That was the day I'd been with Barry in the Press Club, the day before he dropped out of sight. I ground out my cigarette and put the ashtray on the stand next to the chair. "Did he say what the book's about?"

"He was reluctant. I think that's why I wanted to see a sample. I assumed it's autobiographical, but maybe that's just because he's led such an interesting life."

"They're a lot more fun to read about than to lead," I said. "I don't know where Barry is. I'm not alone. His employers have hired me to try to find him. He may have gone underground because of a hot potato he was working on. The hot potato may be the book. It may be he's trying to duck a grand jury investigation. He's had some personal problems lately and it may be those. In any case you could be the last person he had contact with before he slid off-stage."

"I have an alibi. I was in New York at the time."

I stared at her.

She colored just a little. "Sorry. I plead jet lag. Do you think you can find him?"

"I've been in this line a long time, Mrs. Starr. I get asked that question twice a week. I'm fresh out of answers. I can't see through walls or read the future in sheep intestines. I'm pretty good, but I'm not that good."

"It would be worth a great deal to the firm I work for if you could answer the question," she said. "It would be worth a great deal to me."

I sat there for another second. Then I stood and picked up her empty glass. "More juice?" She shook her head. I took the glass back into the kitchen and rinsed it out and wiped it off and put it next to the others in the cupboard. I didn't even look at the fresh bottle of Hiram Walker's on the same shelf. Back in the living room I sat down and said, "Your job's that thin?"

She crossed her ankles in that way she had that could empty a gentlemen's smoker across town. "I edited a biography of a dead movie star by the movie star's daughter. It contained two lines on the movie star's affair with a captain of industry I'd thought was dead. The biography was a Book-of-the-Month-Club featured alternate and two producers were bidding for motion picture rights. Then the captain of industry came out of the woodwork with a battery of corporate lawyers and got every copy yanked off the stands. The publishing business isn't the automobile industry; it isn't equipped to handle a one hundred percent recall. Yes, my job's that thin. Thin enough I don't dare put this trip on the pad. I'm just hoping that when I get back I won't find some bright young thing who cut her capped teeth editing westerns sitting at my desk."

"How do you stand it?" I asked.

"I put myself through college proofreading mathematic

texts for a small academic house in Boston. After graduation I spent four years as a reader for a senior editor at the house I'm working for now, one of these self-styled Max Perkinses with a red beard who thought his writers should clear every apostrophe and semicolon with him before they submitted a word. He went on to greater glory condensing books for a national magazine, but it was another two years before I got my present desk and half a window looking out on the screw top of the Chrysler Building. In the meantime I corrected other editors' spelling and once talked a former Great American Writer who was sitting in a furnished apartment with the telephone in one hand and a revolver in the other out of pulling the trigger on himself. Now I go to sleep at night reading typescripts and spend four-hour lunches listening to would-be Norman Mailers mewing about essential punctuation and one bad review written by a free-lancer with hemorrhoids for a regional magazine no one ever heard of, when I should be in front of the board going to the mat for a first novel by an unknown writer of rare genius. I hold their heads when they're blocked. I canvass the bars and police stations when they're on a binge. I listen politely to counter-offers by literary agents who think their clients are working for them, and when I'm not doing that or brushing up on the American League standings in case I should find myself in the elevator with the man who owns the firm I work for, I sometimes squeeze in a few minutes to edit someone's book. And all the time I'm counting the months since I delivered my last best seller and wondering how much longer the dry spell will last before they show me the door."

She recrossed her ankles the other way. "I don't know how I stand any of it, Mr. Walker. But I do, and if I ever had to stop I suppose I'd become the mistress of someone in the publishing business just to stay near it. Will you accept me as your client? Just me, this time. We won't bother the boys on the top floor."

I grinned. "That's some pep talk. I bet it sounds good Monday mornings at the dressing table."

This time she didn't flush. "When you read too much you tend to talk in soliloquies to anyone who will let you get away with it. Are you working for me?"

"I'm already working, Mrs. Starr. One client at a time will do. Otherwise the paperwork would kill me."

"You're too honest."

I moved a shoulder.

She stood. I got up with her. "Will you call me when you've found him?" she asked. "After your client, of course. I'm staying at the Book Cadillac. Appropriate, don't you think?"

"Last time it was the Westin."

"Last time I flew first class. That's one of the reasons books cost so much. You'll call?"

"I'll call." I got the door for her.

"I'll be there through the weekend." On the threshold she looked at me. "You promised me a tour of the city last time."

"How's Mr. Starr?"

"In New York."

I said nothing again. She waited a little, then said good-bye and went out trailing jasmine.

15

ACME COLLISION CLANGED AND RACKETED INSIDE A hangarlike building with a hip roof and lime-washed barn siding and its name painted inexpertly over the doors in red letters spidering down the front in streaks. The sun was warm on the asphalt outside, where a row of hulks with accordioned front ends squatted on blocks. In the corner nearest the street, two boys of about eleven were peering through the windows of a fresh wreck with a head-size hole in the windshield on the driver's side and brown stains on the upholstery. While I was locking my car, a loose length of redheaded man in greasy coveralls came out of the building with a wrench in one hand and chased the boys back to their bicycles. They kicked loose the stands and when they were rolling they turned in their seats to gesture obscenely back with enviable choreography. The redhead lunged forward, shaking the wrench. They leaned over the handlebars and pumped their legs like pistons and pulled away fast. Their pursuer stopped, spat. "Little bastids." I recognized the Kentucky accent from my telephone call yesterday.

I intercepted him on his way back inside and asked where I could find Wally Petite. His eyes traveled over my suit. They were a baked-out blue under pale brows as thick and as straight as an accusing finger. Finally he pointed his wrench through the spread doors. "Office."

I entered ahead of him and paused while my eyes grew accustomed to the dim light inside. Most of it was coming from a dropcord hooked on the edge of an open pickup hood, where a broad back was bent in gray coveralls with ACME COLLISION stenciled across it. On the far side of the big room, another set of coveralls whooshed clouds of acrid-smelling blue paint from a spray gun over a white Lincoln with masking on the windows and trim. A third worker had a door panel clamped in a wooden vise on one of the steel workbenches that lined the room and was banging out the dents with a short-handled sledgehammer in time with the music blasting out of a portable radio at his feet. He was naked to the waist and his arms bulged when he swung back the heavy hammer. Every time it struck home he said, "Huh!" Sweat rolled off his slick torso, overpowering the odors of stale grease and turpentine sunk into the walls.

The office was a glassed-in cubicle to the left of the doors. The door was propped open with a brick and I went in without knocking. It wouldn't have been heard over the music and pounding anyway.

"Have a seat, Walker. Close the door."

I kicked the brick out of the way and pushed the door shut. The noise level went down a notch.

The man who had spoken was hunched over an old Adler on a stand behind an oak desk with a cracked veneer, plucking at the keys with one index finger and taking all the time in the world to select his next letter. He had on a salmon-colored shirt with puffed sleeves and the collar spread over a tight black vest with gold fleurs-de-lis on the back. A gold chain glittered among the dark hairs on his swarthy chest. He wore his brown hair long and full on the sides in styled waves to bring out his high cheekbones, and the one eye I could see in profile had lashes long enough to trap a bird. A black jacket with peaked lapels faced in velour draped a wooden hanger on a hook on the door I had just closed.

"Mr. Petite?"

"With you in a minute. Sit down. I usually have someone fill in these applications for title for me, but she's out sick. Funny how many employees take ill these last few weeks of good weather."

His voice was absolutely smooth, not so much polished as lathed down, with no hint of geography or origins and only so many tones as he needed to make himself understood. A perfect cylinder. I turned a chair made of steel tubing and red vinyl to face the desk and trusted my weight to it. A picture calendar on the one wall that wasn't glass behind the desk showed a gang of gray moustaches in scarlet jackets and jodhpurs leaning horses around a copse of trees in pursuit of a red-brown streak with the hounds in full cry between. Whenever I saw a print like that I wondered what happened to the fox. I decided I didn't want to know.

"There!"

He struck one last key and rolled the sheet out of the typewriter. When he turned my way I saw that his left eyelid drooped a little, as if a nerve or a muscle had been severed. It spoiled his girlish good looks. "I'm sorry about the condition of the place," he said. "We're moving to larger quarters end of next month. My office will be on a different floor from the nuts and bolts, air-conditioned and soundproofed."

I said, "The body game must be booming."

He didn't take the bait. "It's always good. When the economy's rolling so are the cars, and the more cars on the road the more likely they are to run into each other. Then when money's tight everyone saves by holding on to the old wreck and they bring it in here to keep it looking good. You should see some of the crates that limp in. By the time we're done stripping them to the frame and replacing the rusty parts with sheet metal and pounding out the dents and repainting and rechroming them, their owners might as well have bought a new one hot off the line. But we earn it, and there's real satisfaction in turning a clunker into a classic."

"Kind of like surgery," I said. "Only more fulfilling."

That time his face shut down. He leaned back in his chair and steepled his fingers, and Lou Gallardo was wrong; there was no grease under his nails. A gold ingot flashed on the third finger of his left hand. "You wanted to talk about Phil."

"I think the man I'm looking for was investigating his murder when he disappeared. Maybe you've seen him." I described Barry.

"No one who answers that description has been in here. No one has come around asking about Phil. You're the first in more than a year."

"Maybe he spoke to one of your employees."

"I'd have been told. What makes you think he was interested in what happened to Phil?"

"He had a file folder full of newspaper clippings in his

office. The piece about the cops finding Niles's body was among them."

"That's all?"

"Amigo Fuentes told me a blond man with a limp was in asking about Niles last week."

"Amigo Fuentes." He made as if to crack his knuckles. "That son-of-a-bitch greaser killed Phil and got clean away. Maybe he killed your friend too."

Something about the way he said the Cuban's name. Not the way someone whose ancestors came from a cold climate would have said it. I got out my pack and offered him a cigarette. He hesitated, then took one. I struck a match and lit it and one for me. "In that case he wouldn't have told me Barry had been there," I said. "And Fuentes was in Florida at the time of the murder."

"He had it catered."

Our smoke curled and mingled in the air. Smoke doesn't care what kind of company it keeps.

I said, "How hard did the police question you about your partner?"

"Pretty hard. When I was younger I was pretty wild. I have a record for theft. But that's behind me, and I could account for all my movements. They wanted Fuentes worse. I guess you know about Acme's reputation."

"A little."

He scraped some ash off on the edge of a Styrofoam cup on the desk. "I'm not making any confession today. But small businesses have a steep hike the first year or so. You tend to get involved in things you wouldn't if your old age didn't depend on them."

"You're no longer heisting cars?"

"I never said we were."

His voice presented no ethnic or environmental handles

107

whatsoever. Someone had put in his share of hours on this one. I used the cup. "Anyone can cater a kill. Five grand will buy the best talent Hazel Park has to offer, complete with a virgin piece and a new demonstrator model borrowed off a Ford lot for the get-gone. If you're strapped you can go down Woodward and hire it for the price of a lid, but the quality will suffer. There's a whole range of working muscle in between."

"The point being?"

"The point being that if, say, a former mechanic with a police record, in partnership with a businessman who won't see the profit in certain trade practices, wanted him gone, his partner's involvement with a loan shark could stir up some useful dust."

"I think I've just been accused of contracting a murder," he said. "I wouldn't know, of course."

"I'm just poking at the haystack. All I've got is a newspaper clipping and the word of a shylock."

"We're through talking now." He swiveled his chair and turned a knob with exposed wires running up the wall, like an antique light switch. A loud burring ring like an amplified telephone bell echoed through the building. It was still fading when the door opened and two men came in. One was the lanky redhead who had chased the kids away from the wreck out front. He still had the wrench. His companion was the man I'd seen beating the door panel in the vise. He had a bald head and a matted black tangle of beard that spread into the hair on his chest and the muscles of his torso bunched and squirmed as he worked his hands on the sledge across his thighs. "Make sure this gentleman finds his way out," Petite told them. To me: "Unless you bend a fender, don't come back. A man that doesn't know his way around the equipment in places like this . . ." He gestured with the cigarette between his fingers.

"I have to admire me." I got up. "I'm unstoppable. They bounce jack handles off my stomach and throw me in with the big cats and I keep coming. I don't even pause to count my teeth. So long, Mr. Petite."

"Good-bye, Walker. Thanks for the smoke. I'm trying to cut down."

"That's what I was counting on."

After unlocking both offices and throwing away my mail I didn't know what to do next. I looked at Barry's typescript, which I'd brought with me from home, but I didn't feel like reading. I didn't even know why I'd brought it. It wasn't doing me any good.

The first lead never leads anywhere. You spot a bright thread and pick at it, hoping the whole dense fabric will come apart in your hands, and then it catches and you tug and it snaps and there you are staring at the frazzled end. But there was still the blond cripple Fuentes had said was also curious about the Niles murder. The shark might have known those things about Barry from his column, but even crooks don't lie just for practice. I called Jed Dutt at the *News*.

"Any sign of the boy reporter?" I asked.

"None. Which answers *my* question. Anything else?"

"You remember who got the Philip Niles case?"

He went to get his notes. I listened to a lone typewriter somewhere clacking out its last days amid creeping technology. They used to argue about sex and politics at parties. Now they talk software. He came back on the line.

"Sergeant Ysabel, with a Y, of the Royal Oak Police

109

Department. He's with Detroit now, Major Crimes. Or was last I heard."

I mouthed gratitude and punched off and dialed Detroit Police Headquarters. The switchboard put me through to Major Crimes. "Sergeant Ysabel," I said.

"You mean Lieutenant Ysabel," a woman's voice corrected. "He won't be in until four. Can I take a message?"

I said I'd call after four. Replacing the receiver, I looked at Barry's script again.

There is a specialist with the First Air Cavalry, a large fellow with football shoulders and gentle brown eyes who grins easily and wears his helmet tipped forward with the strap buckled under the bulge of his head to keep it from skidding over his eyes. The prostitutes in town, whether or not they are out with other men, are always making excuses to touch him and stand close to him with their eyes sliding sideways to look at his profile. He is popular with the men of his unit, but officers do not like him, as he has a quick mouth and even when he is carrying out an order behaves as if he just thought of it himself. We met some weeks ago by accident during a shelling. I like him and think he is the reason I have stayed in this area so long rather than moving ahead with the main column.

Last week while on patrol he came upon a Vietcong standing over what remained of a specialist with whom he'd gone through basic training. He went on spraying lead into the Cong seconds after his body stopped twitching, until his M-16 clicked empty. None of the other Americans who witnessed the incident dared step forward before then.

Today we went into town together for a drink. He smokes heavily, and through the haze his grin is as quick and his eyes are as gentle. His repartee is as lively and he is no less responsive to the admiring glances of the prostitutes.

It is not in the little ways we show change.

Well, what did you expect, Barry? It's like when you see a movie or read a book you liked years before, and not only do you not like it, you can't imagine ever having been the sort of person who would. And basic training or no, I had never been all that close to Spec-4 Michael Valducci, who ate his squid raw and cleaned his rifle with whoever's jockstrap was handy. He was just a constant face in a shifting sea and then he wasn't.

They sent us halfway around the world to a place where our fillings rusted in our mouths and declared open season on jungle creatures with leaves on their heads and bags of rice on thongs around their necks. Russian MIGs shrieked overhead in formations no farther apart than spread fingers and American F-111s sprayed villages with a gelatinous mass that caught fire with a sucking sound when it hit the air. We hunted Charlie and we plowed the girls in Saigon and it was like one of those lost continent pictures with rubber dinosaurs and midget actors made up like ape men, that you hoot at in the theater and then when the lights go up you go outside and breathe cold air and listen to tires swishing down the street and already it's fading. Six months later you put your hand in the pocket of a jacket you haven't worn in a while and come out with the stub and then you remember. Jesus, but that was a lousy picture.

Only it wasn't a ticket stub that brought it back, but a

glimpse of the neighbor's Asian gardener weeding the lawn or a traffic helicopter chattering over the house or the sunlight coming green through leaves in a park at a moment when you're thinking about anything but Vietnam. Then you think about nothing but, and then you get mad because the whole thing has ruined you for those moments, and maybe forever, the way learning of the death of a close relative while your favorite song is playing on the radio will have you thinking of the death every time you hear the song from then on. It wasn't at all like a bad movie, or even like a bad dream. It was like nothing for anyone who wasn't there.

I restacked the typewritten sheets and pushed them to one side and thought about what I should do next. I was suddenly thirsty and thought about the bottle in the bottom drawer of the desk. It seemed a corny place to keep a bottle; why didn't I have a bar? But Mr. John T. Molloy said professionals who want to look professional didn't have bars in their offices. A careful man, Mr. Molloy. He would wear pinstriped pajamas to bed and line up his slippers with the toes pointed out and when he had breakfast he would take his coffee and his toast first and then his eggs and bacon, one strip, fried not too crisp, because that was how professionals slept and ate breakfast. I thought of all that and then I wasn't thirsty anymore. I said to hell with Mr. Molloy and his pajamas and bacon and got out my little sheaf of Xeroxed clippings. On top was the long piece about Alfred Kindnagel, the Jewish labor chief.

The main photograph was one of these flattering studio jobs shot through a Kleenex, of a man with a large dome, jug ears, a comfortable set of chins, smiling eyes, and twelve black hairs strung across his scalp. He wore a brown suit with a stripe that was almost invisible and a

112

softly shining sepia necktie. It was the kind of thing they frame in heavy gilt and hang in the boardroom with a brass plaque reading OUR FOUNDER. The others were more casual: Kindnagel, much younger and slimmer but already losing his hair, conversing earnestly in his shirtsleeves with a group of mortar-smeared bricklayers during the labor crises of the Depression; Kindnagel, aging, sitting on a bench outside a congressional committee hearing room, slumped in his overcoat with the brim of his hat turned up and a bodyguard seated on either side; Kindnagel in retirement, broad, bald, and beaming, pale belly hanging outside his swim trunks, tossing a ball for his six-year-old granddaughter at the beach; Kindnagel at his brother's funeral, tired and emaciated-looking, leaning on the arms of his wife and middle-aged daughter. The caption said that was his most recent photograph. It was probably his last, as he died shortly before the article appeared.

The story concentrated on his early years and the quiet methods by which he had obtained power among Jewish workers while the nation was watching the brawls and sit-down strikes at River Rouge and the machine guns atop the Ford plant, and on the efforts of the FBI, once it had belatedly taken notice of him, to harass him into retirement because of "leftist leanings." But 117 hours of telephone taps at his home and office had yielded nothing more instructive than a crash course in the Yiddish vernacular and his mother's matzoh recipe. Twelve years later he bowed out of public life for reasons of health and thereafter divided his seasons between the family home in Bloomfield Hills and a small estate in Miami.

His widow's name was Grete. Just for fun I looked her up in the directory. A G. Kindnagel was listed in Bloomfield Hills. I looked at my watch. I had four and a half hours to kill before Lieutenant Ysabel reported for duty.

"Hello?"

An elderly woman's voice. "Grete Kindnagel?" I asked.

"This is Grete Kindnagel. Please, who is speaking?"

"I'm a Detroit private investigator looking into the disappearance of a man who I think may have been researching your late husband's life when he vanished. I wondered if I could come over sometime and talk to you about it."

There was a little silence before she asked the question. "Is this Mr. Stackpole?"

16

A TISSUE OF CLOUD SLID PAST THE WINDOW, GRAYING OUT the square of yellow on the desk and floor. I waited until it passed.

"My name is Amos Walker," I told Grete Kindnagel then. "Has Barry Stackpole been in contact with you?"

"He called. Last week sometime, I don't know what day just. They have to tell me when it's Saturday so I remember not to cook or clean house. He asked could he come over, talk about Alf, just like you. I told him to come ahead. But he didn't." She paused, and I heard her breath trembling. "Is it about Alf's pension?"

I assured her it wasn't. "What did Stackpole say?"

"What I said. He said he didn't want to talk about it over the phone. I made tea and put some cookies on a plate. I always have refreshments when visitors come. Only he didn't."

"Is it all right if I come over now? I have some questions to ask. It won't take long."

"I guess. But I'm not putting the water on until you get here."

I got directions and cruised on out.

The feudal lines are softening around Detroit. In the old days, the blue collars and lunch pails kept to the city, with its weatherworn apartment buildings and miles of housing developments as alike as hiccups, while the gold collar pins and silver fox furs breathed the bottled air in Grosse Pointe. But then wages rose, drawing itinerant field hands up from Kentucky and Tennessee and Georgia and Alabama and Mississippi in their rattletrap trucks and touring cars to the automobile factories and creating a new class among the workers already on the scene, who fled north and west and staked out their own communities with names like Birmingham and Beverly Hills and Madison Heights and Pleasant Ridge, places with country clubs and basements with walnut paneling and blue shag rugs for the neighbors to sit around in sipping gin rickeys and talking about lawn edgers and orgasms. Bloomfield Hills was one of these, grown up around a sprawl of half-timbered buildings established by newspaper magnate George G. Booth in the 1920s, inspired by Hearst's castle at San Simeon and including a church, private schools, an art school, and a science museum, under the name of the Cranbrook Institute. The homes were laid out in kind: bricks of hedges and redwood fences around backyard swimming pools, gaslights and Neighborhood Watch decals in the windows.

The address Grete Kindnagel had given me belonged to a large brick house with wings on either side and red-painted shutters on at least a dozen windows facing the street. It had a half-acre of front lawn with one of those marble birdbaths on it that are made to look like Roman ruins and a circular composition driveway containing a

116

gold Continental Mark IV glittering in a puddle of water that reflected the clouds skidding overhead. I parked behind it and mounted a fresh concrete slab in front of the door and used the knocker. It was shaped like a ram's head with a ring in its mouth. Somewhere a motor with a long piston stroke was making a noise like pea soup coming to a boil.

"Yes?"

I looked at a tall man in his thirties with dark hair combed forward over an advancing brow and dark eyes I thought looked familiar without knowing why, and then I remembered the portrait of Alfred Kindnagel that had accompanied Jed Dutt's article. He had on a white tennis shirt with a chesspiece embroidered on the left breast, rumpled gray cotton slacks, and black oxfords. He kept his hand on the knob of the open door.

I explained who I was and why I was there. As I spoke, a little of the suspicion on his face skinned off. "Yes, Grandmother said she was expecting you," he said. "I'm Jack Kindnagel, Alf's grandson."

"Jack?"

"Jeremiah, originally. Come in. Grandmother's out back."

I wiped my feet and entered. He closed the door and I followed him through a sunlit room with paintings on the walls into other rooms with leather-bound books on shelves and antique tables holding up china clocks and porcelain figurines. The place was immaculate. Jack Kindnagel caught me looking around. "Grandmother does all the cleaning herself. She won't have a housekeeper."

The motor noise got louder as we walked, and then we stepped out onto a screened-in porch with wicker furniture and bright cushions. Beyond the screen stretched an expanse of grass twice as big as the one in front. At the far end a tiny figure in a flowered dress under a broad straw hat wheeled a baby tractor around the corner of the lawn, towing a cutter spraying green clippings out the back. The air smelled sharply of cut grass.

Kindnagel said something to me that was lost in the noise, but which I took as a request to wait, and went out through a screen door. At his approach the woman on the tractor reached down and hauled back on a handle, then flipped a switch or a key on the dash or whatever it was called. The motor sputtered and died. She climbed down. Facing the young man at ground level she came barely to his shoulder. The straw hat bobbed up and down and the two started walking back to the porch.

"Mr. Walker?" While her grandson held the screen door, Grete Kindnagel stepped through it and held out her hand. It was tiny and full of blue veins and gripped mine like a pair of pliers wrapped in a damp cloth. "My, you got here fast. I hoped to get done the mowing before you came. You met Jeremiah."

I said I had.

"He's a great disappointment to me," she said, shaking her head. "All he does is wash the car and play golf."

"I'm a professional golfer." He said it without rancor.

"You smack a little white ball into a hole and call it work. Any schlemiel can do that."

"Grandmother keeps all my trophies in a glass case upstairs," Jack told me.

"Out of sight."

Jack said, "I'll put the tea on."

"You keep Mr. Walker company. The male half of this family can't boil water without burning it." She went inside.

118

Her grandson waved me into one of the wicker chairs and took the bench for himself. "She's quite a lady," he said. "Everyone thought she'd dry up and blow away when Alf died. She just got stronger. It took not having him around to make a real Jewish mother out of her. She's eighty-seven now. She was a child bride."

"You call your grandfather Alf?"

"Everyone did. He insisted."

We ran out of polite conversation then. I shifted my weight on the wicker. I felt like Sidney Greenstreet.

"Why are you here?" asked Jack. "Alf's been dead almost three years."

"You're asking the wrong person, Mr. Kindnagel. Two other people are dead, one for almost as long as your grandfather, and I don't know why I was asking about them either."

"It's a strange way to go about conducting a missing person investigation."

"In my line I have to go looking in the tall grass. I can't go where the light's better because what I'm looking for won't be there. Being a golfer you should understand that."

"I'm going to stay if you don't mind," he said. "And even if you do. To make sure Grandmother doesn't get hurt."

I moved my head noncommittally and looked out through the screen. A line of half-grown maples separated the end of the yard from the beginnings of the one next door, the leaves turning copper.

The old lady returned carrying a tray with a silver teapot and white china cups and a dish of oatmeal cookies. She set it down on a latticework table and began pouring. I stared at her. She was thick-waisted but not fat, and her face was round and tan without a wrinkle. Without the hat, her white hair curled back in thick waves behind small flat ears with amber buttons in them. The backs of her hands were burned red. She handed me a cup and saucer.

"I hope you're not one of these people that take sugar," she said. "Alf did, until we went to England and they almost deported him for it."

"Thank you. I don't take sugar in anything."

"You didn't look to me like someone that would. Have a cookie." She sat down on the bench next to her grandson, balancing a cup and saucer in her lap.

"Where's mine?" asked Jack.

"You're not staying."

"Yes, I am."

"Whose name is the house in?"

"Grandmother—"

She patted his knee. "Run along, Jeremiahla. Practice your bogies."

"You don't practice bogies, you try to avoid them." But he stood up. Bending to kiss her upturned cheek, he let his eyes rest on me for a second. I ate a cookie.

When he had gone inside, she said: "He eagled the fifteenth at Metropolitan Beach last Saturday, finished four under for the tournament. Alf would have been proud."

I fed my grin some tea. "Can I ask you about Mr. Kindnagel?"

"That's why you're here, isn't it? Do you like those cookies?"

They tasted like pressed newspaper. "Very much. Did Mr. Kindnagel have any dealings with a man named Philip Niles? He owned half of a body shop in Royal Oak."

"I don't think so. He leased his cars from a company that took care of the maintenance."

"Union business?"

"It's eight years since a Kindnagel had anything to do with the union. Alf didn't want anyone else in the family involved. He said labor racketeering was getting to be on the wrong foot. It's why he left."

"I thought it was for his health."

"That's what he told everyone. The truth is he came home one night and said he looked around and realized he was the last member of the board of directors that had ever held a trowel. All the younger men around him went to business school. They thought a callus was something you got on a clay court. I said, 'Quit.' He announced his retirement next day."

"He sounds like a man of principle."

"Yes." It was a sigh.

I played my hole card. "Did he know a Lieutenant Ray Blankenship of the Detroit Police Department?"

"I can't say. We met a number of police officers once the FBI started persecuting him. They searched his offices in Detroit several times. We knew they were cooperating with the federals. I don't know that he knew their names ever. He didn't bring them home for dinner."

"What about all that? Was your husband a leftist?"

"You mean was he a Communist. Is this the home of a Communist? Well, he voted for Eugene Debs once. Who didn't, who wasn't born in this country? What can I tell you of a time when a quarter was so big you could trip over it? No, Alf was no leftist."

"Searches aren't lieutenant level," I mused. "Any other circumstances that might have brought him head to head with the authorities?"

She freshened my tea. "Mr. Walker, my husband made his living in those what-do-you-call circumstances."

"The police specifically."

"Well, in the old days, when he was getting started, he had to cooperate with the Purple Gang, let them know what he was doing and was it all right with them. They had everything nailed down to do with the Jews around Detroit. He spent time at their homes and the police knew that and they came to talk to him now and then. And later he talked to some Jewish police officers about organizing them separate from the D.P.O.A., but that fell through. That's too far back probably. I can't think of anything else. Well, the murder."

"Which murder?"

"Which murder. The murder. How many do you think we have? This isn't the Teamsters. A shop steward in a bearing plant on Eight Mile Road. I think it was Eight Mile. It doesn't matter because it's closed now. He was shot. I don't remember his name. It wasn't long before Alf retired. The police talked to him about it, but he didn't even know the man. I don't know if they ever found out who did it or why." She watched me writing in my notebook. "Do you think it's important?"

"Maybe. Probably not. The odds of being in the same union with a murdered man aren't encouraging. These Purples you say your husband was in tight with; some of them kept their hands in after Prohibition was repealed. Did he maintain contact?"

"I don't know that he'd have reason to. Those boys lost their hold when the country went wet."

"That's it?"

She shook her head, smiling with a little shrug. "What has this to do with Mr. Stackpole?"

"If I knew that I wouldn't be out here breathing your air." I flipped the pad shut and picked up my tea. The cookie was lying like a hockey puck on the floor of my

122

stomach. First Amigo Fuentes' jack handle, then Grete Kindnagel's cookies. When the cup was empty I set it down and made leaving movements and she said:

"Please stay a minute. I don't get many new visitors, just the family. You get tired of looking around and seeing your own eyes looking back at you. Alf and I outlived all the friends we made."

"You did well doing it." I sat back.

She looked out across the broad sweep of lawn and at the young maples. She had a profile like a little girl's, all round with no sharp angles. "I spend most of my time out here when the weather's nice. It's the only place where I can feel it's my home. When we built the place Alf brought in an interior decorator, a tall young woman in leopard pants and a scarf hanging down around her ankles. She decided antiques and old books fit someone of Alf's gravity. That's the word she used, gravity. So our furniture and my mother's knickknacks went into storage and we made the place over into a museum like one of those Great American Homes they're always painting in commercials on the TV. Sitting in the living room I always feel like I'm waiting to go somewhere else. I guess nothing's stopping me from changing back now. But Alf liked it. Don't ever let them take your home away from you, Mr. Walker."

"I won't."

"I came over in nineteen-eleven," she said. "My father smelled a pogrom coming and put together everything he had to send me. I made the trip all alone, a girl of fourteen, and stayed with my Uncle Max, who owned a fruit stand on Brush. I stayed a week, then he tried to do a terrible thing to me and I moved out. He said I'd become a whore or starve. I got a job waiting tables in a restaurant on Beaubien. I was a good waitress. I made my salary all over again in tips. Then the owner fired me and hired his daughter in my place, only she didn't make one third as much in tips. I got another job waiting tables uptown. Three years I waited tables, and then Alf came in all covered with mortar dust. He looked like a young prince."

She was staring at the spot where the trees met the sky. Then she shook her head. "I'm sorry. When most of your life is the past you spend too much time in it. I've watched my people move past Twelfth and Fourteenth Streets into Oak Park and Southfield, and now they're leaving Bloomfield Hills for Farmington. It's a lot of past measured in city blocks like that."

"Not so much an exodus as a migration," I put in. "Over here, anyway."

"I guess. Mr. Stackpole is a friend of yours, isn't he?"

I had to scramble to jump the gap. "Yes."

"I know by the way you talked about him over the phone. Is he in trouble?"

"I don't know. Probably. He almost always is. We're a lot alike that way."

"I had a brother. The Nazis put him on a train to Poland. I heard about it later. By the time I wanted to help he was gone."

"I'm sorry."

"They were talking about it on the radio the other day. They call it the Holocaust now. For thirty years it didn't have a name and now they've given it one. I guess that makes it something they can handle. It's wrong. You can't give a thing like that a name, like a pet you can make do tricks. It's a horror without a shape. You try to step back so you can see it all, but there isn't that much room in the world. It's too big to call big."

I agreed by saying nothing.

"Amos," she said. "A good Old Testament name. He was the shepherd who warned Syria and Palestine of the wrath of God."

"I've heard."

She looked out through the screen. "'Hate the evil, and love the good.' What else? Oh, yes. 'Let justice roll down as waters, and righteousness as a mighty stream.' Are you Jewish, Mr. Walker?"

"No. I was named after 'Amos 'n' Andy.'"

"I didn't think so." She refilled our cups. "The name means 'burden,' you know."

"I didn't know."

"Well, the Bible is like the Talmud. You can make it say what you want."

My stomach hurt, so I let it ride. She sipped tea and watched the leaves turn.

17

A COUNTY WAGON WAS SKINNING AWAY FROM THE CURB in front of my building as I cruised past looking for a place to park. With its light off and its sirens still, it made all the noise of embalming fluid filling a vein.

I felt my heart give a little hop. It was like driving home and seeing a column of smoke rising over your neighborhood. I doubled next to an unmarked car I recognized and walked back. Sergeant Grice was just coming out of the building. He had on a yellow shirt like the one I had seen him in at the blind pig, under a red tie and his three-piece. The crinkled flesh on the right side of his face glistened in the sunlight. When he saw me his brows bunched. "You must have a scanner. That, or you're following me. Which?"

"Neither. This is my building. Who's dead?"

"A connoisseur of the grape that called himself Willy, according to the super. We probably never will know his real name if he don't have a record."

"Black, army coat, knit cap?"

"That's him. One of your neighbors tripped over him in the stairwell an hour ago."

"You made good time."

"I was in the area when I got the squeal."

"The slasher?"

He grinned with one side of his mouth. The burned side didn't move. "Which one, Philo? We got at least four, way the M.O. pisses all over the lot. No, this one was a bad call. He took a pull and missed the stairs. Folded his head neat as you please and stuck it in his pocket. Or he would of if he didn't already have an extra bottle in it. Someone got generous."

"I slipped him a five yesterday."

"You didn't do him any favors. Or maybe you did, depending on how you look at it. I bet you feed pigeons too."

"Rats with feathers." The white cop with the thin moustache and snapbrim hat appeared from inside. "Bastards shit on every hat I got."

"What you get for dressing like Dick Tracy," Grice said. "Let's go, Waddell."

They started toward the unmarked car. I fell into step. "An employee of a bearing plant on Eight Mile Road was shot to death about eight years ago. That's the Fourteenth, isn't it? Blankenship's old precinct?"

"I don't know. Maybe. Go down to headquarters, look at the map. This your bucket?"

"I'll move it." I got out my keys.

He watched me get in and start the engine. "That where we met? Headquarters?"

"Could be. I'm down there a lot."

"No, it wasn't headquarters. I'll get it yet."

He was rubbing the jaw I'd slugged. I took hold of the

127

inside door handle. He stopped leaning on the door and I pulled it shut. I put the Olds in Drive but kept my foot on the brake. He was still staring at me through the open window. I said, "You know a lieutenant in Major Crimes named Ysabel?"

"Yeah, I know Izzy."

"What sort of cop is he?"

"A killer, like the rest of his detail."

Major Crimes had a big room to itself on an upper floor at 1300 Beaubien, Detroit Police Headquarters. A row of windows made of the same tough bullet-resistant plastic that they cover telephones with overlooked the corner of Macomb, across from an American flag tacked to the plaster wall above the wainscoting. In the center of the room rose a square pillar paved with wanted circulars, duty rosters, interdepartmental communiqués, and hand-printed advertisements selling used cars and registered puppies. The light came through frosted panels in the ceiling, and the floor was covered with squares of linoleum with a marble pattern under a glaze of dirt. There were too many desks in the room and too many detectives for the desks.

I buttonholed a big sergeant in uniform shirtsleeves, who glanced at the visitor tag on my breast pocket and pointed out a dark man sitting at a desk on the far end of the room. On my way there I passed a plainclothesman at another desk polishing the chambers of a Colt Cobra. It had four notches in the handle.

When the old STRESS undercover unit was disbanded under the present administration, most of its veterans were shunted into a special squad created to handle priority cases—terrorism, hostage situations, transportation for the mayor's sister—anything that could cost votes in an election year if not handled properly. Nothing else had changed, and it was still pretty much the same cast doing pretty much the same things, atlhough fewer black fugitives were getting blown away in boxcars. If there was a man in that room who had never killed anyone it was the guy emptying wastebaskets near the windows.

The cop who had been pointed out to me was on the telephone. He was all squares and hard angles in a suit and tie with no more color in them than the well-trod floor. He had a broad dusky face set off by a thick moustache and brown hair cut in bangs. His features had a Mediterranean look, but more Greek than Italian. He spoke low into the receiver with his eyes cast down and his elbows on the desk. The desk was big and old and relatively uncluttered, with arrest forms and file folders and blank sheets arranged in separate stacks and a battleship-gray manual typewriter on a sliding wood leaf at his left elbow. His nameplate read LT. K. YSABEL.

I moved a straightback chair to a spot where I wouldn't feel so much like a job applicant and sat in it and lit a cigarette. I had it half smoked when he said "Okay" and cradled the receiver. He was one of those who put it down backwards, with the cord looping around in front of the instrument.

I said, "K?"

"Konstantin." He looked at me. He had liquid brown eyes, and for a change they had more depth than a pair of soup stains. "You're Walker?"

I said I was Walker. I had called at four and caught him as he was signing in. He said:

"I talked to Alderdyce in Homicide like you said. He said you were good for a favor. Right now I can't picture any fix bad enough I'd need private help to get out of it,

129

but in this business the one thing you know is you never know. I have to go from memory on the Niles burn, though. When I came down here my records stayed in Royal Oak."

"I always said a cop's memory is as good as a bulldog's handshake."

"Too true."

"I talked to Amigo Fuentes, the shark, and Niles's partner, Wally Petite. I wondered which one you liked for it."

He leaned back in his chair, linking his hands behind his head. Even his elbows made a square angle. "Detroit handed us Fuentes. We questioned him. I took along a Hispanic officer just in case he wanted to trot out that *no hablo inglés* shit, but he didn't. That little spick can talk like an English lord when he feels like it. I hated his pepper-burning guts. But he didn't kill Niles. Those boys don't step on the clientele no matter what you read. Re-hang their noses, maybe, when they don't pay through them fast enough, but they don't even do that anymore, much. Hell, some of them are demanding collateral up front these days. It's getting so you can't tell them from the suits in the bank buildings, as when could you ever. It wasn't Fuentes. Why take the loss when you don't pay taxes in the first place?"

"Petite, then."

"I like Petite," he said. "I like him a lot."

"He had an alibi?"

"Couple of buying trips for parts upstate. Nothing we couldn't blow down. But he was a cool order. He had some old priors for embezzling and petty theft, did ninety days at Cassiday Lake for cannibalizing parked cars at public access sites. He knew the routine. We couldn't budge him."

"You figure he had it done?"

"Yeah. You don't go from Larceny Under a Hundred

Dollars to Murder One without something in between. The cells are full of law-abiding citizens that suddenly turned Lizzie Borden, but damn few petty thieves kill in cold blood. I could show you the stats. But we couldn't link him to any of the known local talent and we keep an eye on the stone killers in from out of town. The case was still open when I left. Nobody was doing anything about it."

I watched him squaring off the edges of the stacks of paper on his desk. He was a neat cop. I wondered if he read John T. Molloy. "Has Barry Stackpole been in asking about Niles?"

"That's the guy from the *News*?" I nodded. "He hasn't talked to me. He the guy you're looking for?"

"Yeah."

"You find him, ask him for me where that guy in the City-County Building found that silk wallpaper. I want to show it to my wife. Maybe she'll get the hint and go easy on the tile in the new bathroom."

I said I'd be glad to, and got up. "Oh, would you know anything about the murder of a factory worker on Eight Mile Road about eight years ago?"

"Not me. Eight years ago I was chasing skinny-dippers out of the community swimming pool in Royal Oak."

"Would Eight Mile have been Ray Blankenship's territory when he worked out of the Fourteenth?"

"Could be. Funny you should mention him."

I waited.

"Blankenship was the arresting officer on one of Wally Petite's priors," he said, flicking a shred of paper off the top file folder on the desk. "I don't know which one. I wouldn't have remembered except he's been on my mind since he croaked himself yesterday."

I thanked him and left one of my cards.

The foyer of my building smelled of lemons from the floor wax the building superintendent used. He had rushed the season this time because Willy the Wino had landed on his jug when he jackknifed down the stairs and splashed Tuesday's grapes over the linoleum. At this rate the tenants would have to chip in and buy the super a new can in five years or so.

I crossed the spot where the old man had landed and went upstairs. I didn't feel any manifestations. If he'd had enough left of himself to bequeath the place a ghost he wouldn't have spent my whole five bucks on wine, but would've held out some for a new old coat or a pair of socks to keep the corrugated insides of his shoes from rubbing holes in his feet. But he hadn't come for the five. All he'd wanted was a place to snooze where the neighborhood brats wouldn't set fire to his beard. Instead, Big-Hearted A. Walker had bought him his last ride to a broken neck. No, someone had handed him fare for that several stops back. Big-Hearted A. Walker had just called out his destination. Last stop, West Grand River Avenue: Pimps, whores, rummies, and Michigan State licensed private investigators. Everybody out.

You see them poking through cans in alleys for a piece of twine to hold the soles on their shoes and standing back out of the sidewalk traffic muttering to themselves and occasionally snoozing in a fetal position in the middle of Cadillac Square at rush hour with thousands of pairs of feet whispering around them, which is like a hunger-crazed coyote wandering into the middle of a busy village with its tongue dusty and eyes bright with fever, only not quite, because you'd look at a coyote. They don't want your

132

help. They wanted it back when the plant they worked for twenty-two years closed and their son needed bail and their wife walked off with the meter reader and the joint savings account, but when they came to you you told them things were tough all over and go try food stamps. Now all they want is your spare change and your back.

They sleep in weedy lots and abandoned cars and cardboard boxes lined with rags, and on bitter December mornings someone has to rip open the boxes and place the clenched cold corpses like gnarled apple limbs into the county wagon and bury them the way they are in children's coffins rather than attempt to straighten them out. They have to sleep in those places because the city council voted to combat rape by tearing down the empty buildings, and don't tell the city council about burning the barn to get rid of the rats because they'll understand about rats but not about barns. So the buildings came down and now when it starts to get dark the homeless gravitate toward the tall weeds and the deep doorways, and the five percent of them that are women, the lucky ones who are not yet all the way hags anyhow, smooth their ratty coats and adjust their men's hats and trade the only thing they have to trade for a few hours out of the wind. Then in the morning those that get up start scouting for a place for when it gets dark again.

Well, Willy had a place now. They'd lay him out for a while naked on a steel table with a drain hole at one end and his rags in a paper sack between his legs, and when nobody came to claim him he'd go into a cold drawer and when nobody came then he'd go into a hole in county soil. He'd get more attention in the coming week than he'd gotten in ten years. All on five dollars.

I didn't have any loonies or anyone else in my waiting room. I let myself into the office and sat down behind the desk. The half-drawn blinds sliced a bar of dusty sunlight into stripes in the corner next to the old-fashioned water closet, where the stripes lay in that motionless pattern that suggests a stopped clock and a spider dozing in its web, an autumn afternoon with nowhere to go and no pressing need to get there this week, the moment hung in time like a miner's hat on an oaken peg in a saloon abandoned ninety years ago. I spoiled it by picking up the telephone and calling my service for messages. I had a message.

18

"MRS. BLANKENSHIP?"

She jumped a little when I spoke. I'd caught her at a corner table in front of the segmented front window, looking out at the street in front of the restaurant. I'd walked right past her nose and come in the door and glanced around and come up to her without her noticing. Her eyes flicked from my face to my shoes and back to my face in a meaningless little darting movement, and then the corners of her mouth bent to form a smile. "Mr. Walker? I'm sorry. I didn't know what you looked like."

She raised a smooth hand with cherry-colored nails and we touched fingers and I slid into the chair opposite hers. She was a trim woman of about forty-five and she had been handsome, but her face had gotten too thin, the skin tugged into sharp lines from her nose to her mouth, and dark thumbsmears had filled the hollows under her eyes. She wore her wavy auburn hair swept behind her ears and pinned loosely in place with a black hat the size and shape

135

of a cantaloupe quarter nested on top. It was the only black thing she had on. Her blouse was royal blue and her skirt, what I had seen of it coming in, was dark green. Hasty mourning.

The restaurant was on West Davison, one of those places with a striped awning out front and captain's chairs inside and the Catch of the Day paper-clipped to the menu. When a hippy blonde waitress cruised by to refill Mrs. Blankenship's cup from a steaming glass pot I righted the cup at my elbow and she filled that too, leaving me with a sealed thimbleful of what passes for cream in restaurants on West Davison with captain's chairs and awnings.

My companion was looking outside again. The street had that coppery glow you see a couple of times a year just before dusk, that interrupts conversations and has everyone glancing toward the windows.

"Beautiful, isn't it?" she said. "I was admiring it when you came. I guess that's why I missed you. It looks like an old tintype."

I said, "It's supposed to precede bad weather. A storm. Something about the nitrogen in the air."

"The meteorologists can't let pretty light just be pretty light." She sipped her coffee.

We watched the pretty light for a while. Soon the gray sifted down and we stopped looking. She played with the foil on her cup of ersatz cream.

"You said Sergeant Grice gave you my card?" I started.

She nodded jerkily, her eyes on my left lapel. "He said you wanted to talk to me about Ray's—about Ray."

I picked up my spoon and stirred my coffee. There wasn't anything in it to stir. "You found him?"

"The paper boy did. He rang the bell to collect for the

month. When no one answered he looked through the window in the door." She stopped.

"Were you separated?"

"I guess that's what it was." She was speaking rapidly now, getting away from it. "I've been living in Grand Rapids with my sister. I couldn't stay and go on watching him lose pieces of himself."

"He was depressed?"

"'Despondent,' I think, is the word. That's what they call it after you've killed yourself."

"Did he kill himself?"

She met my gaze then. "Are you investigating his death? Sergeant Grice told me they were closing it out."

I rotated the spoon in the cup one more time and held it above the liquid, waiting for the quivering drop on the end of the bowl to fall. "The article on your husband's retirement was among the items left behind by a man I'm looking for. There were other clippings with it, including one about a corpse found in the trunk of a car parked at Metro Airport and another about the life of Alfred Kindnagel, the Jewish labor czar, you should pardon the expression. The murdered man's name was Philip Niles. He ran a body repair shop called Acme Collision in Royal Oak with a man named Wally Petite. Does any of these names mean anything to you?"

She shook her head. "Well, Alfred Kindnagel. I'd heard of him. On TV and in the papers."

"Your husband once arrested Petite for petty theft. Caught him yanking a carburetor from a new Camaro in a supermarket parking lot. I got that from Records down at police headquarters."

"He didn't discuss his work with me."

"Records also told me a union shop steward named

Morris Rosenberg was shot down behind the Wenk Bearing Company on the Detroit side of Eight Mile Road a little over eight years ago. He was connected with Kindnagel's organization. Your husband commanded the detective squad that investigated the shooting."

"Same answer, I'm afraid," she said. "My thought would be that when you find the man you're looking for you'll know what all those things have to do with each other."

"I'm hoping it will work out the other way. So far, your husband is the only thing linking them. I think finding out why he killed himself would go a long way toward tying up this whole mess. If he killed himself."

The waitress came up with the pot and I stopped talking. She leveled off Mrs. Blankenship's cup, glanced at my full one, and glided away. Mrs. Blankenship picked up an open pack of Virginia Slims from the table and shook one out. I lit it for her. She tipped smoke down her throat.

"I thought at first Ray was having trouble adjusting to civilian life," she said, letting it curl out from under her upper lip. "He just sat around the house, smoking cigarettes and drinking too much, though I never saw him really drunk. We started arguing about a lot of little things we'd never argued about before. All the arguments ended the same way, with the two of us screaming at each other and me getting into the car and driving away. Ten days ago I did that and didn't come back. I just kept driving. I guess I put the gun in his hand." She picked up her cup and drank quickly.

"Why'd he leave the department?"

"He never said. One morning he just looked at me across the breakfast table and asked how I'd feel being married to a civilian. I thought he was playing a game. You know: Do you regret not having married so-and-so? That kind of thing. But he was talking about himself."

"What did you say?"

She smiled the bent smile. "What every woman who was ever married to a cop would say. Anyway, he didn't bring it up again, and two weeks later he put in for his pension."

"You didn't ask him why?"

"I thought I knew why. You'd have to have known Ray, Mr. Walker. He was as high as he figured he could go in the system and still look at himself in the mirror. Maybe one step higher. It got so when we met someone and they asked him what he did he would change the subject. It never used to be like that. I remember when he got his gold badge. He went right out and bought a can of polish. He wasn't going to let it turn green before he had a chance to earn it. That was a whole different Ray. I couldn't have screamed at the Ray he was then and gone to stay with my sister. The Ray he was then wouldn't have made me. That's the Ray I'm wearing black for. I'm ten years too late."

Her face clenched then, and I watched the shadows start their slow crawl across the street while she clawed a handkerchief out of the blue bag she had with her and made repairs. Then I said:

"Could something have happened that made him feel that way? That he'd climbed one step past where he needed to be to like himself?"

"I don't know what it could be." She snapped the bag shut and retrieved her cigarette from the tin ashtray. "I'm sorry for making like the grieving widow. I'm not crying just because he's dead. I wonder if it's always this much of a shock when you start surviving the people closest to you."

"It is."

"Oh?" She cocked her eyebrows, waiting. After a couple of seconds she put them back down and stubbed out the cigarette. "I always thought I'd be the one to beat death," she said then. "What am I supposed to do now?"

"Live."

"Easy for you to say. You're a young man. That graying hair doesn't fool me."

"No one's young, Mrs. Blankenship. It's an old world."

"Bullshit," she said. "Excuse my French, but bullshit. I had enough of that from Ray. You're a detective. You spend all day looking at the side of rocks no one is supposed to see and then you run around hollering the whole world's covered with slugs and green slime. Writers put it in books that win all the awards because green slime and slugs are supposed to be real and blue skies and flowers and pretty paintings are not. Bullshit."

She wasn't speaking loudly, but her voice carried in the small restaurant. A white-haired woman in an orange tailored suit two tables over put down her menu and slid on a pair of glasses on a chain around her neck to glare at us. I lifted my cup to the white-haired woman and drank lukewarm coffee. She took off her glasses and stuck the menu back in front of her face.

"I'm chastised," I said.

Color scaled Mrs. Blankenship's cheeks. "Sorry. I've been kind of floating since yesterday morning. Nothing's real. I talk about things I wouldn't otherwise."

"I'm grateful you talked to me. Why did you?"

"I guess I thought you knew something. I've been asking myself why Ray did what he did. I've been afraid of

140

the answer. I hoped you'd have one I could get along with. Or maybe I'm just buying an expensive coffin with solid brass handles for someone I should have been more patient with when he was alive. Oh, God." She put a hand to her mouth.

The waitress returned, saw she was crying, and started to leave. Mrs. Blankenship asked her to stay and we ordered dinner. When it was before us, I said: "Do I have your permission to look into your husband's death?"

"Do you need it?" Looking in her compact mirror, she used her handkerchief to remove the ruined mascara.

"Not officially. I'm licensed and I have a client. But whenever a P.I. starts rooting around in the lives and deaths of police officers he's apt to draw lightning. Your blessing could deflect some of it. Cops place a lot of store in police widows."

"Widow." She tasted the word. "That takes getting used to. It draws a picture that doesn't look like how I see myself. Yes, you have my permission." She poked at her chicken with her fork. Then she put it down and looked at me. "Do you think Ray didn't commit suicide?"

"I have nothing to base that on. As a general rule when a street cop like Grice says another cop killed himself you can take it as holy writ. They get pretty Old Testament when one of their own is murdered. On the other hand, I'm not satisfied that a couple of fights over who forgot to screw the cap back on the toothpaste tube and a simple case of burnout are grounds for putting your gun in your mouth."

"Well, there were more than a couple of fights, and they were more serious than that."

"Still."

"My husband was an honest man, Mr. Walker."

"It's the honest ones that kill themselves usually," I said.

We finished our meal and I thanked her again and asked if she needed a ride. She said no. I snatched up the check over her protests, left too much money for the service we'd gotten, and saw her out to the curb. Under a street lamp I took down her sister's address and telephone number in Grand Rapids and promised to get in touch if anything came up about Blankenship. Then we said good-bye. I watched her walking away in the light coming through the restaurant window and from the Budweiser sign in the window of the bar next door, a tall woman and not ashamed of it, straight-backed with her high heels double-clicking on the sidewalk. I drove home. The lamps were glowing along Woodward with that slightly pinkish cast unique to Detroit. The wandering homeless would be settling into their temporary shelters now, those that had found them. Maybe some of them would be asking about Willy, but I doubted it.

The evening air was cool and dew glittered on the grass as my headlamps raked the front yard. I parked in the garage and pulled down the door and let myself into the house through the side door. Just then the telephone started to ring. I went into the living room and caught it on the third stroke.

There was a hollow silence after I said hello. Then a man's voice, trying hard for flat and expressionless, said:

"Tough break, Walker."

The line clicked.

I stood there holding the receiver for a while, more like a weapon of defense than an instrument of communication. Finally I replaced it. For the thousandth time that year I swore that I would learn to get along without a telephone at home.

19

I FOUND MY *FREE PRESS* LYING SQUARE IN THE MIDDLE OF
the front doormat next morning. The kids don't hurl them
from moving bicycles anymore, but get off and walk up to
the door and lay them down as gently as puppies in a bas-
ket. I figure they're being paid by the hour now. When I
had the paper in my hand I closed the door and put away
my gun.

Blankenship had made the second section. FORMER PO-
LICE INSPECTOR KILLS SELF. Three inches, on an inside
corner. It didn't tell me anything I didn't already know.
They got his age wrong. I folded the paper and put it aside
and used the telephone to call the Book Cadillac. While the
desk was ringing Louise Starr's room I stood back away
from the windows.

"Well, hello," she said, when I'd identified myself.

She sounded wide awake. I said, "I thought editors slept
late. All that reading in bed the night before."

"I played hooky last night, went to see the show at the
Fisher Theater and retired early."

143

"Alone?"

"Alone what?" she asked after a second. "Went to the theater alone or retired alone?"

"We're coy for this early. I meant the theater."

"Andrei took me. You know, I almost never go in New York. You just take it for granted it's going to be good, so why go? It's like gambling when there's no chance of losing. But no one told me the theater was so good here."

"We got rid of the Indians too."

She passed that one. "Have you found Barry Stackpole?"

"Barry's still out there in the forest somewhere. Right now I'm up to my ears in trees. I was thinking of taking the morning off, or has Andrei shown you all the sights?"

There was another little hesitation before she said, "Is that something you do often? Take time off from a case you're working on?"

"No. I just have to step back from this one, read the whole billboard. I'm starting to feel like one of the blind men with the elephant. Also I got my life threatened again last night."

"You talk as if it's happened before."

"I lead a popular life. Everyone wants it."

"You're not telling me you're afraid."

"I'm not sitting with my back to any doors, if that's what you mean."

"It's just that I don't think of you as the type that scares."

"Everyone scares, Mrs. Starr, except maybe Gary Cooper. I'm afraid of decaying hands reaching up from under my bed in the night and rats scurrying over my shoes when I take out the trash and that tingly feeling we men get standing at a public urinal when the door opens behind us.

Most of all I'm afraid of lying stripped in the Wayne County Morgue with my eyes open and someone saying, 'Yes, that's him,' although right now I can't think of anyone who would bother. But if I thought any cracker with two dimes in his pocket and ten seconds to kill could dial my number and frighten me off a case I'd paint my toenails and become an exotic dancer."

"You'd make a good one," she said. "Are they trying to frighten you off the case?"

"I thought so last night. It's getting interesting enough. This morning I'm not sure. It's been a long time since I've had to shake friends off my lapels. It's been never. Have you had breakfast?"

"No. It's a funny thing, but I don't seem to miss it when I'm away from home. Should we meet in the hotel dining room?"

"Hotel dining rooms are the same all over. I'll meet you in the lobby in twenty minutes and we'll go somewhere where they serve food."

She said okay and we hung up. After that I lit a cigarette and thought about the connection. It had seemed good, but then we've come a long way in tapping lines.

I was a few minutes late, probably about the same amount of time I had spent inspecting my hood and doors and under the dash for unfamiliar wires. With a fresh shave and a suit just back from the cleaners I felt good enough to be seen in the lobby of the Book Cadillac, though I might not have before they'd covered the Petoskey stone facings on the walls with washable paneling and dropped the cupolaed ceiling. Little by little they are bringing Detroit down to the level of the people who are running it now.

She wasn't hard to find. All you had to do was follow

the glances of the men standing in business suits in the humming lobby. Today she had on a heavy silk gray-blue blouse with puffed sleeves and a blue neckpiece, also silk, loosely knotted in a bow under her collar. Her gray skirt was split as if for riding and she wore gray suede boots. Her hair was down to her shoulders and she was holding a blue purse with a silver clasp and looking at a tiny watch strapped to her wrist. She was wind in the pines, blue shadows on snow across a moonlit valley, the sudden scent of fresh flowers on a zephyr. She glanced up as I approached. Chimes rang.

"Sorry. Have you been waiting long?"

"Five minutes," she said, smiling. "But half the lead time in the publishing business is spent waiting. I'm used to it."

"Me too. Are we going to start right in with what's wrong with the book industry?"

"No." She took my arm. "It's my morning off too."

We went out past the other men in the lobby. Their eyes followed us out like wind-drawn leaves.

The morning was a degree or two cooler than the one before, but still shirtsleeve weather if you kept to the sun. I closed the car door on her and went around to the driver's side and got in and we introduced ourselves to the morning traffic on Michigan Avenue.

Downtown was lively. The sidewalks were anthills and if you drove defensively the way the signs say you got to sit behind a string of buses all day and watch the lights change. I closed up behind an empty haulaway and squirted across Randolph to catch Monroe on the pink. A Caddy convertible with sixteen black Errol Flynn gang members in the back seat laid down horn as I skinned past its custom chrome. Its driver waved at me with a single digit.

"Is it always like this?" asked Mrs. Starr.

"Not always. It gets crowded around noon."

She looked at me. "You don't ever turn it off, do you?"

"It's been called a fault."

"By people who don't have it, I bet."

"I like you, Mrs. Starr."

"Louise. Where are we going?"

"We're there."

She turned in her seat to look around. We were entering the block between Brush and Beaubien, with produce markets and restaurants and coffee houses on both sides displaying bright red and yellow hand-painted signs. Pigeon-splattered awnings overhung racks of tomatoes and radishes and heads of lettuce, where squat women carrying bushel baskets chattered at aproned proprietors whose heads rotated from side to side negatively as if mounted on swivels. An old man wearing a cloth cap and tobacco streaks in his white moustache leaned in the doorway of the steamship office, glaring around between pulls on a brown paper-wrapped bottle that probably contained retsina.

"It looks significant," said Louise.

"Greektown," I said. "What's left of it, anyway. When you're hungry in Detroit, here is where you come."

I hung a right onto Beaubien and bumped over the broken paving in a lot behind one of the markets, parking near a stake truck where two young men in workclothes were unloading crates of rutabagas onto a dock. We walked back to Monroe, cutting between buildings with the smells of stuffed cabbage and fresh baklava mingling outside the kitchen vents.

"It reminds me a little of the Village. Only not as big."

"It was bigger once," I said. "It started here and held the line for fifty years against the blacks and Germans and Arabs along Macomb and Randolph. Now it's just this one block. The city hasn't gotten around to tearing it down yet to make room for a steering gear plant or something equally colorful."

"There's some construction going on there." She pointed at a brick warehouse on the corner, where scaffolding had been erected and a man in coveralls was sandblasting soot off the front.

I said, "They're going to make it into an indoor mall. To revitalize Greektown. Sell pine cigarette boxes made in Taiwan with pictures of Achilles inside the lid and T-shirts with the Athens skyline silk-screened across the front. We'll meet here two years from today and order a roast lamb's head through a microphone at the curb." I touched her arm, steering her through the open door of a storefront with waisted curtains in the windows.

It was a restaurant inside, with a bare plank floor and a narrow aisle running between a row of turning stools at the counter and some wobbly-looking tables and chairs flung about the room. The floor canted upward slightly toward the rear, giving the impression of space. The entire establishment seated thirty if no one objected to intimacy with his neighbor's elbow. At this hour there were two diners at opposite ends of the counter and three more at the tables, two of them together. A speaker at the far end was tumbling frantic violin music out into the room.

"You said this is better than the hotel?" Louise inspected the rump-polished vinyl seat of the chair I had drawn out for her before sitting down.

I took the chair facing hers. "I hear in New York they

148

charter buses to a roach hatchery in the South Bronx because the Vagabond Gourmet gave it some stars."

"No one goes to the Bronx just for—oh, I see." She played with a corner of the tri-folded napkin in front of her. "Has anyone ever told you you're something of a snob?"

"Once. If she looked like you I'd have taken it."

We were looking at each other when the waitress came and set two glasses of water on the table. She had fenders like a GMC truck under a knobbly white uniform, and a watch smaller than Louise's rode her bare wrist like a rubber band around a leg of lamb. Her eyes were dark and angelic, trapped in balloons of flesh. She wore her hair in a net. I asked her how the moussaka was today.

"You'll think you died and went to Mount Olympus."

"I thought that was just for gods."

"What do I know, I'm from Warren."

"What's moussaka?" Louise asked.

"Stuffed eggplant, ground beef, green peppers in tomato sauce," said the waitress.

"For breakfast?"

"Greeks don't eat lunch." I handed up the menus. "Moussaka twice, and two bowls of egg lemon soup."

"Ouzo?"

"No. Too early in the day to risk losing the rest of it."

"Iced tea, please."

The waitress rolled off. We sipped our water and listened to the music. Louise glanced around, at the scoured interior and fishing scenes on the walls. "They won't go broke on atmosphere."

"Atmosphere's to keep your mind off what's going on in the kitchen. The food's good here. It always is when a Greek's in charge, for some reason."

"Do you know the owner?"

"I did a job for him once."

She didn't go after it. "Have you lived in Detroit all your life?"

"I was born here. My father had part ownership of a garage on West McNichols, but most of his money came from the pumps out front. Then two companies that were listed on the exchange got into a war and inside of six months he and fifty other independents were looking for work as curbside attendants, read that gas jockeys. He finally shipped me out to a burg an hour's drive west of here and I grew up there."

"What happened to him?"

"Twenty years later he died."

Her lips parted, showing an even line of fine white teeth. Her tea came. She made a thing of removing the wedge of lemon from the lip of her glass and laying it down just so while the waitress withdrew beyond earshot. Then: "I take back what I said before. It can be a fault. What are you protecting yourself from?"

"I'm a detective, Mrs. Starr. Louise. People pay me two-fifty a day and expenses to find things out. After you've been doing it a while you get to thinking of information as a commodity. Ours is not a giveaway society."

"I don't think that's it. I think you like to keep people at arm's length from what you are. You're divorced, aren't you?"

"And you're married. Between the two of us we reflect the entire adult population in microcosm."

She laced her fingers together under her chin. "You know, you've never asked me about my husband."

"What about him?"

"We're very close. We've been married for five years and when I'm away from him I miss him. He's a vice president in a firm that manufactures and sells office copiers, very successful. All his friends are successful vice presidents. Their wives own antique shops in Connecticut and go to aerobics classes out on Long Island."

"You don't."

"Who has time? When I'm not away at a sales conference or helping some tortured young Marxist with a literary bent kill martinis at a club with a fifty-dollar cover, I play a little tennis. Stooping and stretching to Rod Stewart is not my idea of a sound time investment."

"Your body isn't your temple?"

"If it were, it would seem sacrilegious to cover it with sweat, don't you think?"

Our moussaka came. The green peppers and tomato sauce seduced our nostrils. She took a forkful and made sounds of ecstasy. I said, "How come you don't wear a wedding ring?"

"I'm allergic to gold."

I grinned.

"No, really. I break out."

"You're the perfect woman, Louise."

"That's disrespectful of women."

"The hell with that. It's getting so you can't pass along a compliment without looking it over first to see if something's sticking to it."

"I'm sorry. I thought you were making a joke."

"It started out as one."

We ate. She laid her knife and fork in her empty plate. "You haven't told me about this threat you received."

"I get them from time to time, probably not as often as you think. I don't even know that this one has anything to do with what I'm working on. If I started listening to them I'd never get anything done."

"You're not getting much done this morning. On the case."

I left a third of my moussaka untasted and rinsed my mouth out with water. It was a little early for so much spice after all. "Telephone threats, the ones that mean anything anyway, are usually followed by tails. Just to see if it took. Sometimes they're made just to get someone mad enough to do the exact opposite. If I do nothing for a while maybe I'll see which way they want it."

"In other words, if they are watching you and you both do nothing, the threat is genuine."

"Put that way it sounds pretty stupid. But yeah."

"And if it's something else they want, they'll do—what?"

"They'll call me again, or maybe send someone to pay me a visit, and spell it out.

"With brass knuckles?"

"You've been editing too many detective novels. They don't use knucks much anymore, except for parades. You can buy three months in the school of locks just for having them in your possession. Nowadays they run to jack handles and rolls of quarters, things no cop that stopped you for forgetting to signal a turn would look twice at. But to answer your question, no. The hard lessons come later."

She watched me for a moment. Then she shook her head. Her hair threw off soft sparks in the light. "You move in a whole different world."

I said nothing, and she returned to her iced tea. I touched the lip of my water glass. "He went to work in a steel foundry," I said.

"Who did?"

"My father. After he sent me away to live. He died of a

coronary in the heat treatment plant the year he would have retired."

The hectic violins played. After a stretch she smiled and laid her fingers on my hand resting on the table. They were cool from the glass of tea.

20

THE OLD CLOCK IN THE LIVING ROOM CHIMED ELEVEN, grinding and wheezing between the strokes like a fat old man climbing stairs. It made me want to go out and help it. Almost.

Louise undressed with the bedroom window at her back. I had drawn the shade and curtains, softening the light in the room to a medium gray. Pale double shadows fluttered on the wall as she drew off the silk blouse and then stepped out of the long skirt. The teddy she had on underneath was a very light blue, almost eggshell-colored, and shone softly. I went over and helped her out of that. She was golden all over.

"I didn't know busy editors had time to scout out nude beaches." My voice sounded scarcely louder than the quiet in the room.

"Far Rockaway," she said, and hers was even quieter. "I bought one of those suits that don't block the ultraviolet rays. But I think I'll go back to a regular bikini. I like to see how my tan is doing."

"I like it this way."

We kissed. Our tongues touched and I felt the warmth of her through my clothes. Her naked back was smooth under my palms. The air was sheathed in jasmine. When we finished kissing she undid two buttons on my shirt and traced my collarbone lightly with her fingers. "Do you have music?"

"What do you like?"

"Something appropriate. And not under twenty years old."

"Lady, you came to the right place."

In the living room I took Bunny Berigan down from the shelf and started him turning on the cheap stereo. The first notes of "I Can't Get Started" crept out of the speakers— the good version, no singing, just his trumpet playing like raw silk sliding over polished stone. I turned the volume down to heartbeat level and walked away from it.

She was under the covers now, the sheet outlining her in a way even the soft light couldn't match, falling away in a gentle pyramid from one raised knee. Her hair spilled over the pillow in a fall of muted sunlight. I stood in the doorway and stared. After a long time she smiled. "I don't bite."

"Like hell you don't," I said.

She laughed. In the next room the clock with the tired chimes listened for pointers. I went to her. She cried out softly in the half-light.

I slid out of bed, put on my robe and slippers, and sat on the edge of the mattress to get a package of cigarettes and a book of matches out of the drawer in the nightstand. Louise sighed and stirred as if she'd been asleep. A hard-nailed finger went up my spine, making me shudder.

"That's a cliché," she said,

I got rid of the charred match, blew smoke away from

the bed, and resettled myself so that I was facing her. "What is?"

She nodded at the cigarette. "First the sex, then the smoke. I strike it when I see it. If the manuscript's worth saving at all."

"Clichés don't get to be clichés by being wrong."

"Books aren't like life. They can't repeat themselves." She was looking at me. "It can't mean anything, Amos."

"I never thought it could."

"It could if I let it. That's why it won't. I've finally got all my furniture arranged just the way I want it. I'm not going to start breaking it up and moving it around because of one nice morning in Detroit."

I went on smoking. She was still looking. "I'll bet you were thinking I was going to say I love my husband."

"I wasn't thinking anything."

"I don't know that I love him at all. It's a final-sounding word, like death. You'd think it would be as definite. Have you ever been in love?"

I grinned. "That's worse than smoking after sex."

"You don't have to answer."

"Once."

"Your wife?"

"No. I thought I was but I wasn't. Someone else. Someone recent."

"Was she here?"

"Yeah."

"Should we have gone to the hotel?"

I shook my head. "I thought about not bringing you here. Then I thought it'd be like when someone dies and you get a chill every time you walk past her room and it made me think of the old lady in the rotting wedding dress still waiting for the guy that left her at the altar."

"Miss Havisham. *Great Expectations*." She saw me looking at her and colored. "Sorry, but I am in the business. Did she leave you?"

I stubbed out the cigarette in the china saucer I use for an ashtray. "I've got Barry's manuscript."

It took her a second to catch up. She drew up her legs with the sheet over her breasts and clasped her hands around her knees and rested her chin on them. Naked, she looked more like an editor in that moment than she had in any of her tailored suits. "How long have you had it?"

"Since day before yesterday."

"Wasn't that the day you were hired to look for him?"

"For him. Not his book."

"May I see it?"

"No."

"Why not?"

"I stole it. If he wanted me to have it I wouldn't have had to steal it and if he doesn't want me to have it he doesn't want me showing it around."

"But he called me, wanting to sell it."

"He wanted to sell a book. It might not be this one. Chances are it isn't, because this one looks fairly complete and he told me he was taking the time off to finish a book. But none of that means anything because I don't have his permission to show anything."

"Well, why'd you tell me you have it?"

"I don't know. Maybe because it's the damnedest thing and I had to tell somebody."

"What's the book about?"

"Vietnam."

"Vietnam books are big," she said after a space. "If I told the board I had a line on one by Barry Stackpole I

157

wouldn't have to worry about my job until the next dry spell."

"You won't, though."

"What makes you so sure?"

"Because if you promise them a book and then something happens and it doesn't come through they'll empty your desk drawers into a suitcase and send it to you."

"That's not how they work. But I see what you mean." She tossed her head so that her hair fell behind her shoulders. "Why did you steal it?"

"I don't know that either. There's something about it. I keep thinking that if I read it closely enough I'll find out what's been bothering Barry."

"Isn't it the story you think he was working on? The hot potato?"

"It goes back further than that. I think. We haven't been in touch on a regular basis for a long time. Eleven months ago he took up with the sort of person you don't take up with unless you've stopped liking yourself. Then he started drinking hard. Not that he ever drank soft, but this time it was hard enough to land him in AA. Something happened. Whether it was something new or something further back, I don't know, any more than I know what it was. Maybe it's in the book."

"Maybe it *is* the book. All those memories coming back in the writing. The war."

"Maybe."

"But you don't think so."

"That flashback thing's been done and done," I said. "Every time a guy knocks over a gun shop and it turns out he's a vet, his lawyer says he thought the counterman was Cong and the street outside was mined. Barry's too original for that. It's a cliché like sex and cigarettes."

She said, "I've spent most of my adult life around writers, a lot of them hacks and a couple of authentic geniuses. Even the geniuses couldn't manage to live lives that were wholly original."

"It's not like it is in books."

"That's why people read them. What are you going to do?"

"Find Barry."

"Such a simple goal," she said. "For such a complex character."

"I am an anomaly."

Her eyes were pure lavender in the gray light. "Hard to get close to."

I took the hint and shifted closer. She ran a finger down my jaw, letting the sheet fall from her breasts. Her hand kept going, following the line of my throat and the lapel of my robe down to where the belt tied.

I saw her to the lobby of her hotel, where a neat black security man in a gold blazer took his attention from the row of closed-circuit television monitors over his desk to glare at me. I glared back unitl he looked away. "Call me?" Louise asked.

I said I would and pressed the button for the elevator.

"Not just if you find something out," she said. "Any reason will do."

The doors opened and she stepped inside, past a man coming out who hesitated for an instant, wondering whether he should get back on. But by then the doors were closing on a dream in blue and gray. The security man hadn't asked to see her key before letting her go up. With me they unbutton the flaps over their holsters.

I used one of a bank of pay telephones off the front desk.

"Acme Collision."

This was a new voice, youthful, male, gum snapping. In the background a welding torch hummed and splattered sparks. I asked for Mr. Petite.

"He's at lunch. Back at three."

"Where can I get in touch with him? It's urgent."

"Hang on."

The radio was playing loudly under the noise of the torch. I held the receiver away from my ear until he returned.

"Curly's, on Fenkell in Highland Park. Know it?"

"That's a bar."

"I never said he was eating, ace." I got hung up on.

I drove to the low brick building on Fenkell, which was just five minutes away from Acme. It was a few minutes past one and the parking lot was filled. Not a lot gets done in Highland Park after lunch. I circled the place twice before a yellow Cavalier convertible pried itself loose from a space near the door. A green Charger that had been waiting leaned on its horn when I swung into the opening. The driver saluted me with a finger when I climbed out. I waved back.

The interior was cool and lighted only by the rosy lamps behind the bar. They didn't reach far enough to show anyone inside who you were leaving with. Guitar music floated out of a hidden speaker. I was still standing in the entrance, getting used to the change in visibility, when a red-faced character in a blue silk bowling shirt with *Ed* stitched over the pocket swung through the door, banging me with the handle. When I turned, tiny eyes lit on me.

"That was my space you took, fucker."

160

"Sorry."

He rocked back on his heels and came forward on his toes. I had six inches on him, but he was built like a sack of angle irons. "I didn't hear that, fucker. Let's hear you say it again like you mean it."

I turned the rest of the way so that I was looking down on him. I really needed a scene. Like a cover girl needs acne I needed a scene. I took hold of the collar of his bowling shirt and twisted.

"Don't mix up good manners with no guts," I said. I didn't speak any louder than the general whisper of conversation in the room.

His face got redder. His eyes lost focus. At length he nodded quickly. I let go and he turned around and went out, muttering, "All a guy wants is a drink."

I went to the bar, set at an angle to the door. The bartender, a big black with a moustache and gray in his natural, was looking at me with his hand wrapped in a chamois inside a glass that was already sparkling.

"Trouble?"

"The guy was right," I said. "I just wasn't in the mood for him to be right. Wally Petite here?"

He went on looking at me with his hand in the glass. I got out my wallet and laid a five-dollar bill on the bar. He didn't look at it.

"This is a good bar, mister," he said. "Maybe not the best bar in the world, but not the kind of place you seem to be used to either. You want to see a customer, you give me your name, I ask him does he want to see you. Otherwise buy a drink or get out."

"A hundred tap-jockeys in this town and I had to draw an honor graduate of the Dearborn School of Bartending Arts. Pour me a Stroh's and deal me change."

He did that, pocketing the chamois, and that was when I knew there had been something in it besides his hand. I sat on the end stool, sipping and watching the smoked-glass mirror that ran the length of the wall near the ceiling, tilted forward to take in the entire room. I spotted him finally near the windows. He was sitting at a table with the red-haired hillbilly and the bald man with the great beard and another man I didn't recognize, a graying number in gold-rimmed glasses and a tan suit with a windowpane pattern that was so faint it almost wasn't there. I saw the light glinting off the gold chain around Petite's neck before I saw anything else. He was wearing a burgundy jacket today, over a pale blue silk shirt open to his ribs. It would be like a former mechanic with sudden money to dress out of *California Today*.

He and the gray-haired man were talking and laughing in a relaxed sort of way that suggested the business part was over. The two other men from the body shop drank beer and said nothing. They had on clean shirts and jackets that didn't match their trousers. They were amateurs. Professional bodyguards were more successful at not looking like bodyguards.

I was still sipping and watching the mirror and thinking when a white man twenty years younger than my bartender but dressed the same, in white shirt and black clip-on tie, came in through a door at the end of the bar buttoning his shirtcuffs. My bartender said something to him and he nodded and then my bartender took off his apron and stashed it under the bar and went out through the same door.

I finished my beer, signaled his replacement for another, left a buck for it, and got down to find a pay telephone. There were three in the hallway to the men's room. I took note of the number on the dial of the one in the center and went to the one farthest from the bar and dropped two dimes and dialed the number.

Leaning against the wall with the receiver to my ear I watched the young bartender set down my beer and a fresh napkin where I had been sitting and come over, mopping his hands on his apron. I turned my back. When he answered I said, "Mr. Petite, please. Wally Petite."

"See if he's here."

The bartender laid the receiver on the ledge under the instrument and went back to page Petite. I hung up, stepped to the telephone nearest the bar, picked up the handset, and waited with my back to the hallway entrance.

21

I SMELLED HIS COLOGNE FIRST, ONE OF THOSE STICKY brands with jungle names that smell like burnt leather. As he walked past me with his hand out to pick up the vacant receiver I looped the cord of the one I was holding over his head and pulled. The cord drew tight around his throat before he could get his hands on it. He tried anyway. They always do. He said, "Gkkk!"

"Amos Walker," I said, next to his ear. "We spoke yesterday. Now let's say something."

"Gkkk!"

"Three years ago, Lieutenant Ray Blankenship of the Fourteenth Precinct arrested you for stripping a parked car. You pulled some light time, then lucked into a partnership with a guy that got killed by someone who knew how to do it. Two days ago, Blankenship pulled his own plug. You're bad luck, pal. I want to know how come."

He said it again. I glanced back over my shoulder. The bartender was leaning on his forearms on the other end of the bar, talking to a brunette in a dark red shift and pearls. From where he stood we were two guys using the telephones. I turned back to Petite and loosened the cord a little. He sucked in air loudly.

"You son—"

I pulled the cord tight. He grunted and tried to elbow me in the ribs, but he didn't have the room to do it right. This time I hung on until he started to go slack. When I relaxed, his lungs creaked.

"I got friends here," he gasped. "They'll bust you good."

"Wally, your grammar's slipping. You won't be here to see them bust me, get it? You'll be too busy holding your breath."

He made no reply. I started to tighten the cord again. He said, "Don't! We'll talk."

"Start with you and Blankenship."

"I was boosting a couple of things. It was while I was working at the dealership. The sons of bitches weren't paying me anything. A guy's got to live. I didn't see Blankenship. He was off-duty, picking up something for his wife on the way home, something like that, I don't remember. He came up behind me and asked if I had car trouble. I tried to bluff it out, said it was my car and it wouldn't start. He wanted to see my license and registration. I got three months and a day."

"Records gave me that much. Skip to Phil Niles. Why'd you have him killed and what did Blankenship have to do with it?"

"I didn't have him k—"

I leaned back hard. He struggled, relaxed. I held on. He struggled again, and then he relaxed for real. His face went black and the only thing holding him up was the cord.

When I let go his knees gave. I got an arm around his chest under his arms and let the receiver dangle while I slapped his cheek. He was pale now, paler than his shirt. His color returned in patches. I looked back toward the bartender, who was topping off the brunette's glass from a bottle of Chianti.

"We go on," I said. "Alfred Kindnagel. Where's he come in?"

"I don't know anybody by that name." His voice came through six layers of gauze.

"Wally..."

"I don't! I swear! Who's Alan Kindnagel?"

"No good, Wally. Either you remember the name or you forget it entirely. If you got it wrong it wouldn't be the Alfred part. What about Morris Rosenberg? He ate some bullets on Eight Mile Road eight years back. Kindnagel was his union boss."

"Christ, eight years ago I'd never seen this town."

"Okay, let's just for now say it was before your time. Who killed Niles for you?"

"Niles?"

"Niles. N is for the nasty names you call me. I is for the illness you'll go through. L is for the lies you try to tell me. E is for—"

Cold air from something that had plenty of it to give prickled the down on my neck behind my right ear. I stopped singing.

"Mister, I'm going to blow your face clean off you don't let go the man."

The voice belonged to the black bartender. I opened my arms. Petite fell to one knee. I turned around slowly with my hands in plain sight and looked at the shiny nickel plating on a square .25 automatic at the end of the bartender's outstretched arm. His big hand was wrapped almost twice around the butt with less than half an inch of pistol showing. His expression was flat. Behind him loomed the figures of Petite's men, Redhead and Blackbeard. The gray-haired man in the windowpane suit stood behind them, and behind him, crowded out into the bar proper, was the young white bartender. The hallway was very full.

"You okay, Mr. Petite?" Blackbeard wanted to know. He was staring at me the way he had when I'd last seen him in the body shop holding a sledgehammer.

"Yeah." Standing now, Petite dusted off his knee and straightened, adjusting the rumpled collar of his burgundy jacket. "I was just directing Mr. Walker to the exit."

"I think we'll order some law," said the black bartender.

"No, it's okay. Isn't it okay, Walker?"

I didn't say anything. I was watching the black bartender. He hadn't moved, just stood there turned sideways to me with his arm stretched out level with his shoulder and the gun in the end like an extension of his hand. He looked like a Charley Russell sketch of an old-time gunfighter.

"I take him outside, show him where he went wrong," drawled Redhead.

"No, it's okay." And Petite backhanded me across the cheek.

It made a noise like a pistol shot in the confined space. I backed up a step as if staggered. Then I kicked him in the crotch hard enough to lift him off his feet. He made a sound like a sick cat and wheeled out of my way, hands clasped between his knees.

Blackbeard roared. He and Redhead lunged forward.

167

The black bartender swung the gun their way. They stopped.

Over Petite's mewing, the bartender said: "We don't escalate, okay? Man had it coming. Everybody out. Pay the man at the rear." His hooded eyes moved my way. "You first. Don't come back."

I didn't move. "Cop, right?"

"Bodyguard. Teamsters. Out."

He gestured with the gun and the gang in the hallway parted heavily to let me through. I passed Blackbeard closely enough to smell the clam chowder on his breath. Behind me, Petite was sucking wind in long therapeutic drafts.

In the parking lot I walked around a man on his way inside. He had his shirtsleeves rolled up and carried a plaid sport coat under one arm. His hands were filthy. After he got a look at what was on the way to the men's room he'd find a better place to have a flat.

I got into the Olds and put my key in the switch but I didn't turn it. Instead I adjusted the rearview mirror to take in the door of the bar. A grim face with a hot red patch on its right cheek looked back at me from the corner of the glass. At one-thirty it had already been a long day, and sunlight coming warm through the windshield made me drowsy. I cracked the window for fresh air and waited.

After five minutes, Petite and the gray-haired man came out followed by the two body shop employees. Petite had straightened his clothes and restored the layered waves in his hair. He walked with the gray-haired man to a Chrysler Cordoba parked a few slots down from my car and the two shook hands. Then the gray-haired man opened the door on the driver's side and got in. Petite stood back while he pulled out, lifted his hand in a short wave, then jerked his head at the bodyguards and the three started my way.

I slid down below the back of the front seat, my hand going to the butt of the Luger I kept under the dash. A moment went by, and then a car door opened a few yards away. I raised myself a little to peer through the passenger's window and the windows of the car parked next to mine as Petite climbed into a blue Mercury two vehicles over. Redhead got in beside him on the driver's side and Blackbeard let himself into the back seat.

I waited until the car had swung out into the aisle before starting the Olds. As the Mercury hit Fenkell I backed out and followed. I let a couple of cars get between us. It was a sunny day and the terrain was flat. The Merc was large by today's standards. It was a textbook tail job.

Petite had been frightened under my grilling, and not all of it had been because of me. I had to wonder why he'd risk being strangled over giving up the name of Philip Niles's killer. Finding out meant getting him away from his hired help and the odd nosy bartender.

At Schaefer the blue car waited for the light to change, then turned right. When I got to the corner I rotated the wheel that way. The Olds kept going straight and the wheel came all the way around in my hands.

22

I ROLLED ACROSS SCHAEFER WITH MY HANDS LOCKED ON the wheel for no good reason. It was like clinging to a noodle in a high sea. I put my foot on the brake, but they had thought of that too. The pedal went all the way to the floor with a sigh and stayed there. The emergency brake pulled back without effort in my hand and the car kept moving. I thought about the man I had seen going into Curly's on my way out.

Louise would probably have called it a cliché.

I had slowed down for the turn, but the street sloped a little and the speedometer needle was climbing. I cut the motor and shifted into Neutral. If I could bring the speed down far enough to shift into Park without doing a double jackknife through the windshield, if.

That wasn't going to happen. I was up to forty now and still picking up speed. Also, Fenkell was taking a lazy curve to the north and the Olds was heading east with all the blind machine faith in its pilot of an Aztec holy man walking into a volcano.

Forty-five. I opened the door on the driver's side.

Forty-eight. A small shopping mall came up on my right. The curve sharpened and I could read the USA TODAY logo on a newspaper box chained to one of the posts that held up the roof of the mall. It was in front of me now.

Fifty. I leaned out. The slipstream sucked at my jacket and sent my necktie flapping around my left ear.

Fifty-two. I jumped.

There was no traffic coming up on my left. I was the only motorist exceeding the limit in this block today. For a long, hanging moment I had a sensation of flight, and then the pavement shot up and white light raked me from the top of my skull to the soles of my feet. My lungs made a noise collapsing and I rolled and banged my knee and rolled and scraped my hand and rolled and barked my shin and rolled and hit my head and rolled and then I stopped with another jolt of light.

Sky and earth did one last slow turn and wobbled to a halt like a coin coming to rest on a bartop. Beyond all that, beyond me, a great painful silence came down, as after the ringing of a church bell, and in that silence I heard the echo of the crash. Then pain welled up in my knee. It was a pain I could see, all white and glowing, and it was the kind of pain I'd have traded ten years of my life to be over. I rocked back and forth with my hands clasped around the knee until the pain changed color and spread out and settled into a reassuring throb.

I had landed across the street from the shopping mall with the curb cutting me in half across my lower back. I rolled over onto my left hand to push myself up, winced, and looked at the palm. My slide had ground a dozen tiny pebbles into the heel. I plucked out the worst of them and tried again. That time I made it to my feet. I did a quick bone check and decided I'd heal okay alone. A triangular flap of torn material hung from the knee of my right trouser leg, exposing my worst injury. The knee was bleeding in ten tiny places, as if I'd shaved it with a rusty razor. I tried bending it. It went the right way.

A crowd was gathering across the street, where my Olds crouched on the sidewalk with its back humped like a bull getting set to charge, only its charging days were over. It had squashed the newspaper box and wrapped its grille around the steel post the box was chained to, springing the frame and releasing clouds of steam from the smashed radiator. The headlamps were staring at each other.

"You all right, mister?"

I looked at a tall old man standing on the sidewalk on my side of the street, in jeans and a checked shirt buttoned at the neck. He wore a black string tie with an Indian totem snugged up under his large adam's apple. He had a leash in his hand and a Schnauzer at the other end of it, relieving itself against an overflowing city trash can. Everyone else on the block was looking at the wrecked car. "I'm swell," I said. "Wait for the cops, will you? Tell 'em I'll be back."

"Wait, mister! You shouldn't ought to be leaving the scene of an accident."

But I was already moving, hobbling back the way I'd come.

It was only a two-block run, but I hadn't got back all the wind I'd had belted out of me and the knee made me clench my teeth every time I put weight on that leg. I hadn't banged my head hard enough to raise a lump but it

172

hurt, throbbing fit to burst in time with my accelerated heart rate. I was puffing like a leaky valve when I made Curly's Bar.

"Thought I said don't come back."

The black bartender stood with his hands spread on the bar and the shiny little automatic under one of them. He wasn't bothering to wrap a cloth around it now.

"Guy came in here a few minutes ago," I said between gasps. "Probably used the men's room. Had his shirt-sleeves rolled up and his hands were greasy. Where'd he go?"

"Why, you want to strangle him with a phone cord too?"

"Son of a bitch rigged my steering and brakes. That's why the grease."

He looked me over again, took in the dirt on my face and clothes and the tear in my pants. "Man, you lead a hard life."

"Skip the eulogy and tell me where he went."

"Didn't see the man."

"The hell you didn't, Hawkeye."

"There was some confusion here, you remember. Couple of guys come in, use the bathroom. I was too busy to get their prints. Your man in here now?"

I took a slow turn. Not a few of the faces at the tables were turned my way. He wasn't in the barroom. I went down the hall and into the men's room. I wasn't wearing a gun. In the mood I was in I didn't need one. There was no one standing at the sink or urinals. I squatted, favoring my injured knee, and looked under the stalls. One of them was wearing a pair of brown loafers. I straightened and rapped on the painted plywood door.

"I'll be through in a minute."

I took a step back and threw a heel at the lock. The door

173

flew open and banged the inside of the stall. I looked at a bald man in his sixties sitting on the toilet with his pants down around his ankles and that day's Detroit *News* in his lap. He stared back over the tops of his bifocals.

I flashed a grin. I guess it was sheepish. "Sorry. That damn Mexican food."

By the time I came out the bartender had put away his gun. I spread ten dollars on the bar. "You need better locks on the stalls."

"Man wants to see you." He inclined his head.

I followed the angle and nodded at a young uniformed cop standing just inside the bar entrance. He had a thumb hooked in his belt near his holster.

I got away from Highland Park with a citation for careless driving and a reprimand for leaving the scene of an accident. I hadn't told the police my car had been tampered with. It sounded screwy even to me. A tow truck with a city contract hauled what was left of the Olds down to the garage where I have all my service done in Detroit. I rode along. There I paid the driver and stood by while the owner, a German named Schinder, gave my transportation its last rites. He said he'd see what he could do for me in the matter of wheels.

"What'll you allow me on the Olds?" I asked.

"Depends on what you left in the glove compartment."

I wrote him out a check for a hundred dollars by way of down payment on another vehicle, rescued my Luger from the special pocket under the dash, and took a cab home to change.

I showered, washing my knee carefully and the scraped hand, from which I plucked the remaining pebbles with tweezers. I applied iodine. The knee felt as if it were wearing a sheet of gauze, but a light brush started it tingling. I decided not to bind it, and put on dress pants and a sport coat over a knit shirt. Then I locked up, walked four blocks, and waited forty-five minutes for a city bus for the fifteen-minute ride to the office.

No line of eager clients was loitering outside the locked door to the reception room. I glanced at the party-colored envelopes on the floor under the mail slot and left them. There were no messages at my service. I missed Willy. I wondered if I could find out where they were going to bury him and if I should put flowers on the grave. Somehow I thought he'd prefer a bottle of carbonated Beaujolais poured over the fresh sod.

I suppose I should have been looking over my shoulder a lot more than I was. But they'd made their move, whoever they were. If it was a warning they'd wait to see if it took before they tried something else. If it was a legitimate try they'd be busy rigging another one. I could have been wrong; I already had been once, thinking they'd spell out last night's threat before they did anything. But my knee hurt and I had a headache and the hell with them, whoever they were. Whoever they were, they were good. I hadn't even spotted the tail.

I reached for the telephone to call Louise. The damn thing rang while I had my fingers on it.

"Walker, this is Arthur Rooney. Today makes three days you've been working on the Stackpole case. I was wondering if you'd learned anything."

"I have and I haven't, Mr. Rooney," I said. "I've got a pretty good idea what Barry was looking into when he vanished. The rest is a tangle. Can I get back to you?"

"Tomorrow's Friday. Monday the *News* starts kicking in a thousand dollars a day to the grand jury in his place."

"If you were counting on me finding him by then you're not as smart as I know you are. Tracing a missing person is tough enough without doing it by someone else's watch."

"I'm leaving tomorrow for a weekend in Jamaica. I'd like some sort of report by five o'clock."

The buzzer went off, telling me that someone had just entered my reception room. I switched it off and said, "You forgot 'or else.'"

"Look, I'm not making any ultimata." His tone was suddenly conciliatory. I was the grieving widow again. "It's just that the *News* has placed the matter in my hands and they'll expect me to have some information for them before they start paying fines. No one's hurrying you. I just want a rundown on the progress you've made so far."

"I'll be in tomorrow. I need more working capital anyway. The expenses on this one are running high."

"How high?"

"I need a suit and a new car."

Pause. "You're wising off again, right?"

"Not this time. Any explanations would run as long as my whole report. I'll be in before five."

"Make it four. I've a plane to catch at seven and I have an idea we'll be talking a while." He clicked off.

I got the Luger out of the top drawer where I'd stashed it, slipped it into the side pocket of my coat, and kept my hand on it while I opened the door to the outer office. A woman of fifty, trim and tall in a tweed suit and glasses with big round lenses, her graying hair cut short and streaked blond, was sitting on the bench with her ankles crossed, reading a two-month-old copy of the *Saturday Review*. She closed it and returned it to the coffee table with a tight lipsticked smile and I held the door for her.

Her name was Mayanne Latimore, Dr. Mayanne Latimore, and she was a licensed psychologist with a practice in Grosse Pointe Woods. She had two grown daughters, both married, and she had been divorced six years. Eighteen months ago, she said, she had begun treating an inmate named Oscar Klave at the Wayne County Jail, who was serving ten months for fleecing some doctors in Dearborn on a phony moon shuttle project. The therapy was one of the conditions for parole. After his release they had gone on seeing each other, but not as doctor and patient, and he had promised to marry her as soon as his divorce came through. Meanwhile she had advanced him several sums of money to tide him over while he looked for a job. A week ago he and his estranged wife had pulled up stakes and left the state, violating his parole and neglecting to inform Dr. Latimore that they were leaving. She was concerned about what would happen to him if the law caught up with him and wanted me to find him first.

I played with the pencil I had been using to write all this down. "How much money did you lend him?"

"Roughly five thousand dollars." The eyes behind the big lenses didn't flicker.

I wrote that down too. "Do you have a picture?"

She gave me a Polaroid snap taken at the beach. Dr. Latimore, looking awkward and matronly in a one-piece white sharkskin suit, was standing next to a lean dark muscular number in his thirties with a hairy arm wrapped around her waist and that broad white smile you see on doorsteps and in insurance offices. He was wearing one of those black jockstraps that are always the rage in Europe. I put the picture in the drawer next to the gun.

"I'll put out a line on him, Dr. Latimore. But I wouldn't count on him coming back any way but in bracelets."

"I just want to talk to him," she said.

I got some more information out of her and she wrote out a check for my three-day retainer. We stood.

"I guess I look pretty foolish," she said.

"He's a professional, Dr. Latimore. He gets his living making people look foolish."

"And me an expert on the human mind."

"It's the personal equation. They don't teach it in college." I saw her to the door.

The case was nothing. I traced him to a Milwaukee address through the firm that had sold his house and gave it to Dr. Latimore the next day. I don't know where it went from there, but I had an idea. You can go to school six years longer than anyone else and not know as much as a kid in a video parlor on Gratiot who can barely write his own name.

After the psychologist had left the first time I called Louise and asked her how was the world of letters.

She laughed mellowly. "You got me just in time. I'm reading a scene in a first novel that has Pulitzer Prize written all over it. The hero is a bum and he's negotiating with a flophouse manager for a bed for the night over the manager's wife, who's sitting on a chamber pot."

"Realistic."

"Oh, yes. Everyone receives visitors on the toilet. Where are you taking me for dinner?"

"We're confident today," I said.

"This morning was very nice."

"I knew you'd like Greektown."

"Who mentioned Greektown?"

I grinned at the wall. "You won't mind getting picked up in a cab."

"Car trouble?"

"Not anymore. Ten o'clock okay?"

"Why so late?"

"I have something else to do first," I said. "After dark."

23

IF THE U.S. ARMY ELECTED ITS OWN OFFICERS AND the election were held tomorrow, Sergeant Mark Harney, no middle initial, would be commander-in-chief of all Southeast Asian operations by sundown.

Harney is the type they used to cast as the leading man's best friend in college pictures—the ones about finals and the big game, not the one you saw last week about shower rooms. He is a chipmunk's smile in the center of a broad pink face topped by creamy yellow hair, with rings of wobbly flesh around his chest and middle and a piping voice that cracks when he gets excited, and no one has ever seen him calm. His bell shape is instantly recognizable against a landscape of emaciated orientals and reedy youths in uniform. Harney has done three tours in Nam and has service stripes to his shoulders, but no two of us can agree on whether he has ever seen combat, though the consensus is that if he has, it has been a long time. He lives in a two-story hut on the edge of the base outside Hue, where he has strung sound equipment worth several thousand dollars stateside, but which he acquired for the price of a month's supply of C rations from a Tokyo dealer with ties to the black market. When he is not there he can usually be found in the officers' club, which is off limits to enlisted personnel and noncoms except for Sergeant Harney.

Until recently it was a simple business transaction to deal heroin and cocaine from the sergeant. But of late he has moved his store upstairs to officer country. Soon, it has been said, he will do business with no one of lesser rank than first lieutenant.

That is speculation, however. Because last night someone rolled an incendiary grenade through the door of Sergeant Harney's hut while he was sleeping overhead, and this morning he is in the infirmary with third-degree burns over three-fourths of his body and the ends of the blood vessels on his head tied off like Farina's pigtails. He is not expected to live.

That was the last page of Barry's manuscript. I went back and read the passage again. It seemed a strange place to end a book. But then it wasn't the end or he wouldn't have complained to me about never being able to finish anything. I laid the pages on top of the stack and lay fully clothed on the bed looking at the ceiling. My bed, my ceiling.

It was after 6:00 P.M. and the star pattern scattered across the ceiling paper was growing dim. When I could no longer see it, it would be time to go out. The window was

181

open and one of my neighbors was edging the weeds in his lawn with a power trimmer that hummed like an electric razor. I hoped it cut better. Farther off someone else who had his window open had a television set tuned to a Pistons exhibition basketball game. Last year's season had ended the week before. A prop plane droned somewhere, an excruciatingly lonely sound. A woman called to someone named Brian and a screen door whacked a wooden frame. Under all this the hollow whooshing of heavy traffic drifted in from downtown; a muted roar like distant surf.

The sunlight slipped a little, or it seemed to. Images turned over in my mind like old rotted timbers rolling in deep water. I thought about old labor men like Alfred Kindnagel, who get out because they don't recognize any of the faces around them, then die. About cops, not old, like Ray Blankenship, who get out because they can't look someone in the eye when asked what it is they do, and who maybe because of that close their lips around the cold blue oily barrels of revolvers in the ultimate act of self-degradation and squeeze the triggers. What do they look at? The wall? Pictures of their wives? Or do they watch their fingers contracting slowly, the cylinder starting to turn?

I thought about bloodless bodies jammed into the trunks of automobiles with their wrists and ankles bound and holes in the backs of their heads, left to decompose and attract eventual attention in the long-term lot at the airport. Until that happens there is no grave more anonymous. You lie there getting waxen, your eulogy a litany of arrivals and departures gurgling unintelligibly out of the P.A. system in the concourse, your mourners bored redcaps leaning on their luggage carts on the sidewalk arguing about the Lions' bench. I thought about walking blonde dreams that the men who have them are not meant to keep. About friends that were more trouble than they're worth. About wars, and how each one always seems worse than the one before because more things come out that were part of all the others but just waited their turn to be talked about. I thought about dead partners on dirty pavement and wives' notes that don't get thrown away and wait to be found again, like corpses walled up in the basement. About loan sharks named Amigo and pushbutton killers named Wally. I thought about a lot of things, and then the patch of sunlight was gone and I couldn't see the printed stars.

I got up, the rotted timbers of my thoughts spinning away in clouds of splinters, and padded into the kitchen in my stockinged feet. I was out of Scotch, but there was a swallow of vodka left in the company bottle. I poured it over ice and left it to steep while I took a shower. Afterward I got ready to shave, had a hand full of lather before I decided I was better off with a shadow and rinsed off the lather and dressed in dark clothes. I chose blue jeans and a dark gray sweater, colors that are harder to see at night than straight black. Last I put on thick brown socks and blue sneakers and went back into the kitchen and drank the vodka, watching my reflection in the window over the sink. It was gray out now. By the time I got to Barry Stackpole's house in Harper Woods it would be dark enough.

I called for a cab. The dispatcher, a gravelly voice with a Middle Eastern accent, said one was cruising the vicinity and would be at my door in a few minutes. I drained my glass, chewing the ice, washed it, dried it, and put it away in the cupboard. I looked at my reflection again and smoothed back my hair with both hands. Two more years of cases like this one and they'd be calling me the gray fox.

A horn blew out front. I cut a Z in the wall and went out and mounted up.

Harper Woods is strictly for local residents who don't want a Detroit address. The bigger city presses against it on two sides, with Grosse Pointe Woods to the east and St. Clair Shores and East Detroit squatting on its head like Siamese gargoyles. It has no history and no business section to speak of, just rows and rows of houses and a school or two and some trees to justify the second half of its name and more churches than you can shake a prayer book at. I had the driver let me off three blocks short of my destination and tipped him a buck. He took it with a noncommittal smile. A diplomat.

I walked the rest of the way. My knee was feeling pretty good, the way sore muscles feel good after an honest workout. The evening was cool. Someone was burning wood—hickory, by the smell. The sky wasn't as cloudy as I'd have liked and a moon several days off the full stared down at me like an occluded eye. You can't have everything. If you could you wouldn't want it. Philosophy has it all over detective work; no one ever knows if you're any good at it. Light shifted from star to star, like moths seeking a hole in a screen door. Two miles to the southwest, the rotating beacon at City Airport swung a smoky bat through the blackness.

The house took some finding. I had been there only once, more than a year before, and then by daylight. At night the houses looked even more alike than their designers had intended. But the hour was early, and it was the only building on its block that wasn't lighted. It was a brick one-story with garage attached and nonfunctional shutters on the windows. On the stoop I got my pencil flashlight out of a pocket and cupped my hands around the beam to read the number on the mailbox. It was Barry's, all right.

Just for the hell of it I pushed the bell. It chimed a lonely double stroke far back in the house. After a couple of minutes I tried again. Nothing. I opened the screen, tried the door, and trained the light on the lock. It was a dead bolt. I had hardly expected less. He would have another one on the back door and bar locks on the windows. Just because he was no longer living out of a suitcase didn't mean he had gotten careless.

I retraced my steps down the front walk. The street was empty. Across from Barry's house stood its twin, but with everything reversed and a border of painted rocks to protect its prize lawn from motorcycles and pedestrians. Each rock was the size of a small coconut. I pried one loose, struck a Denny McClain stance, and hurled it like Grandma Moses.

I was running when it hit, in a long silvery jingle of collapsing glass followed a half-second later by the clanging of a commercial alarm. This time I paced myself, running with head high and my arms pumping and my feet drumming the sidewalk in a steady rhythm. I was heading toward what passes for downtown in Harper Woods.

I had made three blocks before the siren started up. It made a long thin tearing noise in the night air, yelping at corners and cross streets. Rubber scraped the curbs. The car passed me a block over, flashing its popcorn popper and shining its spot at doorknob level down both sides of the street. By then I was walking. My breath rasped and my heart hammered in my skull and my sweat dried to an icy shroud against my skin.

Nearing the little business district, I stopped to comb my hair and adjust my clothes, using a darkened window belonging to an empty real estate office for a mirror. On the corner I entered a Cunningham's and went to the magazine rack. I shared the premises with the pharmacist, a counter girl reading a paperback book with a groping couple on the cover, and a woman in her seventies in a red blazer and a black beret studying the label on a jar of cold cream. I slid a copy of *Newsweek* out of the rack and started reading. In a little while it was just me and the pharmacist and the counter girl. I flipped through an account of the President's trip overseas, glanced at the Book and Cinema sections, read an article that said the sexual revolution was over. I was surprised no one had consulted me. I put it back and tried *Time*. The pictures were different.

The girl at the counter had put down her book and was watching me, sighting down the aisle between the rows of greeting cards and pantyhose. A hand-lettered sign taped to the rack read NO LOITERING IN THE MAGAZINE SECTION. I chose a copy of *Gentleman's Quarterly* and brought it over to her. She looked from it to my rumpled sweater and lowslung jeans.

"It's for my brother," I said.

She rang it up. I paid for it and left. There was a coffee shop on the next corner, where a group of Thursday night bowlers in green silk shirts were having their own little party at a back booth. They reminded me of the guy whose parking space I'd taken at Curly's Bar and I grabbed a booth at the opposite end of the room. A waitress brought me coffee and a doughnut. I spent the next half hour dunking and sipping and grinning at the men's fashion ads in *GQ*. A piece on grooming had some shaving tips I could use and I read that and a profile of Jack Nicholson and then the clock over the counter said nine o'clock. I folded a dollar bill under my saucer and settled the bill at the register. Walk twenty feet in any direction in this country and there is another place to eat. At any hour there are enough griddles going to heat Greenland.

I rolled the magazine into a tube and jammed it into a city trash can, where the swarthy Italian number on the cover smiled amid crushed Styrofoam cups and wads of tissue. He reminded me of Wally Petite. Then I began walking back to Barry's neighborhood. My knee had stiffened up some and I walked slowly to avoid limping, but not slowly enough to attract attention. I passed an elderly couple out for a stroll, the woman taking little nibbling steps with her hand on the man's arm and his other hand on her back for support. It's possible to do that on well-lighted streets that far north of the Renaissance City.

Even taking my time like that I pushed it a little. A uniformed cop was standing on the lawn in front of the smashed window with his hands on his hips, looking around, while his partner leaned on the roof of the cruiser, speaking into the radio mike. I turned and walked down a side street before either of them spotted me. If they collared me and looked at my ID it would be tough explaining what a Detroit P.I. was doing walking in Harper Woods after dark. After two blocks I turned again. I was heading back in the right direction when the blue-and-white rolled away up the street with its roof light off and no siren.

Just in case someone was watching I circled the house, then stepped over a low grille fence in back. The back door was dead-bolted as expected. I stood in front of a window and pulled off my sweater and jabbed straight out from the shoulder with my other forearm across my eyes. The glass caved in with less noise than the window in front had made. I hesitated, poised to run, but no sound came from inside. The police had found the turnoff switch to the burglar alarm and used it. They were peace officers, after all. I cleared away the rest of the glass and let myself in over the sill.

24

THERE IS NOTHING QUITE SO QUIET AND REMOTE-FEELING as an empty house at night. The air lay in room-size blocks and didn't move. Where I was, moonlight reflected flatly off triangles of glass at my feet. Somewhere a section of foundation settled under the new weight with a noise like a human palm makes dragging across an inflated balloon.

I was in one of those damp-smelling unfinished chambers that get called utility rooms, although except as a place to hang a mop and stack cases of dusty empty deposit beer bottles, this one wasn't being utilized at all. I got bored with it quickly and mounted a step that took me through a vacant doorway into a fair-size kitchen with a stove and refrigerator built into one wall and a sink and drainboard that extended into a half counter. A row of glasses stood bottomside up along the edge. I drew a finger down the side of one. A faint streak showed in the pale light.

The tiny refrigerator bulb rinsed me in blue when I

opened the door. The inside was empty except for a six-pack of Molson Canadian with a bottle missing, an open package of sliced bologna with the top slice starting to curl, and a quart of milk in a cardboard carton. The freshness date had run out two days before. I sniffed at the open spout, took a swig. It hadn't started turning yet. Well, it had only been nine days. I put it back and closed the door.

That was it for the kitchen. Moonlight threw barred patterns across the floor of the living room, where the rock I'd thrown lay in a litter of broken glass. The cops hadn't come inside to retrieve it. Other cops who had helped themselves before calling the owners had made them wary of internal investigations. The room reflected Irene's arid taste: scoop chairs, a sofa that could ruin the man who tried to stretch out on it, a pale rug with a stripe along the edges, set at an angle like a baseball diamond in the middle of the floor, pedestal tables with round glass tops holding up nothing. One of the framed canvases on the walls was blank except for a dot that was a little off center. When you looked again it was in the exact center. Then it wasn't. Hours of fun. Fashion and architectural magazines were spread in a fan atop the coffee table. My finger made a streak on those too. Barry hadn't touched them since Irene left.

The bed was made in the bedroom and the dresser contained men's shirts and slacks and socks and underwear. I had no way of knowing if anything was missing or how much. I used my flash to examine the stuff on top, Comb, brush, loose change, some ballpoint pens. No wallet. A couple of suits hung in the closet. I went through the pockets and came up with a handkerchief and a book of matches from the Peacock's Roost. In Barry's case a lifetime of traveling light was a long time going away.

The bathroom was clean. No interesting drugs in the medicine cabinet. Barry didn't use them.

I had seen most of this before, of course. But not after dark with the only light sliding in guiltily through two smashed windows and me alone in mid-felony. On the first day of sleuth school they tell you what tools you'll need: camera, fingerprint kit, eavesdropping paraphernalia, arch supports. They never mention the latchkey, the jimmy, the well-placed heel. No room for that stuff in the display case with the blank affidavits and the FBI-approved portable lab. I had found my way around more locks than a balcony rake in the age of chastity belts. I had spent more time in other people's homes and offices without their knowledge than a fly with a muffler. I had housemaid's knee from climbing through windows and when a burglar alarm went off anywhere in the city I started running, like a punch-drunk prizefighter throwing left jabs every time the telephone rang. It's funny work for an honest man.

I went into the only other room in the house. Barry's study.

It had been a second bedroom and it still had that look, but he had moved out the bed and moved in a cheap desk and chair and a steel bookcase jammed with reference material and a wicker magazine rack to hold his file folders and hung a framed eight-by-ten blowup of an angel-faced young man nattily dressed in wide lapels and a Panama hat with a broad silk band. It was Jerry Buckley, the crusading radio commentator slain by Purple Gang killers in the lobby of the Hotel LaSalle in July 1930. The picture had kept Barry company everywhere he had lived for no matter how brief a period. I never knew if it was because he felt a kinship with another journalist who had fallen victim to the underworld or if because on later investigation, Buckley had proven as corrupt as a factory second. The Stackpole sense of humor didn't run to anything so simple as pratfalls and seltzer.

I flipped through the folders in the magazine rack. Mob stuff, mostly tearsheets from published sources. He had crossed out a lot of the information, sometimes drawing X's across whole pages, and added corrections in the margins in his hasty block printing. Some of these were pretty interesting, but I wasn't learning any dangerous secrets or he wouldn't have left the stuff out in the open. I saved my batteries for something better.

A Smith-Corona portable, out of its carrying case for maybe the first time since he had acquired it, shared the desk with a stack of blank sheets in an ocher box. There was nothing in the machine. I tried the top drawer of the desk. Locked. I sighed and broke out the picks I'd brought.

I was sitting in Barry's chair hunched over the lock when a shaft of hard white light rammed through the window over my left shoulder.

I fought down a nearly overwhelming urge to throw myself to the floor, and froze. My shadow, black and solid, leered at me from the wall. For a long time the shaft remained motionless, lying across my shoulders and the back of my neck like a bar of white-hot steel. Then the light moved on, sliding across the wall until the window frame cut it off. The door to the living room was open and I watched the beam glide over the furnishings there. After another long interval the shaft vanished. An engine started up and purred away.

My night vision returned slowly. I looked at my watch, turning its face to the moonlight. Quarter to ten. With luck the cops wouldn't patrol the place again this shift. But I started working faster.

The lock was all show. There was just the one keyhole, which indicated a rod affair that secured all three drawers, and those never are much. The tumblers shifted and I put away my picks and tugged out the drawer. Inside I found a divided steel tray cluttered with pencils and erasers and paperclips and jars of rubber cement. Nothing underneath the tray. The second drawer held more blank sheets and carbon paper. The bottom drawer contained a lead strong-box.

The metal's in disrepute now. It connotes poison, which some people think is communicated by biting. But for safe places to keep things, it has it all over steel. You can pound on it with a sledgehammer and pry at it with a jimmy and it will just keep changing shape and never let you inside. But this one wasn't locked, or even closed. The papers jammed inside wouldn't let the lid down. I hoisted the box out of the drawer and placed it on the desk and snapped on my flash.

It was all financial stuff, pay receipts and old passbooks and check stubs. Overstuffed though the box was, it wasn't much for the average person living in the age of Xerox and American Express. Barry owned no credit cards and had only started a checking account to keep his tax man happy, preferring to deal in cash rather than leave a trail of paper for his enemies to follow. The passbooks told me nothing, other than that the pattern and size of his withdrawals had stepped up considerably during the months Irene had been living with him. None of them was big enough to agitate my jaded mind. The deposits jibed with the sort of income a journalist with a column syndicated across the country would be making. I should have felt like a kid with his ribs exposed peering through a window at a turkey dinner with all the trimmings, but they were just numbers to me. When you get above the poverty level, everything's in the abstract.

Most of the odd receipts were deductible expenses: typewriter repair, telephone, books for research. I riffled through the little bundle of check stubs bound with a rubber band and found more of the same and one that interested me. It was made out in the amount of three hundred sixty dollars to "Z Travel," and dated September 23. That was the day I'd gone to the Detroit Press Club with Barry, the last day anyone had seen him. I pocketed it, went through the rest quickly the way you do when you figure you've found what you're looking for, put it all back, and returned the heavy box to its drawer.

That was it for the study. I closed the drawers and flipped off the flash and went back into the living room. A low bleached cabinet stood in one corner. I tugged open the door, used my light to read some labels, and lifted a bottle of Scotch off a shelf. I uncapped and tilted it. The liquid slid down my throat and landed with a dull thud. I took another drink to cushion the blow. My mind started clearing, as from a draft of clean mountain air.

The desk was awfully neat for Barry. I hadn't known many writers, but those I had known weren't the tidiest people I'd met, and even the tidy ones left clutter. There wasn't a scrap of writing in the study. Someone, probably Barry, had been through the place with a new broom. I drank again. My mind was getting clearer by the minute. I screwed the cap back on and put away the bottle and went back into the study.

The wastebasket was green plastic and tucked away in the kneehole of the desk. I untucked it, upended it. Baseball-size crumples of paper cascaded out and bounced all over the bare floor. I tossed away the empty wastebasket and sat on the floor to inspect my booty.

The first three pages I uncrumpled and turned this way and that in the moonlight were blank. It seemed a waste of paper. I saw Barry sitting and staring at a sheet in the machine just so long before he yanked it out and balled it up and tossed it, just to be doing something. He would go on that way until there were words on one of them. The fourth had a piece of a paragraph starting about a third of the way down the page. In the upper right-hand corner he had typed "Steel/ Lead, 1."

The doctor's name is Willard. He is a tall man with a tan and a rumbling bass and gray curling hair at his temples, the rest of it chestnut. He asks me how I am, and there is just the right amount of concern in his tone. He says he has brought

The passage ended there. I laid the wrinkled page aside and picked up another crumple, smoothed it out on the floor.

The doctor's name is Willard. He is tall and tan with chestnut hair curling and going gray at the temples. He asks how I am, and there is just the right amount of concern in his rumbling bass. He says he has brought something for me. He places it on my lap and hinges back the cover and I am looking at a book of noses.

I straightened out another ball of paper.

. . . and I am looking at a book of noses. Hopes and Barrymores, Durantes and Eckstines, pugs and roman hooks, they are all there in front view and profile, a mug book of probosci. My puzzlement must show through the chinks in my bandages, for Dr. Willard says, "We don't often have as much lee-way as we have in this case. The extent of the damage to your face calls for substantial restructuring, and as the taxidermist said when the poacher brought him an eagle he blasted with a shotgun, 'How do you want it, duck or eagle? I can go either way.'" And he chuckles.

That finished the page. I rooted around until I found page 2.

Using old photographs, Dr. Willard rebuilds my face along the old lines and when at last the bandages come off he places a mirror in my good hand and I look and say that he has done a wonderful job, which he has. Not a scar is visible. But the face is not mine, more like a close relative's. Little things have changed, and I know that it will take some getting used to. I

The rest of that one was blank. I dropped it and went through the others, looking for the thread. All I found were pieces of what I'd already read and something else, a close mass of single-spaced lines smudged on a torn sheet without a number or identification.

I wear a Judas face but I am Cain. Cain ably killed Abel in a canefield and trod to Nod to find a wife and a new life without strife. Instead he lost his face and even Abel wouldn't know the face he placed in its place. No tied-off blood vessels or gray cooked flesh stuck to the sheets for Cain, the swain. Just new sheet metal work and fresh trim and a coat of paint, a Detroit makeover for the man who burned the candy man. Candy Cain.

It was nutty stuff, a college freshman's idea of stream-of-consciousness. It didn't sound like Barry at all, but it had been typed on the same machine as the other stuff. I got up and rolled one of the blank sheets into the portable on the desk and pecked out something original about a quick brown fox, then unrolled it and compared it to what I had just read. It was the right machine, all right. I figured he was drunk when he wrote it. They say that a complete personality change is one of the signs of alcoholism. They say a lot of crazy things that don't hold up outside the laboratory where they torture monkeys and white mice. I folded both sheets and put them in different pockets and scooped the remaining crumples back into the wastebasket and parked it under the desk. Then I let myself out of the house through the back window.

I walked back downtown and used a pay telephone to call the operator and ask her to report a fresh disturbance at Barry's address to the police. This time maybe they'd put an officer in front until morning and keep some opportunist from getting inside the way I had, someone whose moral character was not as high as mine. I hung up while the operator was asking my name, then used the quarter that had come back to dial Louise's room at the Book Cadillac and tell her I'd be late and to meet me in the hotel dining room. She said okay and didn't ask any questions.

There wasn't much chance of catching a cab cruising Harper Woods at that hour, so I started walking west. My knee was good. Cool air touched my face like a hand carved out of ice. That's when I realized I was sweating.

25

THE DINING ROOM AT THE HOTEL WAS ONE OF THOSE places where a waiter named Armand, snowy hair and crepe soles, sets the little silver-plated coffee pot down at your elbow and ghosts in every five minutes to empty the ashtray. There wasn't much business in the place late on a Thursday night and he was all ours. He was going to be disappointed by my tip. Dessert was a cold pink cloud in a stemmed glass with whipped cream and half a strawberry on top. I finished mine, Louise ate her strawberry, and we went out to hail a cab. We weren't going anywhere, just riding around.

"Why, this is a beautiful city." She watched the lights sliding past the windows like colored glass on a black satin lampshade.

"At night," I agreed. "And depending on where you are in it."

"What's that blinking light?" She pointed.

"Broadcast tower on top of the Fisher Building."

"It looks like a landmark."

"The Lone Ranger was born there, the Green Hornet too."

"It is a landmark."

"Was. WJR's moving."

"Into some flat dull box, I suppose. Like the churches they build now."

"Steeples have no resale value." I pointed south, where a spidery span strung with colored lights seemed to hang in space. "That's the Ambassador Bridge. Windsor on the other side."

"Isn't that the wrong direction for Canada to be in?"

"There's a little neck of it down there hiding out from the Queen."

She sat back. Light from the street lamps along Michigan fluttered across a shimmery off-white thing to her ankles. A light shawl draped her bare shoulders and she had on a silver band around her neck, so thin it showed only when the light struck it. Her hair was up. I'd cleaned up and shaved and put on a suit before meeting her and I was just barely adequate. "You like living here, don't you?"

"You can get used to being stuck in the eye with a finger if that's how you wake up every morning," I said. "Yeah, I like it."

I told the driver to take us along the river and we jogged over onto Jefferson and turned east. The lights from Windsor scalloped the choppy surface. Ahead and to the right, the glittering canisters of the Renaissance Center seemed to be turning with the play of light like huge interlocking gears. The place had all the sinister beauty of a stiletto with a jeweled handle. If you had an infrared scope you could

200

look out through any of its windows and witness two crimes of violence per night.

"You haven't told me what made you late," Louise said then. "I've been wonderfully patient."

I reached up and slid shut the safety shield between the front and back seats. The driver's eyes flicked to the rear-view mirror, then back to the road. I lowered my voice to a murmur.

"It takes time to burgle a house."

She picked up on it quicker than expected. "Barry Stackpole's?"

"Yeah. He's started a new book."

"Did you bring it out with you?"

"I didn't see it. Just a couple of rough opening pages I found in the wastebasket in his study. It has the same title as the Vietnam book, only this one's not about Vietnam. I don't think."

"What's it about?"

"It doesn't matter. It won't tell me where he is. I found something else that might, a record of a payment to a travel agency. I'll check into it tomorrow."

"Is there something wrong with your leg?"

I had shifted positions a couple of times. The cab wasn't a Checker and there wasn't room to straighten the knee. "I hit it with Fenkell Street this afternoon."

"This has something to do with what happened to your car, hasn't it? Were you in an accident?"

"I wrecked it. I wasn't in an accident."

She crossed her legs and propped her chin up on her elbow, looking at me. The shawl slipped three inches. "Are you being a confidential character again?"

I met her lavender gaze. "I bet the young Shakespeares clap their hands and bark like seals when you do that.

Show them a creamy shoulder like alabaster under a Cairo moon."

"Damn thing's always down around my ankles." She adjusted the shawl.

"Better," I said. "Someone monkeyed with my steering and brakes. I aimed for the softest and cheapest thing I could find and took the air."

"My God."

I made a shrug. "I should get a new car out of it. The *News* will be happy to pick up the tab when they find out I trashed a *USA Today* box with the old one."

"Did you talk to the police?"

"No."

"May one ask why not?"

"One may."

"I see," she said after a moment. "We're in the hero business this week."

I said, "I've wrecked cars before. I've been hit over the head and pumped full of drugs and jailed and shot and worked over with brass knuckles and lied to a lot. Maybe I will be again, though I really hope not because my head's not as hard as it used to be. Certainly I'll be lied to again. But if I start running to the cops, getting my name in the papers with theirs, I'm on the street. My livelihood depends on a profile no higher than curb level."

"You talk as if private investigators don't have rights like everyone else."

"We surrender them when we sign the license application form. It's part of the ceremony."

"This has something to do with the warning you got last night?"

"I hope so. Any other answer would be too complicated."

"You scare me."

"Not you."

"Yes, me. I'm not half as tough as I like to make out. There's a whole universe between facing down a fat publisher who hasn't read a book since *Black Beauty* and dealing with people who kill people, actually kill people. I couldn't exist in your world."

"Nobody asked you to."

We had passed the RenCen by this time and were heading northeast, where the river broadened and the foreign skyline disappeared behind the long dark bulk of Belle Isle in the middle. The street lamps were spaced out farther now. The intervals of darkness between them were longer. She rested a hand on my sore knee. "Coming back to the hotel? I'll put some ice on this."

"Run that gauntlet of clerks, hops, and dicks?"

"They're grown up."

"All the way up to blackmail."

"We could go back to your place."

I laid my hand atop hers. She smiled. I patted it.

"A funny thing happens to a man when he passes thirty," I said. "He finds out he can live without a warm body next to him in bed. It changes his whole outlook."

"What do you mean?"

"I mean Freud was only a little bit right. It can be the driving force in your life, but only after lunch. Preferably on an expense account from the publisher."

Her hand jerked, but I hung on. "What's your point?" she demanded, and the warmth in the air was gone. Only the scent of jasmine remained, like incense in an empty room.

"The book's not mine to sell, princess," I said. "Not for money, and especially not for sex. Tomorrow you'd be flying back home with a best seller in your briefcase and I'd just have sheets to change."

"That's disgusting!" Her nails were claws.

"No argument." I let go.

She said, "You wouldn't know an honest emotion if it bit you."

"Most of them do."

"You're a suspicious, vile man. You think everyone else has an angle and you're the only character with any sort of integrity. But someone had to pay you to look for your own friend."

I closed a hand on her bare arm, high up where it can hurt. "It's a business, lady," I said quietly. "Just like yours. A title without any clout, a card that only opens doors when I slide it between the tongue and the jamb. When I have a legitimate client the cops don't stand on my foot so hard. And the missing persons business takes money, lady, money to get lost and money to get found. Clients have money. It isn't at all like opening your thighs to keep a job."

She said, "You're hurting my arm."

I released it. "Don't pay any attention to me. My knee's throbbing."

"Please take me back to my hotel."

I pushed back the safety shield and told the driver. We watched the scenery on the way back. A jet angled in low overhead on its way to Metro Airport, its blinking lights describing a neon cross. It reminded me of a case I'd had once and I thought of an old lady in black living in St. Clair Shores. The old ladies in black were dying out, giving way to sinewy hags with hair bottled in blonde and leathery brown skin burned dry by the sun and that hungry look behind their dark glasses when the beach boys glide past in their tight G-strings. Age didn't matter anymore. Everyone was stuck in gear. The sexual revolution had ended but the refugees hung on.

Louise got out while the cab was still in motion and started across the sidewalk. I told the driver to wait and caught up with her at the door and touched her arm, gently this time. "I wasn't calling you what you think."

The lavender was gone from her eyes They were splinters of blue ice. Very low she said something to me that didn't come from her part of New York, not during the day anyhow.

A character in a burgundy uniform with gold braid on one shoulder and scrambled eggs on his cap pried himself loose from the door and said, "The lady doesn't look like she wants your company, sir."

"You ought to put some nail polish on all that trim," I told him. "The glare's blocking your vision."

"What's that?"

"The gentleman just insulted me," Louise explained.

When she spoke, he looked at her with just the right measure of sappiness to go with a guy who would let his boss dress him like a wedding cake, and when he looked back at me the sides of his jaw stuck out in lumps.

I started to laugh then, and got back into the cab. As we pulled away, the doorman was holding the door for Louise.

A block farther on we passed a little girl hugging herself in a short skirt and knee-length boots in a doorway on the corner. By this hour she would have been in and out of the outfit five times. At night the smog over the city turned to clouds of stale perfume. If the place had a welcome sign it would read "Over Forty Billion Serviced." What they charged, fifty bucks or a book on the *Times* list, had nothing to do with the basic nature of the transaction. We've established what you are, lady. Now we're haggling over price.

On my way home it occurred to me that I hadn't told Louise the real reason I hadn't called the police yet. I didn't half buy it myself.

26

I WAS TOO WIRED TO SLEEP. I STAYED UP PAST THREE reading Barry's typescript, some parts of it for the third or fourth time, and staring at the single-spaced paragraph I had found in his wastebasket, waiting for the axe to fall. It didn't, and when the type started running together I put everything away and went to bed. I may have slept. An hour ahead of the clock I got up, wide awake, and went to the office. The bus was almost empty at that hour.

A note on my desk informed me the building cleaning service had been in. It was the only thing on the desk that didn't have dust on it. I turned the Venetian blinds up and down. I decided they looked less grimy. Then I decided they didn't. My finger left tracks on the tops of the file cabinet and safe. Finally I opened the deep drawer of the desk and lifted out the office bottle. They had cleaned two inches off the top.

The mail wasn't in yet. I put away the bottle and sat down and squirmed around until I'd fitted myself into the groove I'd worn in the seat. That killed a few seconds. I chain-smoked two cigarettes, which killed ten minutes more. By then it was time to call my answering service.

They didn't have anything for me. I hung up and smoked another cigarette. Then I called for the time. My watch was a minute and a half slow. I reset it, and there went two more minutes. This was going to be a snap.

When it was coming up on eight o'clock I opened the Yellow Pages to Travel Agencies and paged to the Z's. The pickings were lean in Greater Detroit. A display for Zodiac Vacations, Inc., took up a quarter of the page, complete with map, special holiday hours, and a row of smiling faces with the agents' names printed underneath. It listed two locations. Next to it Zephyr Travel ran a more modest notice the size of a calling card, just its name in elegant script and a number in Grosse Pointe.

I didn't see the third one until I moved my thumb. It was a one-line entry: "R. Zeitgeist, trvl agnt." A telephone number and a Fort Street address followed.

That was it for the Z's. Zodiac, with its main office on Forest, was the closest. I wet my cab whistle and left.

It was one of those mellow gold fall mornings. The wind had a nip in it and the air was sharp with burning leaves and fermenting cider. Where a tree grew out of a box on the sidewalk and its leaves hadn't gone the way of industrial toxication, those leaves were turning brown and russet and umber and red. It was a morning to ditch the office and go looking for a football game, any football game. I hoped someone was doing just that for me.

Zodiac occupied a storefront on the north side of West Forest near the John Lodge, a large communal office with a suspended ceiling and two rows of walnut veneer desks with a broad green-carpeted aisle running between. A standing rack near the door held colorful brochures and the walls were papered with posters of matadors and hula girls and Times Square lit up like V-J Day and couples walking along deserted stretches of immaculate beach. All the desks were manned. I chose a vacant seat in front of a man in his late twenties balancing a telephone receiver in the hollow of his shoulder while pattering away on the keyboard of a computer terminal on a revolving base next to the wall. The nameplate on the desk read DAVE, no last name.

"I don't recommend that hotel," the young man was saying into the telephone. "Sure, the rates are the best in New York, but we got complaints of rooms getting ripped off and the customers think it's personnel. Yeah. Okay, can I get back to you? Thanks."

"I worked in a couple of hotels," I said, when he'd hung up. "I wouldn't recommend any of them."

The corners of an impressive handlebar moustache turned up jauntily and he relaxed in his chair. He was wearing a plaid shirt and skinny tie under a corduroy jacket with ornamental patches on the elbows. "Hotel people are mostly scum, the upper levels anyway. They know there's an eighty percent chance they'll never see you again and so they gouge you. I rate them down around morticians and sidewalk solicitors. Where can I send you today?"

"My wife says she wants to see some color. Do you arrange tours of the north country?"

"Sure, but you can hop in the car and take off up 23. You don't need me."

"You must own the place," I said.

"No, I just don't believe in picking pockets. I figure my days in the travel business are numbered."

"You're the man I want to talk to, then. Barry said to be sure and look up Dave."

"Barry?"

"Barry Stackpole. He's on a trip he said you set up."

He turned his chair and thumbed through a stack of scribbled sheets on a spindle, hesitated, then finished the job and turned back, smoothing his moustache with a knuckle. "No Stackpole. You're sure he said Zodiac?"

"I'm not even sure he said Dave. But it sounded like that and the place he used had a name that started with a Z."

"There must be several in this area."

"There are three."

He ran a thumb along the veneer of the desk. "What is it you want? You're not interested in any fall color tours. I don't even think you have a wife."

"I'm an investigator." I gave him one of my cards. "Stackpole's come into an inheritance and he has till the end of the month to come forward, otherwise it goes to the government. We found a reference to 'Z Travel' in his records and we thought maybe you were the agency that got him out of town. We need a location or a number where he can be reached."

"What was that story about the tour?"

"A blind. In cases like this where money is involved, our informants tend to want to cut themselves in."

He grinned. A lad with a cookie-duster like his can really build you a grin. "I guess you're not going to tell me what it really is. That inheritance story is older than that poster of Hawaii."

"Force of habit." I grinned back. "Stackpole's got an appointment with a grand jury. If he doesn't show up it's going to start costing his employers. The money thing

210

works the other way too. The smell of green ink loosens a lot of tongues."

"Is there money?"

"If the information's good."

"Makes me wish I knew something. If your boy used Zodiac he didn't go through me."

"He might have used an alias." I described him. Dave shook his head. I said, "What about the other agents?"

"I'm managing the office while the regular guy's in Aruba. I have to okay all checks and I didn't see any signed Barry Stackpole. Unless he has an account under another name?"

"Who said he paid by check?"

"Everyone does. If someone came in here with cash, one of the girls would ask to see two pieces of identification before she'd accept it."

"Yeah."

"He's not hiding under any of the desks," he said. "There's hardly room for our knees there."

"How about your other office?"

"It's just a telephone and a place to drop mail. No agent there."

I got up and tapped the card on the desk with a finger. "You can reach me here if things change. Maybe you can send me on a trip I don't go on and give you back the ticket to cash."

"Hell being an honest man," he said. "Have to go clear around the Horn to make a little change."

"Choice you make."

"Nobody makes the choice to be honest, pal."

"Just testing."

He smiled under the thatch.

Next I tried R. Zeitgeist on Fort Street near the post

office. The first cabbie I got wouldn't even take me to that neighborhood. The second kept his eyes moving and his hand between the front seat cushions while I counted out the fare. He took off with a cheep of rubber as soon as I slammed the door. A couple of cabs had been shot at in the vicinity earlier in the year.

The ground floor of the building sold auto parts. The counter was just six feet in from the door, with a painted partition behind it with another door cut into it. The real stuff would be stored in back. You went up to the counter and asked for a water pump for a '78 Mustang and if they didn't have one in stock they would back-order it from a parking garage six blocks over, preferably after dark,

There was no building directory inside the stairway entrance from the street. From the looks of the entrance I was lucky there were stairs. On the second floor I found the elephants' graveyard for the ninety percent of small businesses that fail within the first two years: credit dentists, disbarred attorneys, auto insurance agencies for the accident prone, easy loan companies, palmists, and karate schools. The rubber-paved hallway smelled of stale hope.

I found the same legend I had read in the telephone book lettered in flaking black on a frosted glass panel with brown grime hammocked in the corners. When I opened the door it bumped against the desk on the other side. The whole place was no bigger than a linen closet and had no windows, but the walls were covered with overlapping posters, orange island sunsets and blue oceanscapes with yellow moons hanging over them. One of the yellow moons was wearing a face with six chins.

The face had a body and the body was jammed into a pink shirt and a green sport coat that gave up where a pair of huge furry wrists began. Two points of a yellow bow tie with red squares on it poked out from under the chins.

While I was staring at this arrangement, the telephone on the desk rang and the moon face stirred and a broad pink palm came up in a holding gesture to me while its mate lifted the receiver to a surprisingly small and well-shaped ear. The other hand came down and picked up a freshly sharpened pencil from a row of them on the blotter and began scribbling on the pad.

"Yeah. Got it. No, I can't repeat it now. Yeah." The receiver went back to its cradle. A pair of tiny black eyes looked at me without blinking.

"R. Zeitgeist?" I asked.

"What it says on the door."

His voice was high and shallow, like a boy's. I got out of the way of the door enough to shut it. He didn't ask me to sit down. There wasn't anything to sit down on. I was giving him the line about setting up a fall color tour when the telephone rang again and the palm came up. He used the next pencil in line.

"Okay, got it." He cradled the receiver, put down the pencil next to the one he'd used first, saw me turning my head to read what he'd written, and moved his hand over it.

This time I finished what I'd started to say and he said, "Color won't be reaching its peak up north before next weekend. Try me in a week."

"Barry Stackpole told me to look you up."

He caught the telephone in mid-ring, picking up another pencil at the same time. "I can't give you that now," he told the mouthpiece. "Five minutes." Hanging up: "I don't know any Stackpoles. You got the wrong agency."

Before I could answer he was on the horn again. I

skinned two twenties out of my wallet and tucked one end under the blotter.

When he finished talking he scooped up the pencils he'd used and fed them one by one into a sharpener mounted on the desk, cranking the handle noisily between a meaty thumb and forefinger. He blew the shavings off the point of the last one, sighted down its length, then reversed ends and used the eraser to push the currency back in my direction.

"Don't let the location throw you, Jim," he said. "I keep a roll of bills bigger than these in the toilet."

"Bet they get used when a twenty-to-one longshot comes in at Hazel Park."

His face turned a darker shade of yellow and his chins started to work. The bell jangled again. I picked up my money and let myself out while he was writing. If Barry was going to book a trip, he wouldn't do it through the road show version of *Guys and Dolls*.

Zephyr Travel was a dish of another order. The building was a colonial mansion built by one of the more obscure auto magnates during the First World War, all white with a shake roof and a balcony running clear around, supported by enough square columns to hold up three more of the same size. Its many windows looked out on a tide of cool green lawn that would make a golf course look shabby, bordered on either side by a line of cedars trimmed into perfect cones. The place had no sign. My driver checked the number on the gatepost and we glided up a broad composition driveway and braked in front of a porch that made the one on the Grand Hotel on Mackinac Island look like a tenement stoop. Ours was the only vehicle in sight. I paid the driver and said he could go.

"Maybe I wait." He snicked up the flag on the meter.

"You don't look like someone that's going to be in there long."

I went right in without knocking. That's one ceremony cathedrals don't stand on. The room I found myself in was a cozy acre, surrounded by windows with thick maroon drapes drawn shut and illuminated by sunlight streaming down through a skylight toward the rear onto a glossy brown floor, where it glimmered like moonlight on calm water. In the center of all this emptiness stood a French desk, all top and curving legs bleached white and then tinted mauve. The extra pair of curving legs under it belonged to a sleek operation in a blue dress with white lace trim around a heart-shaped neckline. Pearls above that, and higher up a gaunt model's face with black hair all around, lots of it. As I approached, my footsteps chuckling in the rafters, she slid a red leather bookmark into a volume that would be Dante in the original or something like that and set it aside.

"Zephyr Travel?" I asked.

"Yes?" Her dark eyes gave up the barest flicker over my J.C. Penney suit.

"I had to make sure. There's no sign."

"We don't advertise," she said. "Our clients come to us on recommendation."

"You have a display in the Yellow Pages."

"Colonel Wheelock, that's the owner, owns stock in Michigan Bell. He calls it priming the pump."

"He in?"

"Have you an appointment?"

"I need an appointment to arrange a vacation?"

"You need a reference to make an appointment," she said. "Maybe we aren't the agency for you. We charter jets and around-the-world cruises and arrange safaris in Africa."

"I might consider renting an elephant."

"Twelve is the minimum." She rested her chin on a red-nailed hand.

"They come in sets?"

"Maybe if you told me what you have in mind I could recommend someone."

I handed her a card. "I'm looking for a man named Barry Stackpole. He's a columnist with the Detroit *News*. He recorded a check for three hundred and sixty dollars to a Z Travel shortly before he came up missing. We thought that might be you."

"Who is 'we'?"

"Sleuth's plural. To make you think I've got a whole organization behind me. I don't get as many doors put in my face when I use it."

"It wasn't us. Three hundred and sixty dollars wouldn't get you out that door."

While she was talking, a gaunt old man came out of the sun-washed section behind her leaning on an ebony cane and laid some papers on the desk. He had a straight back under a tan suit pinched at the waist, crisp white hair against a complexion the shade of walnut, and the general appearance of someone who was used to coming in out of the sun.

"These are fine, Diane. Get them off today, will you?" His clipped British accent held a hint of command.

"You didn't have to bring them out, Colonel," she said. "Why didn't you buzz?"

"I once hiked three miles through enemy lines with a dead sergeant on my back, although I didn't know he was dead at the time. I think I can handle this." A pair of faded blue eyes jerked my way and he stood a little straighter, if that was possible. "Sir?"

I introduced myself and held out my hand. "You have a very famous name, Colonel Wheelock."

He hesitated, then took it. His grip was corded and very strong, but the hand shook a little.

"An ancient war now," he said, letting go. "Not many of you lads born since know anything about it nor care to. Which is only right. The study of war can have no end but destruction."

"Clausewitz?"

"Wheelock. What can we do for you, young man?"

Diane gave him my card. "Mr. Walker is looking for someone he thinks may have used us, a Mr. Stackpole of the *News*. I told him he's mistaken."

"A private enquiry agent. Well, well. You were in Intelligence, no doubt?"

"Military police. Before that I was stationed in Vietnam and Cambodia."

He made a face. It was cracked all over and when he did that he looked like the Mummy. "Filthy little bastard of a war. I was over there as an advisor when the UN first came in. I said then it could never be won. The cancer was too deep."

"That when you got into the safari business?"

"I used to do a little shooting in Africa, but I'm not supposed to admit that now. When it went out of fashion I couldn't see myself crawling through the bush with a camera around my neck. Now, hunting controls the animal population and prevents mass starvation, but what earthly good does photography do the ecology? So now I send others to do what I refuse to do and it's made me a very rich man. I'm so proud of myself I could spit."

217

"Blood pressure, Colonel," warned Diane.

He creaked his cane. "It's hell to be old. I'm not even allowed to get up a good head of steam. I didn't do business with your quarry, Mr. Walker. My clientele is small and select, read that stinking. If he couldn't afford to fly in friends from the Continent for a day on Boblo Island he isn't on my preferred list. Did you know it's terribly gauche to own a jet? One must charter. Those are the sort of interesting things one learns at this level of the travel game."

"All wars end, Colonel," I said.

"The hell of it is the professional soldiers go on."

"To fade away?"

A smile tugged at the pleated lips. "MacArthur. The old rooster knew his strategy, but he certainly let the Japs pull the silk over his eyes during the Occupation. If only it were so neat as the process of fading. But someone has to stay on to pull out the tubes and fill your veins with evil-smelling fluid and paint your face and say words over you before lowering you into a stone vault so you can't return to the earth. Humanity is a messy business. I can't think of one messier, short of fantasy fulfillment, which is the one I'm in." He thought about it a little longer, then shook himself like an old dog. "Good luck, young man. I hope you find your friend."

"I didn't say he was a friend."

The old eyes sparked briefly. "Didn't you? Oh, well. Silly old man. Good-bye."

He turned and walked back into the wall of sunlight, leaning a little more heavily on the cane now, a deactivated warrior with a back that had to stay straight to support the kingsize chip on his shoulder. A hell of an old man. I had never heard of him.

27

"WHAT'D I SAY?" ANNOUNCED THE CAB DRIVER AS I GOT in the back. "But you was in there a little longer than I figured."

I gave him an address in downtown Detroit and said there was another buck in it for him if he didn't talk on the way.

"Okay, buddy." He tucked a magazine with a Centennial Colt on the cover up over the visor, started up, and we turned away from the place where they put up air and sunshine in special bottles and back to the real world.

Hole No. 1 was a challenge the first day out, full of interesting possibilities and the chance to meet new people. It was still that way on the third day if you were young and owned stock in Detroit Edison and Dr. Scholl's. When you were broke and not young and it was the fourth day it was like shaving without a blade, driving a car up on blocks, shooting blanks at ducks. I had a record of a payment to a travel agency that didn't exist and a wacky theory about three seemingly unrelated deaths that may or may not have had anything to do with why I was blowing my old age on cabs. I didn't even have transportation. I was as low as you can get without having to climb a ladder to pull up your socks.

The scenery changed by degrees from gables and wrought-iron fences to six-pack housing tracts and then worn granite making obscene gestures at the sky. I tipped the driver two bucks for keeping our bargain and stepped from warm sunshine into the chill cave of Schinder's garage.

The German was standing in front of the yawning hood of a two-year-old Thunderbird with a green finish worn down to rust-colored primer in leprous patches. As I came near he took a step backward, wiping his hands on a greasy rag, and said, "Start her." The engine kicked in with a roar. He listened for two seconds and shouted to the man behind the wheel to shut it off.

"Lifter," he said. "Number two."

"Just like Paderewski."

He turned and saw me for the first time. "How do you feel about manual transmissions?" he asked.

"We're just good friends."

"Out back." He started walking toward the rear. I followed.

From the neck up, Schinder could have been a successful product of Hitler's early experiments in genetic engineering: blue eyes, square features, and blond hair that was almost white, swept up from shaved temples into a mass of curls. Aside from that he was constructed along simian lines, a long waist and arms balanced on a pair of bent legs with a foot that turned inward sharply. He looked at least thirty years younger than he was.

The foot gave him a rolling gait that was impossible to keep step with. From behind him I asked, "How's Jock?"

"Not too good. They expelled him from Ferris State for setting fire to his dormitory."

Jock was Joachim, Schinder's son. I had helped get him off a Grand Theft Auto charge in return for a lifetime discount on all my auto work.

We went through a tiny office at the back and exited into an asphalt lot with an eight-foot board fence all around and a narrow alley running alongside the building to the street. A row of cars and trucks in differing states of repair stood there and Schinder led the way to an old Buick Skylark with a dull blue finish.

"This the best you could do?" I looked at a parking ding the size of a half-dollar on the door on the driver's side.

He said nothing, but kept walking to the front of the car and threw up the hood. The engine took up all the available space beneath.

"Woman who had it thought oil was something you put on your salad," he explained. "We yanked the block and dropped in an engine from an Olds Ninety-Eight. I was saving it for something special. You're not it. But I'll lease it to you for a month."

"A lot of hoses," I said.

"Camouflage, in case Lansing gets in mandatory pollution checks. Most of them aren't hooked up to anything. She burns leaded gas. Lots of it. Three-fifty for the month."

"I'll go two hundred."

"It just went up to four. We don't bargain, or did you forget?"

"Same service deal as always?"

"I make a deal it's a deal."

"Okay, four hundred. End of the month okay?"

"Week," he said. "Cash."

I put a cigarette in my mouth without lighting it. Wherever Schinder went, the air swam with gasoline fumes. He sweated the stuff. Finally I said okay again.

"You want a test drive before we draw up papers?"

"I trust you."

We went into the office and Schinder started opening and closing drawers. "Your boy did a pretty good job on that Olds, bled the brakes and broke the emergency shoe clean off. Your tie rod ends were just gone. Must have loosened the nuts. No wonder she didn't steer." He found a blank dealer's license sticker and put it on the desk.

"What kind of mechanic do you have to be to do that?" I asked.

"No kind at all. Give me five minutes and I'll show you how."

"Too bad."

"Had somebody for it, huh."

"Yeah, but I didn't like it. Too neat."

When he had the sticker made out he handed it over. "Life is that way," he said. "When things get too tidy you want to go out and mess them up."

"You sound like an old warhorse I was talking to this morning."

"Which war?"

"Yours."

"Other side, I bet." He showed me his brief Wehrmacht recruiting-poster grin. "Keys are in the ignition."

The motor was as smooth as oil.

I let it out on East Jefferson along the route Louise and I had taken by cab the night before. The lights were with me

222

and between East Grand and Conner no one passed me. When I stepped on the gas the bottom fell out of the carburetor with a noise like lions in a pit and the needle jumped ahead twenty miles. Ralph Nader was going to put me on his Ten Most Wanted list.

I played around with it on the expressways for a while. Wind fluttered through the open window on the driver's side and sharpened my thoughts, or tried to. I do some of my best thinking while driving, but today my head was full of cottage cheese. At noon I stopped for lunch and dialed my service from the restaurant. I was to call a number at Detroit Police Headquarters and ask for Lieutenant Ysabel.

"Ysabel."

There was noise on both ends of the line. I stood back out of the flow of employee traffic to and from the kitchen and screwed a finger into my free ear. "Walker," I said. "How's Major Crimes?"

"They just keep getting majorer and majorer. When can you get away?"

"Get away where?"

"The Wayne County Morgue for starters. Then we'll talk about whether we come back here to Thirteen Hundred."

"Who's dead?"

"The idea is you tell me."

I told him twenty minutes and we hung up on each other.

The morgue is hidden underground behind Traffic Court at Lafayette and Brush. Most Detroiters don't even know it's there. I told the attendant inside the door I had an appointment with Ysabel and he said the lieutenant was waiting for me downstairs. I found him standing in the little room where they receive the parents of little girls found in dumpsters with their clothes gone and their faces beaten to bloody pulp. It had a table and chairs for sitting in while watching the closed-circuit TV screen over the table.

Ysabel was wearing the same colorless suit and tie I'd seen him in at headquarters. Standing, he looked smaller, his large head and broad athletic build somehow out of proportion to his five-foot-six height, but it was an illusion; he was all to scale. A black attendant in a white coat too big for him stood on the other side of the blank screen.

"I'm getting the rube treatment today," I said, nodding at the set-up.

"New regs," said the lieutenant. "No one but personnel goes inside. We had a woman freak out last month when she saw her son laid open on the table. Tactful cop, that Cranmer. She may sue."

"Fitzroy's Cranmer?"

"You know him?"

"I rattled his cage once. When's the show?"

He looked at the attendant, who reached up and turned on the screen. It came on instantly, blue-gray with a face in the center, foreshortened a little by the angle of the camera. Waxen skin with a shadow of beard showing under the surface. Damp hair plastered flat to the skull, eyes glittering white semicircles under half-closed lids. Raw like that without music or make-up, it was a sight to make you appreciate the mortician's art.

Ysabel was watching me. "You know him, right?"

It's hard to lie while you're looking at a stiff.

"Yeah," I said. "He tried to kill me yesterday."

After a second the lieutenant stirred and the man in the white coat turned off the switch. The screen went very black.

Ysabel said, "Let's go inside."

28

THE PLACE HAD A LITTLE LOUNGE FOR THE EMPLOYEES, beverage machines and four orange molded plastic chairs around a folding card table with a blue vinyl skin peeling away from bare sheet metal. On the way there we passed through the room where the corpse I had been looking at on TV was laid out under the mounted camera. It belonged to a pudgy naked body with a trail of coarse black stitches from collarbone to groin and a clear line around its middle where a tight waistband had bisected a roll of doughy fat. The genitals were darker than the rest of the body. Through an open door into the lounge. Ysabel bought us each a cup of coffee from the machine and we sat down at the table. I sipped mine and pulled a face. The smell of formaldehyde and dead naked flesh got into everything.

"The attendants eat their lunch in here," he said. "Just open their paper sacks and haul out the hardboiled egg sandwiches and start scarfing. I guess you can get used to anything you hang around it long enough. But I had an uncle that worked in a slaughterhouse and hot days he'd start sweating and the house smelled like the back room of a butcher shop. I wouldn't invite any of these guys to a pool party. I got a pool, you know. Wives."

I said, "I wouldn't know."

"You did, though. You were married. I looked you up."

I lit a cigarette. It deadened the smell a little.

He drank his coffee. "Kids found the body floating in the Old Channel off Zug Island this morning early. We figure it slipped its moorings in Lake St. Clair and came down river. M.E. found indications of rope burn on the left ankle. No ID, but whoever emptied the pockets was in a rush. Your name and office address was written on a piece of paper in the watch pocket of his pants."

"Any idea who he was?"

"We know who he was."

He was looking at me across the table. I glanced around and finally knocked my ash off onto the linoleum floor. It was already paved with burns and old butts. "This the favor I owe?"

"Nope. This is official police business being conducted in an unofficial place. You have to pretend there's a tape machine and a steno in the room. I don't get any satisfaction here, you won't have to pretend. We'll be at headquarters."

"We're all muscle today," I said. "Must be the formaldehyde."

"Caffeine." He tapped his cup. "I'm supposed to stand away from it. But what the hell, I don't use seat belts either. The stiff."

I took another drag and squashed out the butt. It was starting to taste like the air smelled. "On my way out of a bar called Curly's in Highland Park yesterday I passed a guy going in," I said. "He had grease on his hands. Maybe you found some under his nails." He shrugged. I went on. "Anyway, when I got rolling down Fenkell my steering and brakes got up and left. If it was just a warning he came as close to making it stick as anyone has."

"Sure it was him?"

"I wasn't until five minutes ago."

"What were you doing at this place Curly's?"

"Drinking. What killed our friend?"

"Small-caliber bullet in the brain. From behind."

"Twenty-two?"

He sipped coffee. "We're holding that back from the press. But yeah. I don't know when that got to be badass. When I was a kid every boy got a twenty-two squirrel gun for his twelfth birthday. Now we get more of those at Major than anything else. A good axe murder comes in, there's a rush of volunteers to work it just for the change of scenery."

"That why Major got this one?"

"No. What else were you doing at Curly's besides getting shitface?"

I shook another cigarette out of the pack and played with it.

"Keeping an eye on Wally Petite. You and I talked about him before. I was following him from the bar when everything laid down on me."

"What makes you so unpopular?"

"I'm looking for Barry Stackpole, who's not much more popular among a certain element. It's like poison ivy."

"Or maybe it's got something to do with somethin' else you haven't thought about. Or aren't talking about."

"That being?"

"You're the private star. This the first try?"

"Yeah. I got a call at home the night before. 'Tough break, Walker.' Nothing else, just that. Could've been our friend."

"Report it?"

"You boys have enough to do without shaking the goblins out of my closet."

"Where does Petite figure?"

"When I have that I'll tie this one up with a bow." I studied the brand name on the cigarette. I hadn't lit it yet. "What caliber bullet was Philip Niles killed with? Petite's partner?"

"Twenty-two. You know that. What was Stackpole's interest in the Niles kill to begin with?"

"I don't know that."

"Guess."

"I don't make guesses in rooms that contain cops," I said. "And if I did it would be privileged information."

"That withers under a strong light, pal." His tone would etch steel.

"Look it up," I said. "I'm a licensed investigator on retainer to a firm of attorneys. That makes me an officer of the court and entitled to the same confidences as a lawyer and his client. You want more you go to a judge and ask him for a piece of Latin with his signature on it. He'll fondle his gavel and show you the hall."

"Some would, maybe. There are judges and judges."

I moved a hand meaninglessly.

He stretched and clasped his hands behind his head. "Forget about the imaginary steno and tape machine. Pretend we're just two guys. What's your guts say?"

"Just two guys?"

"I bought the coffee."

"Yeah." I pushed mine away with one sip gone. "My

guts say Barry found a link between several scattered killings, including Niles's and Morris Rosenberg's. My guts say the link was Inspector Ray Blankenship of the Detroit Police Department, who once arrested Wally Petite for petty theft and who ran the detective squad in the precinct where Rosenberg was killed outside the factory where he worked, and who blew off the top of his head the other morning because something made him sick. His wife said. My guts say Alfred Kindnagel was involved because he was Rosenberg's higher-up in the union and because an article about him shared a file folder in Barry's office with clippings on the others, not counting some random stuff I haven't run down. My guts are like police detectives. They do a lot of talking and never say anything. Who's the guy on the slab?"

He played with his cup. "This confidence thing—it exclusive to clients?"

"It doesn't have to be."

"Shit, it'll get out anyway. You can sit on a stink like this just so long. A Vice sergeant named Winters was down here waiting on an analysis when he was wheeled in. He recognized him. It speeded things up twenty-four hours anyway. His name was Gerald Page and he spent the last six and a half years in a blue uniform. Guess where."

"The Fourteenth Precinct. Blankenship's."

"You're quick," he said.

"A cop tried to kill me?"

"Warn you, maybe. You said that. You going to light that weed or feed it and put it away?"

I'd forgotten I was still holding it. I set it afire. "Someone, probably Blankenship, was contracting murders out of the Fourteenth," I tried. "Petite and the inspector—he was a lieutenant then—knew each other from that old arrest.

229

Maybe Blankenship had some kind of underground rep by that time. It can happen without his own brother knowing. When Petite went partners with Niles and then wanted to go solo he set up the hit through him. Maybe he had some kind of leverage; there's plenty of it lying around in lockup. Anyway, he rigged it. Deals like that can eat away at a cop. If he has enough left of his self-respect he'll take early retirement and if he still has enough left he might kill himself."

"We're reopening the suicide investigation," Ysabel said. "Whoever inherited Blankenship's black hood might have made him Page's first assignment."

"Where does Kindnagel figure?"

"I sent a recruit down to the basement at Thirteen Hundred. They love browsing through those boxes of dusty files we haven't got around to feeding the computer. The reports he came up with had Rosenberg organizing a separate union to nudge out Kindnagel's. He had some support among the rank and file. If anyone pushed the button on him it would be the old man."

"Or one of his hirelings. Why didn't this come out eight years ago?"

"It's your Supreme Court too," he said. "We had videotape of Kindnagel strangling his wife, if his lawyer said she was choking on a prune pit and he was holding her up until help came, we couldn't prove otherwise. Besides, it was Blankenship's sandbox and Downtown has a policy about deferring to the original precinct."

"It got plowed under."

"Let's say it got stepped over."

"Christ, I love this town."

He started tearing little pieces of Styrofoam off his cup. "You want honest government, hire a dictator. When you own everything you don't have to steal or cover things up. Cops are trained to kill. Claiming you only shot to wound during a fracas is grounds for dismissal from any police department in this country. It's a skill that's in demand and where there's a demand there will always be someone to fill it.

"We're supposed to be better than average. More honest, more patient, quicker to react but slower to shoot. For that we get less money than these guys you see shoveling monkey shit into potholes on Telegraph and a flag on our coffins when we shoot too slow. You say that's the decision we make when we put in our applications, but the longer you go the less you remember of that little speech you make when they swear you in. Maybe we ought to be made to say it again every couple of years. Somehow I don't think that'd help. There are always going to be scroats."

"You should speak at the academy," I said.

"Even if they let me, no one'd listen. They'd all be too busy admiring themselves in the shiny toes of their regulation black oxfords."

"How wide you figure this goes?"

"I.A.D. is hoping to contain it to the Fourteenth. My own thought is for every roach you see there are ten more you don't. But for now I figure you and me are straight."

"It's a place to start," I said. "So when I stirred the coals I got a warning and then a shot at my life, or maybe two warnings. But it makes too much noise and Officer Page has to go. What about Barry?"

"Forget Barry. Barry's holding down the bottom of Lake St. Clair."

"He's too smart for that."

"It's the dumb ones that get to see their grandchildren.

231

Unless us two straights haven't been completely honest and open with each other."

I slid my stub into my cup. It sizzled and bobbed on the cold black surface, going dark. "Can I go?"

He played with the pieces he'd torn off his cup, arranging them in abstract patterns on the table. Then he pushed them away.

"You always could. I just had this nutty idea we could make each other's job easier. I guess not."

I stood, but he wasn't finished. His dark eyes had lost their liquid sheen. They were studs in his face. "Word I get is you play your own game. Okay, me too. Just don't forget who you owe favors to."

"I won't."

He said nothing more and I left. Gerald Page took no notice of me on my way past his table.

Sergeant Grice was smoking a cigarette in the room with the closed-circuit television. The attendant had gone. I asked the sergeant what he was doing there.

"Waiting on a lab report on that bag lady we scraped off Montcalm," he said, knocking his ash off onto the floor. "M.E.'s going to tell me what was in her stomach when she got her throat slit. Like I don't know it was cat food or that glue they serve at the Perpetual Mission."

"They're just getting to it now?"

"In Detroit Homicide you pick a place in line and stand in it. For derelicts you don't even get to stand in the same building. What about you?"

"Visiting a friend."

He didn't hear the answer. He was staring at my face. "You ever turn in a complaint to Vice?"

"For or against?" I said brightly. He didn't react. "No, I never did."

"I didn't think so. I'm still working on it."

I left him.

The Skylark started with a touch and I took off slowly in deference to the dead inside the building.

Cops come in all packages. Federal cops are the most full of themselves: They flip their IDs out of their neat suits with little practiced gestures like headwaiters snapping open linen napkins and ask questions out of the manual while ignoring any you might have. State cops are the most narcissistic; six-foot-two frustrated mounties in tailored uniforms and mirrored glasses, gloves in their belts. They blaze their spots on your rearview mirror when you're going twenty miles over the limit on the expressway and call you sir or ma'am and ask you to sign the citation next to the X. County cops are the most professional, with time in peeling teenagers off trees and chasing stolen cars along twisting scenic highways at speeds over 100 m.p.h. and exchanging fire with prison walkaways and getting dead at a rate three times that of city cops.

City cops vary from city to city, but they are all kinds, from polite precinct commanders in rich towns like Grosse Pointe who know whose names to keep off the blotter if they want to go on being precinct commanders, to private police forces in monied suburbs whose cars follow cars with battered fenders and cracked taillights until they're clear of the limits just in case they might stop, to ex-Marine drill instructors and jaded former beat cops now vegetating behind desks in the big cities waiting to get in their twenty. Small-town cops are the bottom. They include overgrown hall monitors with their first whistle and gun and county turnkeys discharged for raping female inmates and parole officers forced to resign for cutting themselves in on their parolees' take and squad room supermen who wore out their nightsticks every six months even though they hadn't pulled street duty in two years, and they answer only to bored retired former big-city sergeants hired as part-time chiefs. A few hours with any number of them and you'll yawn your way through Steven Spielberg's next big shocker.

I didn't know where Lieutenant Ysabel fit in there. All I knew for sure was that he'd held out an opening, a hole to step through and dump my load and walk away with that clean sense of freedom an artist must feel after he's burned a bad painting. As usual I'd reversed my feet and skeedaddled as fast as my load would let me. The only holes I ever choose to take always lead straight down.

29

THE MAIL WAS IN WHEN I RETURNED TO THE OFFICE. READ some, throw some away, file the bills under the blotter. When it got high enough to wobble, it would be time to pay some of them. No personal letters of any kind, no hand-addressed envelopes or perfumed deckle-edged stationery or postcard pictures of Spanish-style governors' palaces with cheery notes written on the back. If it weren't for Gutenberg I wouldn't have any correspondence at all. Quit bellyaching, Walker. You called it when you hung out your shingle.

I did a little business. I made a follow-up call to the real estate firm to ask if they had a forwarding address yet for the lady psychologist's wandering boyfriend. They had it, but they didn't have a telephone number. Next I called Milwaukee Information, who did. I typed it all into a brief report, sealed it in an envelope, addressed it, and called for a messenger service to take it to Dr. Latimore. I didn't feel like seeing her or talking to her on the telephone. When I thought about it I didn't want to see or talk to anyone. I needed a dead star in an unknown solar system and someone to hold my mail and messages.

It was one of life's little glitches. I didn't want to deal with anyone but I didn't want to be alone either. Being alone meant thinking, and I didn't want to do that more than I didn't want to do any of the other things. I didn't want to think about Clancy the Cop really being Pittsburgh Phil, or of how I would react the next time I saw a blue uniform. The thin blue line had gone sour. We were all late Roman emperors at the mercy of the Praetorian Guard. I didn't want to think about Gerald Page giving the camera that all-knowing look of the very dead. We had passed each other in the parking lot of a bar. How many of those we pass on the street today will be dead tomorrow?

Most of all I didn't want to think about Barry anchored to the floor of Lake St. Clair like so many of the people he had written about, his sandy hair twisting in the current, fish sliding past his dead eyes. I didn't want to think about thinking about it. I didn't need a dead star. What I needed was a vacation. What I had was a drink.

The telephone rang while I was putting the bottle back in its drawer.

"You want to talk about it?" Louise asked.

I lit a Winston and blew a fan of smoke at the framed movie poster hung next to the door. "Talk is no good," I said. "It's communication that gets people into trouble. If pediatricians started sewing shut babies' mouths tomorrow we'd lick war in a generation. Anyway we talked about it last night. Too much. Mostly me. I'm the guy that casts the first stone, then runs."

"Can I take that as an apology?"

"More like a clarification."

"Well, I'll take what I can get," she said. "But you were

probably right, though I never thought of myself as the kind of woman you were talking about. Maybe that kind of woman never does."

"And maybe that's the difference, not knowing or knowing and then doing it anyway."

"Sex is the currency of our time."

"What's that, the epigraph to a book you're editing?"

"It could be. Subtlety seems to have gone out of literary fashion. Have you been out all day, or have you been just not answering your phone?"

I watched the smoke curling in the room. "He may be dead," I said. "Barry may be."

There was a little silence. "How do you know?"

"I don't. I don't even know why I said it. I wasn't planning to."

"Are you all right?"

"Mild shock. It goes away. It always does." I propped the cigarette in the ashtray on the desk and let it smolder. "It's funny, but I never thought about it until just a little while ago. It's one of the things you take into account when someone's missing, but I didn't this time. Maybe that was my mistake from the start, letting myself think I could handle this as just another missing person case. I haven't been or I'd have considered the possibility of his being dead. But the second to the last time I saw him he was talking suicide, and now someone's dead who tried to kill me because I was doing the same thing Barry was when he disappeared."

"Did you kill him?"

The question broke my shock. "Who?"

"You said the man who tried to kill you is dead. Did—"

"No. Whoever sent him did it. Trouble is I can't think where to go from here. I've lost my objectivity and it's like

237

the first day of class and I don't know what room I'm supposed to be in or what materials I'm supposed to have. This isn't the worst day I've had in my life. But my tolerance isn't what it was."

She said, "I think you should get away from it. Maybe drop it. Let some other investigator have it to whom it's just another job."

"If I do," I said, "I'm done. I'll be like a bullfighter gone horn-shy."

"Would that be so bad?"

"That's something I don't care to think about, like where the department store Santas go on December twenty-sixth."

"Then how about a drink?"

"I just had one. Anyway, I'm due at my client's office in half an hour. Call you after?"

"I'm not going anywhere," she said.

I knew the feeling.

I had just put down the receiver when the bell rang again. I let it ring and got up and walked to the window and leaned on the sill breathing warm air from the street. Afternoon sunlight caught the roofs of cars going past, shearing along the edges like a bright dagger tearing cloth. A yellow Camaro with a jacked-up rear paused at the light, leaking loud rock music out its open windows, then took off with a bellow and a shirring of tires on asphalt. I wondered what it was like to have somewhere to go in that kind of hurry.

The telephone was still jangling when I pulled my head back inside. I sat down and answered. It was Barry Stackpole.

30

"AMOS THE SHAMUS," HE SAID.

My cigarette was still smoking in the ashtray. I picked it up, scraped off a column of ash, and drew hot gas into my lungs. I said, "That's old, Barry. I didn't much like it when it was new."

"Sorry. You never said."

He sounded far away. Then he didn't. "I guess this is where I ask where you are."

"Just for now I'm on the other end of this phone. Word's around you're looking for me."

"Zodiac, right?"

"How'd you figure Zodiac?" His voice sounded pleased.

"You don't gamble, which rules out Zeitgeist, and you wouldn't rent a safari from Colonel Wheelock at Zephyr unless a cab came with it. I'm the guy who had to show you how to pitch a tent in Cambodia, remember? My thinking is Dave, the kid with the exotic moustache, was your plant at Zodiac."

"Your thinking is wrong. But he had a hold on my name just like everyone else in the downtown office. You should've checked the other location on McNichols. That's where my man was. The kid gave your card to him and he called me."

"The kid said that office was empty."

"Since when do you believe anything a kid tells you?"

"I had other leads to run down first. Would I have gained anything by going there?"

"Some new scenery. The Cong put this guy in a wheelchair in '71 and he didn't tell them anything."

What I didn't say filled the line at that point.

He said, "Everyone knows you and I are friends. I couldn't risk them turning the heat on you."

"Them being who?"

"That's for the Press Club some afternoon when my column's done and you don't have any keyholes to look through. I just called to let you know I'm still breathing and to ask a favor."

"You're behind on favors now," I said. "I know about Blankenship."

He hesitated a beat. "What do you know about Blankenship?"

"Not over the telephone. I'm behind on favors to someone else. I know you talked to Amigo Fuentes and I know what your interest was in the Niles and Rosenberg murders. A cop I think is good is on it now. He isn't with the Fourteenth."

"It's gone past the Fourteenth," he said. "The rot is in the roots."

"Anyway, it's known. You can come back if that's why you left. It isn't, is it?"

"The favor I called to ask is that you stop looking for me. You're not helping."

"You left that check stub in your strongbox at home and that file folder in your office at the *News* for anyone to find who cared to look. Then you sat back and waited for your man at Zodiac to let you know who was looking. I'd say you're doing more than just staying out of circulation."

He said nothing. I changed the subject.

"You're due in court Monday. Art Rooney is too refined a character to tear his hair. But his manicurist is having trouble living with him about now."

"Art Rooney can take a flying leap at the Milky Way. I'm surprised you didn't tell him to do just that when he came to you. You know what he is."

"That's dead, Barry. As dead as Dale Leopold."

"A lawyer's just a pimp that went to college. If I came back Monday it wouldn't be for him."

"I know about Harney too. Sergeant Mark Harney."

"Who?"

He had paused an instant too long.

"Someone burned him to death with an incendiary in Nam," I said. "Unless he survived."

"Where'd you hear about that?"

"You know where."

"Yeah, I guess I do. I forgot or I would've burned that script before I left. Too much Hemingway. It wasn't his kind of war. No heroes, and the women weren't delicate enough to admire his muscles."

"You didn't forget. You wanted it found. The Harney thing didn't mean anything to me when I first read it, just another fragging. Or it was until I read your wastebasket."

241

"Wastebasket." There was no question mark on the end.

"You're a poetic drunk. 'A Detroit makeover for the man who burned the candy man.'"

"I don't remember it. What's it mean?"

"Come on back and we'll talk about it."

"Talking won't help. I tried it once, went to a shrink for two visits. He kept asking me to join his group. I'm shelling out ninety bucks an hour for a wall full of diplomas and a Greek oath and he wants me to spill my guts in front of a roomful of strangers. I wanted that I'd have stuck with AA. The coffee was better."

"I'm free," I said.

"You're worth less than that, chum. You go to work for a guy who went to work for the guy who murdered your partner."

"Humanity is a messy business. Someone told me."

"Sorry," he said. "I didn't mean that the way it came out. Hell, I did too. You see why I need the time away? I'm dumping all over the only people who mean shit to me."

"Are you drinking?"

"Yeah, but not all the time. I guess I'm really not a drunk after all. No lightning struck when I took the first one in a month."

"It isn't like lightning usually. More like worms."

"Yeah. Well, I just wanted to tell you I'm okay and to stop looking for me."

"You told me."

"The question is did it take."

"I guess we'll have to count our whiskers and wait."

I hung up then. It was a silly thing, the path to satisfaction for fools who have run out of arguments. I waited for

242

the telephone to ring again but it didn't. I left for my appointment.

"You're late."

Arthur Rooney, towering in a blue suit with orange pinstripes, stood with his back to the window overlooking the old county building. The light coming from behind merged his wolf's eyes with the rest of his crisp features. He would manage to have that bright window behind him during interviews with laconic clients.

"Sorry. I had to stop at my bank."

He waved away the apology. "I had to go ahead and call the cab company. The car will be here in a few minutes. Just enough time to tell me what you've found out."

"I won't need that much time. I'm quitting."

"You're not serious."

"I never joke about giving up paying work."

"If it's your conscience, Leopold—"

"It's not my conscience. Not about that, anyhow. Dale taught me never to get emotionally involved in a case. It was a good rule, though I haven't always followed it. If I still asked myself what Dale would do in a given situation, which I haven't for years, the answer would have been that he'd take the job. But it went wrong somewhere and I'm getting out."

"What's happened? Is it what you said on the phone about needing a new car? I can arrange—"

"Barry called me a little while ago."

"Stackpole? From where?" He started around the desk.

"He wouldn't say. I could get it from the telephone company if it was long distance, but he's tricky. He probably used some kind of patch-through."

"Well, what did he say? Will he be back by Monday?"

"He said if he was it wouldn't be for you. He doesn't share my high opinion of lawyers."

"Did he offer you money to drop the search? Is that why you stopped at your bank?" He had on his cross-examiner's tone.

"No, I stopped for this."

From inside my jacket I drew a thick legal envelope and sailed it onto his desk. It landed with a resounding thump. He stared at it for a second before picking it up and lifting the flap.

"There are several hundred dollars here," he said, glancing up.

"Seven hundred and fifty. You can count it. I won't be insulted."

"You don't have to return the retainer. If you want to quit we'll talk about it. But either way you've earned it. If you worked on the case at all."

"No, I'm walking away clean. Poor but clean."

"May I at least ask why?"

"I've been looking for a man who doesn't want to be found and who's committed no crime."

"Yet."

I charged on. "There's a question of rights here. Not your kind—legal rights—but the other. I'm a character with a certain amount of morals and I like to see some of them looking back at me when I shave. Also I think there's some danger to Barry if he's found."

"What kind of danger?"

"The dangerous kind. Explaining it at this point would be like leading the danger to where he is."

"Damn it, Walker, I hired you to enlighten me, not keep secrets from me."

"That's why the seven hundred and fifty. Full refund if not completely satisfied, like the Ginsu knife."

He worked his fists at his sides. They made a creaking sound.

"You're very naïve," he said then. "You see the world in black and white, good and bad, nothing in between."

"There isn't anything in between, Mr. Rooney. Anyone who says there is has had some of the black rubbed off on him. The gray area is a myth. It's when we started to believe in it that things went wrong."

"Do you honestly believe that?"

"Good word, honestly," I said.

He ran an angry palm over the crisp shelf of hair above his forehead. The layered stacks riffled back down into place like new playing cards. "You've cost this firm and the *News* valuable time and thousands of dollars if Stackpole isn't found soon. Suing you would be worth my appearing in court for the first time in years."

"Be my guest, Mr. Rooney. I've got a hat, two guns, and a bottle in the office with the Scotch two-thirds gone."

"Once a month I lunch with the head of the state police. You know your license comes out of that office."

I laughed in his face.

"It must be the movies. Every tin Hitler with a hanky in his pocket thinks an investigator's license is something to grab hold of and twist and the guy that has it will do whatever is wanted. Maybe it was once but it isn't now. You get a chance to tell your side, and if the hearing doesn't go your way you can go to A.C.L.U., and if A.C.L.U. is too busy smashing Nativity scenes you can go to court all the way up to Lansing, and from there all the way up to Washington. Along the way there are a hundred government and private agencies waiting to feed the kitty. You're a lawyer,

Mr. Rooney. You ought to know nothing dies clean in a democracy."

"And while all this is going on you don't make Cent One."

"I'm good at that. I've had plenty of practice."

He drew himself up. The window wasn't behind him now and I saw the pouches and slack indoor creases in his face and the fluorescent pallor under his superficial tan. He was an ugly man in a glossy package.

"I'm glad I defended Earl North," he said. "If I had it to do again I'd see he collected a bounty for killing your partner."

"That's all I needed to hear, Mr. Rooney. Now excuse me while I go out and burn my clothes."

He watched me go and I walked outside past Helen the receptionist, who glanced up but didn't catch my eye, and I rode the elevator down to the lobby without stopping. The sun was behind a cloud when I climbed into the Buick. The seat felt cool.

I started the engine and drove but I didn't go home or to the office. I was too restless for that. Instead I cruised up Woodward for most of its length, past the sleazy bars and topless bars and workingmen's bars and family bars and cocktail bars downtown, past the Detroit Public Library and the Detroit Institute of Arts and the Wayne State University campus, over the Edsel Ford Freeway and past Shaw College and Northern High School and Cathedral Central High School and through Highland Park and along the edge of Palmer Park, where doctors and executives on long lunch hours dotted the greens in loud golf clothes, hitting balls and talking mergers and capital gains. Past the Michigan State Fairgrounds with the tents down now and the animal pens collapsed and in storage, the long Quonset building and rutted brown earth closed off like a concentration camp inside a wire mesh fence. Through Ferndale and Pleasant Ridge and between Huntington Woods and Royal Oak. Beyond them to Birmingham and then Bloomfield Hills, the silver-spoon twins, department stores and good restaurants and well-lighted bookshops and brick houses on side streets with lawns and gaslights out front and an afternoon literary society to every block, pools in back where the guests sat around in bathing suits sipping vodka gimlets and talking about the crime in Detroit and not swimming. After that I began to smell Iroquois Heights, so I detoured left and took Telegraph Road back down.

Twice I passed bright flashers—red for state, blue for city—where cops had intercepted motorists cutting in and out of traffic or turning at no-turn intersections. It was rush hour and the hunting was good. The town that put the world on wheels was the same town that had hung the first traffic light to make a profit off it. Freud was wrong, all right. It was the angle that drove mankind, the angle and what it would bring.

I didn't have one. That made me a pervert, but perverts don't care what they are. I stopped for gas and called Louise Starr from the station.

31

WE WENT SOMEWHERE FOR DINNER AND ENDED UP BACK
at her room at the Book Cadillac. It had a lowered ceiling
and new furniture and carpet, but underneath that lurked
the slight mustiness that all old hotels have no matter how
elegant, a faint olfactory collage of cigarette smoke and
leather suitcases and overnight sex. We sat in comfortable
chairs, drinking the drinks room service had brought—a
highball for her, a whiskey sour for me—and listening to
something soft and unidentifiable drifting out of the radio
attachment to the television set. Twelve stories down, traffic swished and horns honked.

"So you quit," Louise said, cradling her glass in her lap.

She had on a pale gown that buttoned at the shoulder
and fell open just above the knees, with red shoes and a
matching purse she had laid on the bureau. Ruby barrettes
kept her hair behind her ears.

"I quit working for Walgren and Rooney."

She looked at me. "Is that some kind of qualifier?"

"I don't know what a qualifier is."

"Yes, you do."

While I was sitting there thinking, the radio station changed its format and a singing group came on, one of those that hire piano-movers to kick them between the legs when their voices drop. I went over and found the Windsor station that plays old dance tunes and stood near the window watching headlamps winking between buildings blocks away.

"I'm going to go on looking for Barry," I said, turning back. "In my own way, at my own pace, with nobody watching over my shoulder."

"He won't appreciate it."

"Jumpers don't thank you for pulling them off ledges. That doesn't mean you should keep on walking."

"Is he suicidal?"

"He got drunk one night and talked about it, but I don't think he's the kind to do it, not directly, anyway. Did you ever see a picture with Frank Sinatra and Doris Day called *Young at Heart*?"

"I don't think so," she said. "Was it a musical?"

"There was music in it, not the kind where everyone on the street joins in and knows all the words and dance steps. It was kind of a classy soap, with Sinatra marrying Doris and convincing himself he's not good enough for her. Anyway, he's driving through this heavy snow and brooding on it. Finally he just reaches down and turns off his wipers. The snow keeps piling up and blocking the windshield and he lowers his foot on the gas pedal and waits to slam into something."

"Is he killed?"

"No, the movie had a sappy happy ending with Doris and Frank reconciling in his hospital room. The point is he

249

didn't set out to commit suicide, just removed all the stumbling blocks and let whatever was going to happen happen."

"And you think Barry's doing that."

"Probably not with even that much intent. He has a strong sense of survival from having had to exercise it so much. Maybe he's just testing it and leaving the results to fate. It explains why he got himself involved in a hot case, then vanished, but not without leaving a trail for the wolves to follow."

"Why would he set himself up to be killed, even subconsciously?"

"The Old Testament ethic, maybe. I think he thinks he killed someone."

She set her drink on the lamp table between the chairs. "Who?"

"Someone you wouldn't know, a long time ago. It's in his book."

"The one about Vietnam? What's one killing among a hundred thousand?"

"Nothing, then. A dozen years later, something. It takes that long for that kind of hangover to wear off. I'm guessing. I guess a lot. Six times out of ten I guess right. It's a thing you pick up in the business, like flat feet."

"Your feet aren't flat," she said.

It was there in her tone. I drank. "I don't feel like being seduced tonight. If it's okay."

"I see." The temperature in the room fell off two degrees.

"No, you don't. If you did you wouldn't say you did. The kind of guy that likes to keep box scores could do very well in this line. I get offers from clients and informants and housewives and runaways. A good P.I. with a normal libido and no more scruples than you could poke with a sharp stick could while away his whole career in bed. But he wouldn't get a chance at a woman like you.

"It's not that I don't know what I'm turning down," I said. "It's that men get tired too. We just don't admit it as often."

"I do see. Also it's easier to turn down when you've had it once already."

I put away the rest of my whiskey sour and set the glass on top of the television set. "I knew I was just wasting oxygen. I had to try."

The music went on. The station was playing a transcription of a remote broadcast from the ballroom of a hotel in Chicago that was a parking garage by now. The ancient recording made the announcer sound as if he were speaking through a paper tube. Louise peeled off her shoes and tucked her feet up under her in the chair. She said, "I don't know why I'm still here. I finished my work with Andrei yesterday. By all rights I should have caught a plane to New York this morning. I think it's you."

"It's not me."

"Why couldn't it be?"

"I'm an unsuccessful man in an obsolete profession. You're a book editor."

"An unsuccessful one."

"There aren't any unsuccessful book editors. You don't keep up your average you get traded, like a big-league ballplayer. No one calls them unsuccessful as long as they're still playing. Under ordinary circumstances we wouldn't even know each other. If we passed each other on Broadway you wouldn't look at me more than once."

"Nothing lasts."

"If it does it can't, because the more time you have the

sooner you realize it wasn't anything to begin with. Aw, hell."

The dead band had hurled itself into one of those jam sessions that keep starting up again just when you think they're getting ready to stop, like a dripping faucet. I turned off the radio and went to the door.

Louise uncoiled herself and came over on silent stockinged feet. Standing toe-to-toe with me without heels, she just came to the tip of my nose. Jasmine rode the air silkily. "Drive me to the airport tomorrow?"

"I better not. The car would be too empty on the drive back."

"This is it, then?" She touched the corner of my lips with a pink nail.

"Nothing was it from the start. Weren't you listening?"

"Kiss me?"

I took some time brushing loose hairs away from her forehead, and then we touched lips. Hers tasted faintly of wild berries. We pressed foreheads. With her arms resting around my neck she sighed. Her eyes were lowered. She spoke in a hoarse whisper.

"When you find Barry, tell him we'll pay an advance of fifty thousand for his book."

I laughed until the door closed between us.

The weather turned brisk overnight. In the morning I got up shivering, closed the window on a sill white with frost, and broke out my blue regurgitated wool suit. The weatherman on the radio—meteorologist, excuse me—had a high of fifty degrees for us. I made six pancakes and charred a dozen link sausages for breakfast and had three cups of black coffee you could stand a shovel in. If everything worked out it was going to be a long day and I didn't know when I'd be sitting down to my next meal.

I put on a hat for the first time in weeks and walked out the door at half-past seven, into the teeth of a woody breeze that stiffened my face and made the seat crackle when I slid under the steering wheel. The engine turned over a couple of times before starting. I waited for it to warm up before letting out the clutch. I hadn't thought to ask Schinder if he'd winterized the car.

I didn't go to the office. It was Saturday. Travel agencies were open but not investigation firms, not this one anyhow. I took Woodward up to McNichols and swung west. Light Mackinaws and knit caps were starting to appear near the schoolyards. Fallen leaves jumped and skidded along the sidewalks like grasshoppers on linoleum. It was early October and if this kept up we could expect snow by Halloween.

Zodiac Travel kept its west side office in a fairly new building between Livernois and Wyoming, with a small paved parking lot behind. I walked around to the front door and read the building directory and went past the elevators to the fire stairs. On the third floor I passed some darkened glass doors belonging to a couple of bailbondsmen and a bone specialist and knocked on a lighted one with the signs of the Zodiac stenciled in a circle on the glass. When no one answered I tried the knob. It turned freely. "Uh-oh," I said.

The door opened noiselessly into a big square room with a row of windows along the back and bright green plants spilling out of redwood buckets lining the broad ledge inside. The ubiquitous posters made the same old promises on the walls and a stereo in a walnut console like a deep coffin played "Where Have All the Flowers Gone?" at a volume just above breathing. There was a desk with a plastic wood-grain top and a chromium frame and behind the desk a pair of bicycle wheels showed.

I wasn't armed. I didn't need to be. A bathroom with an extra-wide doorway stood open to the left of the desk and from where I was standing I could see all of it and my reflection in the mirror over the sink. I was as alone as alone can get.

I crossed to the desk and looked at the man in the wheelchair. The back rested on the floor and his feet, encased in brown heelless moccasins, were braced against the stainless steel footrest. He wore a striped shortsleeved shirt with a red plastic penholder in the pocket containing three ballpoint pens and the shirt was tucked inside a pair of unfaded brushed cotton blue jeans. No socks. He was lean and freckled and wore his reddish hair over his ears to his collar. The freckles were misleading; he was my age. The blue hole in his left temple looked too small to have done so much damage. But a hole in the head doesn't have to be big. All it has to be is a hole.

I walked around the desk on china legs. There was no need to feel for a pulse but I did that. His flesh was cool but his muscles hadn't begun to stiffen. I frisked him and found a set of GM keys in his left pants pocket and a worn brown leather wallet on his hip containing some cash, a set of business cards, two credit cards, and a driver's license, the license and the cards all bearing the name Edward Sunburn. I smeared everything between my palms and put it back.

The desk came next. The top was pretty clean: a couple of printout trip itineraries, some odd travel pamphlets, a stack of scribbled telephone messages on a spindle. I leafed through those quickly, not expecting to find anything. I wasn't disappointed. There was just one drawer, a long one pulled out a little. I used my handkerchief to pull it out a few more inches. Desk stuff. The drawer was lined with green blotter paper with an oval stain along the edge. I rubbed it with two fingers and sniffed them. An oily smell.

A steel folding chair stood parallel to the desk on the customer's side. I sat in it and practiced my fast-draw with a stiffened index finger. It could have happened that way. It could have happened any one of a dozen others. There are just too many directions to go in a real murder, if murder was what it was.

I got up and wandered around the office. I looked in the planters. I looked in the foot of space between the stereo and the corner of the room. I got down on my hands and knees next to the body and peered under the kneehole of the desk. Then I turned my head the other way and spotted the slim curved silhouette of a High Standard .22 magnum pocket pistol lying in shadow under the base of the over-turned wheelchair.

I left it where it was and sat down on the floor. I put myself in the wheelchair and put a bullet in my brain with my left hand and fell over backwards, dropping the gun between my legs where it would bounce once on the carpet and come to rest under the chair. I lifted Sunburn's left hand and sniffed. Maybe I smelled something burnt, maybe I had it on my mind. A carbon test would find the proper crystals embedded in the skin, I was sure of that.

It was neat as hell, as neat as any self-killing a tired homicide investigator could hope to find. Sunburn was left-handed; he kept his car keys in that pocket. It would be the hand he would use to put a hole in his left temple. Ballistics would fire the gun and match the bullet to the one in his brain. Maybe they would match it to the ones in the bodies of Morris Rosenberg and Philip Niles, but I doubted that. Cops hate easy jobs.

I stood up, brushing incriminating fibers off my clothes, and glanced around one last time. There were no file cabinets or other promising repositories of information. The place was just a telephone number and a place to pick up mail, as Dave had said. Yesterday's mail would have been kicked downtown already and today's wasn't due for another hour. I stooped to pick up the High Standard, dropped it into the pocket of my jacket, and let myself out quietly. No one hollered cop.

32

HOME IS A PLACE YOU CAN GO WHERE THEY HAVE TO TAKE you in. There was no one to take me in but it was closer than the office and there's a long list of things I'd rather do than drive anywhere near downtown on a Saturday morning with a murder weapon in my pocket.

The coffee was still warm. I poured myself a cup, leaving a quarter-inch space on top, then remembered I was out of whiskey and brought the surface level with the rim. I sat in the living room warming my hands around the cup with the pistol lying on the end table and drinking the bitter stuff. Thinking was hard without whiskey.

When the cup was empty I called my office building and let the telephone ring until the super picked it up.

"This is Walker in 307," I said. "Which one of my neighbors discovered the dead bum in the foyer the other day?"

"Which one, how do I know which one?" His voice was

257

thicker than usual. I'd gotten him out of bed. "The police bang on your door, you don't ask who invited them."

"Who did the banging, the black cop with the scar or the white cop with the hat and moustache?"

"The black one. The one was here again this morning."

I uncrossed my legs. "When this morning?"

"When, how do I know when? Early. I got up to fix a busted pipe and he walked right past my door. Didn't say hello."

I hung up, lit a cigarette, and dialed John Alderdyce's extension at 1300.

"Alderdyce."

"Walker, John. I wasn't sure I'd catch you on duty Saturday."

"We never close. What's on your mind that I'd rather not have on mine?"

"I need the personnel file on a Homicide dick. You know him. Sergeant Grice."

"Christ."

"That mean you won't do it, or it's tough?"

"I'd have to know why you want it. Just for my own peace of mind, what's left of it."

"I can't say till I've seen it. I could be way off and I don't want any more enemies on the department than I have now."

"Meaning I do."

"It's a favor," I said. "Ordinarily I wouldn't ask, because it means your talking to too many people. But this one transferred over from Vice not long ago and the file might still be lying around Homicide. If not, forget it. All I've got is a guess."

"Am I in on the kill?"

"I don't think so. If I'm right this is one for Major Crimes."

"Where do I come out ahead, then?"

"Name it."

I didn't like the length of the pause after that.

"I'd rather not," he said.

"Blank check?"

"Call it a blind loan. My favor to call in any time the urge lands."

"You wouldn't settle for dinner."

"Not in any place you can afford."

"Okay," I said. "There's just one thing I need from the file. I need to know if Grice served in Vietnam. Specifically if he was stationed in Hue about the time of the Cambodia invasion."

"Why?"

I told him then, leaving out Edward Sunburn for the time being. After a long silence he said: "You better be right."

"If I knew that I wouldn't be calling you."

"I'll get back to you. You at home?"

I said I was. Twenty minutes slithered by, one by one on their bellies. I poured myself another slug of caffeine, lingered over it. Outside, the gutters clogged with dead leaves. I caught the telephone halfway through the first ring.

"Hue," Alderdyce said. "He was a sparks with ARVN, one of the first in after the Cong bugged out in '67 and he was still there three years later."

"Anything else?"

"Anything else isn't part of our bargain. But that's it. They don't leave much room for biography in those little blanks."

"Thanks, John."

"Who you working with on this?"

It was my turn to pause. "Ysabel."

"Good choice," he said. "Yeah, good choice. Don't get killed, okay? I hate wasting favors."

I thanked him again and broke the connection. With the receiver still in my hand I dialed 911. I didn't know how the Pinkertons did it before A. G. Bell. When a black female voice came on I said: "This is Amos Walker, 614 Russell. There's a dead derelict in my backyard. I think his throat's been cut."

She asked me to repeat the message. I did and gave her my name and address again. She said an officer would be calling on me.

I worked the plunger again and called police headquarters again. An unfamiliar male voice came on after four rings and said Lieutenant Ysabel had stepped out for a half hour. I left a message and had him read it back to make sure he got it straight. I didn't like that part of it at all.

My ear felt hot from the receiver. I got up and walked around, working my limbs and neck. Someday I was going to invest in one of those telephone headsets like reporters have. It was on the list after air conditioning and a desk chair that tilted back and turned into a waterbed.

While I was thinking about it I drew out the live cartridge remaining in the two-shot .22, put the cartridge in my pocket, and got my Smith & Wesson out of the drawer in the telephone stand and made sure there was one in the barrel. For now I would go with the tools I had.

33

MAYBE IT WAS THE CAFFEINE.

Sitting in my one and only easy chair waiting for the door buzzer, I was an insomniac staring at a dark ceiling and projecting pictures on the blank space. Thoughts charged through my mind in a hot string like a thousand-car train barreling through a long black tunnel. In the lighted windows flashing past I glimpsed faces: Barry and Catherine and Dale and John and in the caboose a character with graying brown hair and gentle eyes and a chin that would always be blue, someone familiar, but whose name I couldn't think of because I never called him by it. I wanted to run ahead and get a look inside the engine cab, see who was driving, but by then the last window had streaked around the long curve and the train was gone, chuckling in the distance. I didn't need to see the engineer's face anyway. It would be the same face I had seen in the caboose. I knew now what was meant by the term "waking dream," and why no one much liked them.

When you are small the whole world turns on your axis. Countries are being built up and torn down and people are slashing at one another all around you and none of it means anything because no matter what happens you're safe there in the center. Then when you get to adolescence and the college money has dried up you have to go to work for it and you're part of the turning outer circle. You adjust to that and have a picture of yourself and you think that's who you are. You go out in the world with your new degree under your arm and maybe there's a war on and you get sucked up into it and the world you find yourself in has no axis at all. The sun rises in the wrong place and the little man walking behind the yak in the rice paddy could as well be the enemy as not and there are roads but you can't use them because the roads are mined, so you hack your way through the jungle and if you're lucky you won't run smack into the middle of an NVN patrol or get bitten by a mosquito and drop into a coma, and if you're still lucky you won't find out ten years later that your own army's defoliants have made you sterile or given you cancer.

Say you're lucky and you come out all of a piece. You have a new picture of yourself and you think that's who you are. You prance around for a while in the white helmet and MP armband, closing bars and breaking up fights and scraping GIs and the occasional officer off the floors of alleys, and then you muster out and buy yourself a suit of civilian clothes and have your picture taken and you look at it and you think that's who you are.

Then you use your veteran's points to get into the Detroit Police Department's twelve-week training course. You train harder than you ever did in the army, tightening your gut and expanding your brain and grinding your reflexes down to a granite point. With one week to go in the program you pose for a picture in your new uniform with the shiny visor square over the eyes and the proofs come back and you lay them out and compare them and you think that's who you are. But something happens and you don't finish. Instead you get married and go to work for General Motors security. You're a family man now and your job is to help push the world around on someone else's axis. Then you aren't and it isn't, as suddenly as finding a note on a kitchen table, and for a long time you don't know who you are, you don't even have a picture of yourself. But then someone steps in and shows it to you, and you know better than you ever knew before that this is who you are, know it so well that even when the someone who showed it to you is no longer there, is a bald head and a battered hat lying upside-down in the street, you still know. It's so simple that you wonder why you didn't figure it out a long time ago.

You are the one who takes the pictures.

The door buzzer had been going for a while before I heard it. I shook myself loose with a physical effort, stood, took the High Standard out of my left pocket, transferred it to my right hand, and went over to open the door. Sergeant Grice looked me up and down.

"What's the gag?" he demanded. "I get a call—"

"I placed it. Come in, Sergeant. Where's Waddell, out blocking his hat?"

"It's his day off." He hadn't moved. The burn scar on his right cheek twitched. "I guess you know it's a felony to point a gun at a police officer."

"Here." I reversed ends and thrust the .22's grip at him. His hand closed around it automatically and I withdrew mine.

"What's the gag?" he said again.

"It's an American trait. Push something at somebody, even a complete stranger, and nine times out of ten he'll accept it. People who give out handbills find it valuable. We're letting the flies in."

He entered finally, balancing the gun on his palm. I closed the door and turned to face him with my back to it. He was wearing a blue wool blazer over one of his yellow shirts and a red knitted necktie. Indoors the milky blue in the whites of his eyes was pronounced.

"So why's it so important I take it at all? They told me the bum you found had a cut throat. Nobody said anything about he was shot."

"There isn't any bum, Sergeant. You knew that the minute I answered the door. I called that in because the bum-killings are your meat and I knew they'd send you. And I wanted your fingerprints on that gun. It's the one you used to kill Edward Sunburn."

He didn't jump or throw himself through any windows. I hadn't expected him to, really. He said, "I don't know any Sunburns. And if I was to kill somebody I wouldn't use no twenty-twos. Department issued me a thirty-eight."

"Yeah, but cops that kill for a living on the side don't use department pieces. They use what the professionals use—quiet, efficient guns that don't make enough noise to turn heads. You should've used something heavier on Sunburn, though. Suicides generally place their faith in weapons they know will do the job the first time. And they don't worry about noise."

"That's twice you said Sunburn. Why'd I kill him? I forget."

"You didn't go there fixing to kill him, or if you did you wanted to pump him for information first, find out where Barry Stackpole was hiding."

"I don't know any Stackpoles neither."

"You knew him in Vietnam, where your friend Mark Harney got himself fried for doing dope business with the wrong people. You knew him here, when he started looking into that old murder. Only he found a lot more than he was looking for. Didn't he?"

His face gave up nothing. "You're telling it."

"Asking around about you he found out you were part of Ray Blankenship's murder machine. Maybe that's the handle he got hold of that opened the door on the whole mess. I looked up your record, Grice. You were stationed in Hue when Harney was fragged there, and back home, before you switched to Downtown Vice, you were a third-grader in the Fourteenth Precinct, where Blankenship ran his contract business. Barry got too close too fast and skipped out until things cooled. He's more cautious about such things than the average reporter, as who wouldn't be, given his experiences? You had to find him and take him out before he exposed you as a murderer all the way back to Nam. Remind me to come back to how you found out about the travel agency Barry used.

"Vietnam vets tend to arm themselves," I went on. "Sunburn kept a gun in his desk. Maybe he had a chance to fire it before you killed him. That was convenient for the paraffin test, but it wouldn't have been a twenty-two; that would've been too neat. You took it away with you to cut down on confusion. If he did fire it, the bullet will be found, probably in the wall behind a travel poster. I don't guess you had a chance to get any information out of him before it happened."

While I'd been speaking, Grice had circled the room. I rotated to keep him in front of me. His back was to the front door now. He flashed a quick white grin with no humor in it.

"You spin a good one," he said. "You're a better writer than your friend Stackpole. Only that's all it is, a story. You got nothing to back it up."

"I've got your prints on the murder weapon. It's empty, by the way."

He inspected the barrels, saw I was right, wiped it down his pants leg on both sides, and deposited it on the sofa. By the time he had his service .38 out of its holster I had drawn the Smith & Wesson from my right pocket. I gestured at his cheek with the barrel.

"What happened, your incendiary go off before you could get clear?"

"You're turned around, Sherlock. I got this pulling Mark out of the fire. He was my partner over there. I don't know how you came up with that."

"I didn't. I just guessed. Thanks for the confirmation."

He moved a shoulder. "You want his killer, talk to your friend Stackpole. He's the one threw the bomb."

"That isn't Barry," I said. "If he wanted to kill Harney, he'd have shot him clean, looking at him. Rolling grenades into bedrooms is your speed."

"Lose it, Walker."

This voice was new. I made an effort to react slowly, backing around in a short arc and keeping my eyes on Grice while the rest of the room came into my periphery. Waddell, the sergeant's partner, had entered through the bedroom and was standing in the doorway with his snap-brim hat low on his forehead and one of the new ten-millimeter automatics in his right hand.

A couple of seconds knocked by on the antique clock

behind me. I lowered my arm and let the revolver slide out of my hand. It thudded the carpet.

"I thought I closed that window this morning," I said.

"I opened it."

Grice said, "Toss him."

Waddell threw me up against the wall, patted me down, and stepped back, shaking his head at the sergeant, who laughed suddenly.

"I like it." Grice had picked up the .22 again and was feeding cartridges into it from a pocket. He wasn't the kind of cop to get caught short. "You take your work seriously. When Sunburn wouldn't tell you where Stackpole is you shot him. Then you came back here and shot yourself with the same gun. It doesn't have a history. That's why I left it with him. This is more complicated, but it'll go."

"What about Barry?"

"Him when it's time." He closed the action. "What made you figure me to begin with? I'm a detective and I got to know."

"Can I stand naturally?"

Waddell moved back another step and I pushed myself away from the wall and dropped my arms. The ten-millimeter was trained just above my belt buckle. Grice had holstered his .38 and was holding just the High Standard.

I said, "You were everywhere. You investigated the Blankenship shoot, probably at your request, and you bent around Willy the Wino's death in my building to justify your presence there as part of your investigation into the bum killings. Was he sleeping in the outer office when you let yourself into the private room or what?"

"He came in while I was at it. I drew the piece and he ran. I caught up with him at the top of the stairs and gave him the other end on the back of his head. He fell. Then I called Waddell to come help mop up."

"You bugged my office. That's how you learned about Sunburn being Barry's man in Zodiac Travel."

"No James Bond shit, just one of those little voice-activated tape recorders with adhesive on the back. I snuck it back out this morning."

"I know. The building superintendent saw you leaving. You got kind of careless there. Gerald Page was better at that sort of thing. He hung a tail on me I never did spot. You killed him, right?"

"He went against orders. Your body would of been one too many just then. He was only supposed to warn you off. I threw it up to him and he got pissed, said maybe the department would appreciate him more if he blew the top off the whole operation. Sure, I killed him. Just for the record, though, Blankenship popped himself. I asked in to make sure he didn't leave no mash notes. He didn't. That's why it didn't do no harm to let you talk to his widow. God bless the Old Guard; they always go down alone. Honor, I love it."

"I'm surprised you recognized it," I said. "Let me finish. Before you made the move to Homicide, you were inside man on the raid on the Inner City Action Council a month ago. Barry must have known that was coming, from his sources in the department. He made sure he was there when it went down, to get a look at you in action. He was that thorough. Either he wasn't as drunk as he pretended or his drinking got away from him. I kept tripping over you. I only have to fall down and hit my head so many times before it starts to work."

The scar jumped. "What do you know about the Inner—"

He stopped talking. Recognition crawled into his eyes. He touched two fingers to the jaw I'd slugged in the blind pig. The .22 came up. I took a short step and chopped him backhanded across the throat.

He fell back against the door wheezing. The blood slid from his face and I reached down and wrenched the High Standard out of his grasp. Then I brought my knee up hard enough to lift him off his feet and swept the gun against the side of his head. He was sliding when I spun on Waddell.

I had moved purely from instinct, without thinking. I'd been expecting a bullet in the back any time. But when I came around with the .22, instead of shooting me Grice's partner thrust the automatic out in front of him in two hands and bawled at me to drop it.

It made me laugh. "Why the hell should I?"

"Because Officer Waddell is ours."

Voices were starting to come at me from all over. This one I knew right away, but I didn't move this time.

"Come on, Walker. Even you can count."

I lowered the gun then and turned to look at Lieutenant Ysabel standing on the other side of Grice's twitching mass. He had the front door open and he was just slipping a short-barreled .44 magnum into his armpit holster.

"We've been watching Grice for weeks," he said, nudging him with a scuffed leather toe. "Waddell there was moled in at the Fourteenth for three months and when the arrows started pointing at the sergeant we got him transferred downtown to stay on top of him. Grice was rabbity, though. Wouldn't do anything while Waddell was around to witness."

"So you dangled me for bait."

"Well, we didn't expect him to move this fast. But yeah. I didn't see you shying from the hook."

"It's starting to look like home," I said.

Waddell said, "Better get Grice's pipe looked at, Lieutenant. He's got talking to do."

"If he didn't I'd let him choke. Call the fast-wagon."

While Waddell was using the telephone, Ysabel relieved Grice of his revolver and cuffed him. The sergeant came around groaning. His breath whistled. Ysabel pulled Grice's own Miranda card out of his handkerchief pocket and read:

"You have the right to remain silent, asswipe. If you give up the right to remain silent, fucker, anything you say can and will be used against you in a court of law. You have the right to an attorney, shithead. If, cocksucker, you desire an attorney and cannot afford one . . ."

After that his language got colorful. I fired up a Winston and listened to the music.

34

Monday slid in gray and damp. The thermometer stayed at forty-eight all morning and started the long crawl down just after lunch. Headlamps burned on West Grand River at noon and a couple of enterprising souls in silver disco jackets were hawking umbrellas on the street at five bucks a pop. They had bought them in Greektown for a dollar ninety-eight.

I spent the morning fielding telephone calls. Some Mondays are like that. Others are like listening to an interpretive reading of the Dead Sea Scrolls. Either way they usually set the mood for the whole week. One was from a woman named Raeburn in Ypsilanti who wanted me to look for her husband.

"How long has he been missing?" I asked.

"Eight months."

"What did the police say?"

"Nothing. I didn't go to the police."

"Your husband's been missing eight months and you haven't reported it?"

"Well, at first I wasn't so disappointed he was gone. Living with Howie hasn't exactly been like a movie, unless you count that one with Liz Taylor and Richard Burton, and I ain't talking about *Cleopatra*. But yesterday right in the middle of *General Hospital* they said on TV that the holder of this year's winning Sweepstakes ticket ain't come forward and they give the number, and, well, Howie was always buying Sweepstakes tickets out of the grocery money and I got to thinking maybe that's him. So that's what I want you to do, find Howie and ask him is it his ticket, because if it is I'm entitled to half. I got the number right here."

"What if it isn't?"

"If it ain't he can stay lost. I got all the pets and plants I can feed now."

"Lady, you don't need me. You need a lawyer named Swifty who wears loud checked suits and beats the cops to traffic accidents."

"Yeah? Well, you blew it, mister. I was fixing to cut you in." She hung up in my face.

Most of the calls ran to that sort of thing. I was thinking of taking the telephone off the hook or getting into greenskeeping when the buzzer went off that told me someone had just come into the outer office. I called to whoever it was to keep coming.

Barry looked tan and healthy. He had let his hair grow out a little and the sun had yellowed it so that it appeared almost white against his brown skin. He was wearing a white knit shirt with a soft collar under a dark plaid sport coat and a pair of gabardine slacks whose cuffs touched the tops of his suede shoes. He smiled cockily and hurled himself into the customer's chair, hooking the artificial leg over the arm.

"And another thing," he said.

"Hello, Barry. How was the grand jury?"

"They ought to re-name it. I pled the Fifth from the time they asked me my name and finally they let me go. You don't give them traction they can't run over you." His blue eyes were very clear against the tan. "You were pretty sure I showed."

"I didn't figure you'd give the *News* grounds to can you this year. Not until the book hits six figures anyway."

"Maybe not even then. This being an author is hard work. Are you sore at me?"

"Hell no. Why should I be? I almost got killed for you while you were down in Miami or someplace taking the sun."

"Fort Lauderdale," he corrected. "I rented a little bungalow down there. And I wasn't out in the sun the whole time. I got a good jump on the book. Hell, I got five chapters and an outline."

"Congratulations."

"I'm sending them tomorrow to that editor you recommended."

"You should've come back Friday. You could have given them to her in person."

"Friday I was still clattering away. What do you mean?"

I told him. He cursed. "Why didn't you say something when I called?"

"Would you have come back?"

"No. Probably not."

For a space neither of us spoke. Then his expression changed. "Hey, you owe me for two windows. If it was you that broke them."

"Sorry. Send me the bill. I also have to get your book back to you, the first one."

"Keep it. I like the new one better. I want you to read it when it's finished."

"Why?"

"You're the only person I know who will tell me if it stinks, that's why. Jesus, I thought you'd be interested. You gave me the title."

"No thanks. I'm all read out on you for a long time."

He wasn't listening. "Who scooped me? I bought the Sunday *News* when I got in last night and read all about Sergeant Grice under Jed Dutt's byline."

"You walked away from the story."

"I wasn't hiding. Well, I was, but not from Grice or anyone else. I had to get away, get a handle on the book. You don't really think I ran scared, do you?"

"I think you went away to get a handle on the book."

"So how come you're sore? And what's this crap about almost getting killed? I didn't see your name in Dutt's piece.

"I told Lieutenant Ysabel he could leave it out when he spoke to the press, and I made sure it was Dutt he spoke to. I owed both of them." I lit a cigarette and flipped the match into the ashtray. "I talked to Grice about Sergeant Mark Harney. He said you killed him."

He watched the match smolder.

"Maybe that's the way he sees it," he said.

"You said so too. I read your wastebasket."

"I was drunk when I wrote that. It wasn't entirely a lie, though. You had to have been there."

"I was."

"Yeah, there. But not *there*. Not in that camp outside Hue the night Grice pulled his dope partner out of that hut

274

and rolled him over and over on the ground until the flames gave out." He stopped looking at the match and looked at me. "It took Harney three weeks to die. They had him pumped full of morphine the whole time. You could still hear him screaming clear across camp. Until the last day, anyway.

"I didn't roll that grenade into his hut. But I know who did. He told me he was going to do it and I didn't do anything to stop him. Which I guess makes me an accessory. But you know what it was like over there. All the rules were suspended."

"Who was it?"

"Keith Porter."

I squinted through my smoke. "Who's Keith Porter?"

"You mean who was Keith Porter. I told you about him the last time we were together. At the Press Club."

"The guy that fried himself with a power drill in Colorado."

"That's him. Appropriate."

"That's what got you thinking about the whole thing," I said.

"I never stopped, really. It got worse when I was writing the book. The first version. Then when I heard Keith was dead it got even worse. I was the last one left who knew. I had to go back over it, try to understand it. Grice was my time machine. If I could understand him . . ." He shifted his leg. "Anyway, it's in the book now, the new version. There's no statute of limitations on murder so I guess I'll have to stand some heat."

"Probably not. Nobody cares. Nobody wants to. You'll sell a million copies, though."

"That's not why I wrote it and you know it."

275

"I don't know what I know, Barry. I thought I did going in."

"I'm sorry I left you in the lurch."

"It isn't that," I said. "Me and the lurch are old acquaintances, we call each other by our first names. But I don't like getting frozen out. I don't like that I'm just another grand jury where you're concerned. I figured I was a little more than that."

He got up and walked around, stumping a little.

"I had my head on backwards, Amos. I didn't know who to trust. Most of all I didn't trust me. That's why I left, went somewhere where nobody knew me and where what I said didn't matter. I had no way of knowing this whole thing would blow up in the meantime. It wouldn't if you'd just—well, to hell with all that." He sat back down.

"I got on Grice's case by accident," he said. "We were aware of each other. We knew each other over there because we were both from Detroit, and every now and then we crossed paths back here. I knew he suspected me of having something to do with Harney's death. Maybe it's part of the reason I didn't blow the whistle right away when I found out he was mixed up in Blankenship's action. And maybe that's another reason I left. I was losing my objectivity, and when that happens to a reporter it's time to get out. Or go into television," he added archly. "So I planted that check stub at home and told Ed Sunburn about it so he could let me know if anyone was looking for me. If I hadn't done that there was no telling what direction they'd come from. It was a safety valve. But I never figured you'd be the one doing the looking."

"You know Sunburn's dead. Grice killed him."

"I know. It was in Jed's piece. I guess I'm responsible

276

for that too. I didn't have Grice down as the type to go over the edge. I came into this one a half-beat off and never did catch up to the melody."

"He was over there, Sunburn was. He must've known his chances."

"I never liked him much. He was just a little too arrogant about having given up the use of his legs for his country. But he could be counted on not to talk. See, that's the thing. You've been tested in that area, but not the way he was."

"You don't have to explain, Barry. You don't owe me anything."

"Like hell."

"It's not a thing I want on a paying basis."

I'd spoken sharply. The words hung in the air for a moment. We watched each other. Then he glanced at his wristwatch. "Buy you a drink?"

"You bought the last one." I lifted the bottle and two pony glasses out of the bottom drawer of the desk, got up and splashed water into the glasses in the little washroom. Back at the desk I filled them the rest of the way from the bottle. Barry picked up one.

"Cold steel."

I shook my head and lifted mine. "The death of friends."

He hesitated the barest instant, looking at me, before drinking his down.

The telephone rang and I answered it the usual way.

After he left I locked up and started for home. On the way I stopped in a corner bar, ordered two double Scotches, and drank them back to back. They didn't work any magic so I went out. I buttoned my coat. The air was metal cold and the skyline to the east had a smoky look of coming rain. Westward the sun had gone down under a violet sky. I didn't look at it long. The color reminded me of Louise Starr's eyes, and I never saw them again.

ABOUT THE AUTHOR

Loren D. Estleman is a graduate of Eastern Michigan University and a veteran police-court journalist. Since the publication of his first novel in 1976, he has established himself as a leading writer of both mystery and western fiction. His western novels include Golden Spur Award winner ACES AND EIGHTS, MISTER ST. JOHN and THE STRANGLERS. EVERY BRILLIANT EYE is the sixth book in his Amos Walker mystery series. SUGARTOWN, the fifth book in the series, was presented the Shamus Award for Best Private Eye Novel of the Year by Private Eye Writers of America. Estleman lives in Whitmore Lake, Michigan.